Envy Unchecked

Lady Mary Mysteries, Book 1

Alyson Chase

ARE YOU SIGNED UP FOR DRAGONBLADE'S BLOG?

You'll get the latest news and information on exclusive giveaways, exclusive excerpts, coming releases, sales, free books, cover reveals and more.

Check out our complete list of authors, too!

No spam, no junk. That's a promise!

Sign Up Here

www.dragonbladepublishing.com

Dearest Reader;

Thank you for your support of a small press. At Dragonblade Publishing, we strive to bring you the highest quality Historical Romance from some of the best authors in the business. Without your support, there is no 'us', so we sincerely hope you adore these stories and find some new favorite authors along the way.

Happy Reading!

CEO, Dragonblade Publishing

Chapter One

Lady Mary

London, 1820

I F EVER THERE was a man in need of a sound codswalloping, it was Mr. Enoch Ryder. I tossed *The Times* down in disgust, one corner of the paper landing on my plate of scones and the lavender strawberry jam that was dolloped upon them.

One of the footman of The Minerva Club glided up to my table and discreetly wiped at the jam on the paper. He turned up the wick on my oil lamp, the gesture doing little to battle the gloom that seemed to descend upon my club after closing. "Can I bring you more scones, Lady Mary? We also have a raspberry torte left over from our dinner service."

"No, thank you." I'd quite lost my appetite for dessert. "Have you ever seen a pagan ritual being performed in The Minerva Club, Bobby?"

"I can't say that I have, milady," the young man murmured smoothly, his handsome features remaining even. He began turning down the gas lamps that lined the Oriental papered walls.

I snatched up the paper again, and slapped my fingers on the offending opinion piece. "Or 'bouts of unbridled lasciviousness engaged in between the members'?"

Bobby's lips twitched. "Well, there was that one time—"

"No, you have not." I sniffed. The problem with treating

one's workers as part of a family was the impertinence that came along with it. I'd started The Minerva Club as a way for women to gather for pleasant entertainment as we were forbidden from the hallowed halls of the men's clubs of London. My ladies' club fostered conversation, lectures on philosophy and the natural sciences, tutorials on the necessary amount of oil an arrow was required to be saturated in order to keep it aflame until it hit its target. Routine events like that. Devil-worshipping orgies were not a part of our programs.

"Has that Mr. Ryder written another article about your club?" Bobby narrowed his eyes. "He and that morality committee of his aren't going to get us shut down, are they?"

"Of course not." I grasped the jeweled handle of the cane resting on the chair next to mine and pushed myself to standing. The cane was more affectation than necessity, but I felt it gave me a dramatic flair. It wasn't easy being a woman of a certain age in modern-day London. Women, even the young and pretty ones, were too easily overlooked, and I was neither young nor pretty. I wasn't as old as my ivory hair might suggest; it had lost its color early, in my fourth decade, soon after I'd lost my husband. And though I had never quite qualified as pretty, I did have some claim to still being called handsome on occasion.

I folded the paper and tucked it under my arm. At least I was the daughter of an earl and had married into a good family. A title made it much more difficult to ignore me. That, and my money.

"Is there anything else I can do for you before I go?" Bobby stacked my dishes onto a tray. It was past midnight, and the club had technically been closed for an hour, though I never let technicalities get in the way of people having a good time. The Tea Room was empty except for me, Bobby, and the Lynton girl. It hadn't escaped my attention that the young woman had been darting glances my way all through my late night repast. I did hope she'd gather her nerve soon for whatever she had in mind.

"No, thank you. Have a good evening, Bobby."

"And you're sure we won't be shut down." He nodded to the

paper. "I can go 'round and have a talking to that Ryder fellow, just say the word."

That thought was altogether too tempting. "That won't be necessary. Besides, once people read the other piece in the opinion section, no one will remember what Mr. Enoch Ryder has to think."

Bobby grinned. "That tasty a morsel?"

A standing member of the House of Lords insinuating that another member was a milksop, controlled with sexual intimacies by his hoyden of a wife? Yes, that was just the sort of gossip London society wanted to read about. And as the wife in question was a member of The Minerva Club, I could only hope that the gossip didn't invade my halls, as well.

"That prurient." I pushed my spectacles back up my nose. "Good night." I picked up the oil lamp and stalked out of the Tea Room, Miss Lynton peeling off behind me.

"Lady Mary?" She cleared her throat.

"Yes?" I kept walking, heading on my closing rounds. I checked for damage to the rooms as I turned off the gas lamps and blew out any lit candles. A wave of fatigue drifted over me. I'd suffered from *ennui* before, and opening and running my club had certainly alleviated that problem. But keeping inventory, paying workers, paying off the loans of my investors, and now fending off morality committees was more demanding than I had anticipated. I'd thought running a business would be like running a household, just on a larger scale.

I had been wrong.

Miss Lynton quickened her step and turned, walking backwards to face me as she spoke. "I was hoping to speak with you about my mother's membership. Mrs. Lynton?"

"I know who your mother is." My tone might have been a bit more peevish than it ought, but I didn't like anyone questioning my mental faculties when it came to the management of my club.

There were other situations where pretending a slight softness of the mind could be useful, but not here. The Minerva Club was my second home, the one place in public where I could be completely myself. I knew the names, faces, and histories of every member.

"This is a matter of some discretion." Miss Lynton pushed an errant strand of her glossy brown hair behind her ear. "But my mother and I are facing some financial difficulties." She looked at the space beside my head. "I was hoping…."

I took her elbow and steered her away from the wall she was about to bump into. "You were hoping for financial assistance with the membership dues." I tried to hide my surprise. The Lyntons were known throughout society as having had money troubles years ago. Mr. Lynton's success in logging had taken a sharp turn for the worse a decade past, but these last few years their fortunes had turned once again. Even Mr. Lynton's death last year hadn't hurt the wealth of his wife and daughter, and they'd been members of high society for a while now. It would be a shame if they were struggling again.

"Good Gad, no." Miss Lynton looked horrified for a moment. She recovered quickly. "No, I thank you. I was hoping that you would tell my mother she was no longer welcome at the club. Perhaps that you've decided to limit the number of members and she didn't meet your requirements?"

I stopped walking and stared at her a moment. "You've read the papers. You don't want your family's name associated with The Minerva Club any longer." I cursed Enoch Ryder under my breath.

Miss Lynton's eyebrows shot up. She cleared her throat. "That would be one way of putting it."

My neck ached with how stiffly I was holding it. I stepped through the doorway into the Great Room, the spacious hall we used for large assemblies. We hadn't had any events for several days so all the chairs were put away, leaning on the far wall. It was a quick sweep of the eyes to make sure everything was in order before closing.

I strode for the lamps on the side wall. "Your mother can

make her own decisions about her associations, young lady. If she sees fit—" My hand paused on the base of the lamp, my eyes narrowing. A low stage ran along the back of the room, used for the occasional play or concert. A bundle of fabric lay crumpled in the middle of it.

"My mother doesn't know what's best for her," Miss Lynton insisted. She trailed after me as I made my way to the stage. "She doesn't... Lady Mary? What is that?" Her voice went low with dread.

We both knew. As much as I wanted my eyes to keep seeing a pile of cloth, my mind knew the truth. A kidskin boot pressed out from the skirts of a striped percale gown.

I climbed the two steps onto the stage, my legs heavy as lead, my heart pounding dully.

"Lady Mary?" Miss Lynton repeated faintly.

She had been strangled, the white cravat around her throat a sharp contrast with her purpling skin. My breath stalled. It wasn't the first time I'd seen death, but I'd never witnessed one so violent before.

"Go see if Bobby has left yet," I said. "Tell him to run for the constable. The Viscountess of Richford is dead."

Chapter Two
Lady Mary

THAT NIGHT AND the following morning were a practice in patience. It took over a half hour for the constable to arrive and two more before a magistrate could be roused to pay attendance. The insufferable man, one Sir John Stauncey of Bow Street, had only a handful of questions for me, Miss Lynton, and Bobby, but he repeated them over and over until my temper got the better of me.

"I've told you. Repeatedly. I saw no one except Miss Lynton and my workers after closing." I tapped my fingers against my opposite elbows. "Would you like one of my men to make you some coffee? Your mind seems to want sharpening." Throughout my life, I'd discovered that irritation was a much more comfortable emotion to feel than horror. If I focused on the magistrate being a lackwit, it kept the images of Lady Richford's purpling face at bay.

The magistrate's lips pinched. He was only about my height, so the intimidating atmosphere he was attempting to impart was sorely lacking. He scraped his hand through his thinning brown hair. "If you or the young lady or your servants didn't kill Lady Richford, then someone else was in here."

"It's a club, not a prison." I narrowed my eyes at the constable who sidled up next to the magistrate. "I don't keep guards on all the entrances."

"What?" Stauncey barked at the man, dragging his glare off me.

"We found this on the corner of the stage almost hidden by the curtain." The constable held up a narrow red ribbon.

Stauncey snatched it from his hand. "A velvet ribbon. Do you recognize it?" he asked me.

"It looks like any other red ribbon." I relented at his soft growl. "There is a member who sometimes likes to wear such a ribbon around her neck. Miss Abbott. She held a discussion in the Great Room five days' past on the ideals of the French Revolution." I sniffed. "Well, it was more of a lecture, really." The woman barely let another member get a word in edgewise.

"Did you not sweep your floors between then and now?" the magistrate asked.

"It was a discussion, not a picnic. That ribbon could have been laying there for a fortnight."

Stauncey leaned close, an approximation of commiseration on his face. "Having a difficult time affording decent help, are you? Don't make enough to pay for a maid?"

"I am doing quite well," I said between gritted teeth. "And if anyone is lacking for an attendant, it is you." I pointed at his crumpled neckcloth. "You have mustard, just there."

His face flushed darkly.

I feared the magistrate and I had a small chance of becoming friends. After my pointed comments about his person, he let me return home, but I spent the rest of the night only chasing sleep and eventually gave up when the sun rose.

"More coffee?" Jane, my lady's maid of over three decades, lifted the silver pot in crepe-skinned hands, the lid rattling ever so softly with the effort.

"I'll get it." I took the pot from her and filled both our cups. We were in my morning sitting room, the windows opened to the early morning activity in my tidy garden. The September morning was brisk without being cold, and a robin took advantage of the remaining days of decent weather with a bath in a marble fountain. It hadn't rained for weeks, and the fountains and baths in my garden had become increasingly popular with the wildlife as other water sources dried up.

It looked to be a beautiful day. If only my spirits could match it.

"What are the reasons a person would kill, Jane?" Becoming so angry as to wrap a cravat around a woman's throat and choke the life out of her was an emotion I couldn't quite fathom. I wasn't naïve: revenge, jealousy, greed were always strong motives, but there had to be more. Besides, I had watched as the cocksure magistrate had gone through Lady Richford's reticule. A roll of bills had been inside. At least I knew robbery hadn't been the motive.

Jane blinked. "To remove a competitor for your lover? To punish the person who didn't reciprocate your feelings?"

I pressed my lips flat. Jane was a romantic. Love was always at the forefront of her thoughts. She'd never married, and as such had some fanciful ideas about the hallowedness of the relationship between a man and a woman.

"And how did the killer get into my club?" Needing the extra vigor, I put two lumps of sugar in my coffee. "Men aren't allowed, except for my workers, of course." The two service doors, one next to my office and one off the Great Room where Lady Richford's body had been found, had been locked from the inside. I'd checked while the magistrate had been browbeating poor Miss Lynton. No one had escaped that way. And a man walking, cravatless to boot, through the club would have been noticed. Wouldn't he?

"I need to speak with Lord Richford." I nodded, a bit of my unease settling with the decision. It was the not knowing how to act that was the trouble. Once I made up my mind to do something, life always became easier.

"Poor man," Jane murmured. "Of course you must go express your condolences to him. Though might it be more proper to wait a couple of days?"

I dipped my chin and looked at her from lowered brows. When had she ever known me to do what was proper? Nothing notable was ever accomplished by fretting about improprieties.

She sighed. "I need to change my shoes if we are to go out."

I downed my coffee and stood. "You needn't bother. I don't need an attendant for this call." I made myself ready and asked Mr. Stavers, my butler, to call the carriage.

It was shockingly presumptuous to be calling on the family so soon after Lady Richford's death. I hadn't known Susan Bannister, Viscountess of Richford well, and her husband even less so. But the man had just lost his wife. He would be too grief-stricken to care about the proprieties. And if he wasn't grief-stricken, well, that was something I wanted to know.

The woman had been killed in my club, right under my very nose. A life cut short by the most vicious of means. A killer had been under my roof. I gritted my teeth. And that pompous magistrate didn't have the wit to discover the villain. No, a couple of well-placed inquiries wouldn't go amiss.

One lesson I'd learned well in life was that if one wanted a task successfully managed, it was best to do it oneself.

LORD RICHFORD WAS a handsome man, in the bland sort of way so popular among the peerage these days. In his early fifties, his hair was still dark and trimmed to just above his shoulders. His clothes were well-tailored and without a hint of personality. His physique was neither fat not thin nor muscular. He was the type of person you would look upon pleasantly and forget thirty seconds after he left your view. The only thing to distinguish him was the current anguish that wiped the color from his face.

"Tea?" he asked for the second time, his finger poised to call the footman who stood as still as a ficus tree along the wall of his sitting room.

"No, thank you." I smoothed my skirts and tried to ignore the fact that the silk-upholstered settee beneath my rump was as uncomfortable as a boulder. "I wanted to tell you what a marvelous addition Lady Richford had made to The Minerva Club. She was liked and respected wherever she went." I had no idea if that were true, but it seemed to bring her husband a bit of comfort. I had a vague recollection of when he and Lady Richford had married. He had only been a couple of years her senior, and by all accounts it had been a love match.

He gave me a watery smile. "She truly was amazing. A force of nature. And she spoke highly of you, as well," he added as an afterthought.

I gave him my own smile. It was all terribly polite. We were hitting all the right notes of decorum, but the conversation wasn't getting me anywhere. "I was hoping—"

The inner door swung open, and the butler stepped through. "Mr. Frederick Rollins, my lord."

Lord Richford jumped to his feet and hurried to the young man who entered. He shook Mr. Rollins's hand vigorously. "Thank you for coming. I didn't know what to do."

The newcomer scanned the room, his eyes pausing on me before continuing their perusal. "Of course, my lord. My sympathies on your loss."

"Please, please, sit down." Richford showed him to a chair. "Tea?"

Rollins cautiously lowered himself into the harp-backed chair. Perhaps in his late twenties, he was a tall man, and seemed much too large for the delicate seat. His clothes, though not as finely tailored as the viscount's, were just as well pressed, his black top boots holding a lingering sheen from a recent cleaning. His aquiline nose bent a shade too much to be considered fine, his lips were a bit too thin for current fashion, but even though each individual element of his face was imperfect, they came together as a whole to form a most attractive face.

He inclined his head to me, a lock of dark auburn hair falling across his forehead. "Shall I wait until your meeting has finished?"

Richford sank back into his seat. "Excuse my rudeness. Mr. Rollins, this is The Lady Mary Cavindish. She owns the club where Susan…where my wife…."

"I own The Minerva Club." I ran my finger along the jeweled handle of my walking stick. "And you are?"

"An officer of the Bow Street magistrates." He nodded again.

"A Runner?" I shifted to the edge of the settee. I'd never met one of those before, which seemed like a shocking omission now that I thought of it.

He gave me a brittle smile. "We prefer to be called officers of Bow Street magistrates."

I pushed my spectacles up my nose. "That doesn't roll off the tongue quite so nicely, though, does it?"

He turned back to Lord Richford, effectively dismissing me. "How can I be of assistance? You wish me to look into Lady Richford's death?"

"Yes." Richford picked up his cup of tea, a bit sloshing over the rim. "I don't have faith in that magistrate who came around with the other Runner, er, officer, and I know I can trust you."

So I wasn't the only one who thought the magistrate a simpleton. "Quite right," I said. "Besides, the more eyes looking into this tragedy, the better."

Richford swiped his palm across his bristly jaw. "My thoughts exactly."

"Sir John Stauncey has already appointed another officer to this case, but if I tell him you've requested me, I'm certain there won't be an issue with my replacing him." Rollins rubbed his jaw. "I would like to interview you in priv—"

"It can't have been easy, the same day you lost your wife to read in the paper that dreadful opinion piece by Lord Anglia." I leaned forward. I excelled at making it difficult to dismiss me. I wouldn't let today be an exception.

"Detestable man." A red flush stained the viscount's cheeks. "The lies. The insinuations. I have half a mind to sue him and *The Times* for publishing such tripe."

"What piece?" Rollins asked.

"A strong-willed woman can ruffle feathers." *Of insecure birds,* I thought sourly. "It is of no account if a husband accepts some advice from his wife."

Richford stood and started pacing. "Just so. Susan might have told me her opinion on some legislation, but that doesn't mean she made my decisions for me. And she certainly didn't—" His cheeks flushed darker.

"Didn't what?" Rollins looked between me and the viscount. "What did the opinion piece say?"

"I hate to broach such an unpleasant thought," I began, "but was your relationship with Lord Anglia acrimonious enough that he'd wish harm on your wife?"

Richford lurched to a stop and blinked. "No. He couldn't. Wouldn't. Just because we voted differently?" His chest rose and fell like bellows. "He couldn't."

Not a resounding negation of the idea. I kept my voice even. "Perhaps not. But can you think of anyone else who would want to harm Lady Richford?"

A snort came from the doorway. "That list would be long and varied." A man in his early twenties stood at the entrance to the room, his features similar enough to Lord Richford's to confirm he was the viscount's son.

"Edgar…." Lord Richford's voice was weary, as though he and his son had butted heads over Lady Richford many a time.

Mr. Rollins unfolded from his chair and gave a respectful nod. "Sir. I am—"

"I know who you are." The young man strolled to a wingchair by the window and sprawled onto it, one leg dangling over the armrest. "And I know who this one is, too." He nodded at me. "You look exactly as I remember from childhood."

As it had been near fifteen years since I'd last seen Mr. Edgar

Bannister, it should have been a compliment.

His tone indicated that it wasn't.

"And I remember you, as well." I tapped the end of my walking stick into the Aubusson carpet. "If I remember correctly, there was some incident at the Whitney's house party involving a large bowl of cherries and a handmade blow dart."

Bannister shrugged. "I was eight."

His youth didn't excuse the loss of one of my favorite day gowns, though his ingenuity was to be admired. "This list of your mother's enemies, anyone in particular we should be concerned about?"

"There is no list," Lord Richford said sharply. "My wife was beloved by all."

The silence after that sentiment became awkward.

Mr. Rollins, instead of wedging himself back into his chair, stepped behind it and gripped the backrest. "Sometimes animosities aren't rational," he said carefully. "Lady Richford might have made enemies through no fault of her own. It is best, however, if I gather a full picture of all her relationships."

Richford picked at one of his nails. "She had friends. Many of them. That's why she wanted to join that club." He nodded at me. "I know it was bordering on scandalous, but my darling was always so impetuous. When she wanted something, she dove right in." His smile was faint, reminiscent. "We met when she was but seventeen. I was willing to wait a couple of years to marry, but she wouldn't hear of it. She'd made up her mind, and had her father announce the banns in just three months' time. Edgar came a year later."

Edgar Bannister rolled his eyes to the ceiling. "They don't want your life history, father."

"No." Richford stared down at his clenched hands. "We were so happy. I don't know what to do."

"Any particular friend your wife might have confided in?" Mr. Rollins asked. "Anyone she was worried about?"

"You should talk to that Abbott woman." Bannister flicked at a bit of dust on his jacket. "She came over here incessantly. Still does."

"Abbott?" I tilted my head. "Miss Lydia Abbott?"

Richford nodded. "She considered herself one of my wife's particular friends. I think Susan was just too kind to send her away. But Miss Abbott has shown kindness herself. She's always asking what she can do to help. Just this morning she went through Susan's things to pick out a gown for Susan to be… to be dressed… for the funeral." He blinked rapidly.

Miss Abbott was one of The Minerva Club's most vociferous supporters. She proclaimed to one and all that if men had their own clubs, women should too. A sentiment I appreciated, even though the stridency of her opinions was somewhat off-putting.

She didn't strike me as the kind of woman to impose her presence where it wasn't welcome. And Lady Richford certainly had never been too kind to refrain from speaking her mind.

Lord Richford picked at another nail. "I don't know what to do," he murmured.

All the resolve I'd started with drained out of me. I knew what it was to grieve. I didn't have the heart to intrude on Lord Richford any longer. I stood. "If you think of anyone else I should talk to, please let me know."

Mr. Rollins jerked straight. "Surely you mean anyone whom I should speak to. Lord Richford has engaged *me* to investigate his wife's death."

"And I'm certain you'll do an admirable job." I tugged at the cuff of my gown, the lace trim irritating my skin. "However, as you yourself pointed out, the more eyes looking into this tragedy, the better."

"You said that." Rollins straightened to his full height. "I didn't."

Hmph. I was certain he had agreed.

A devious smile creased young Bannister's face. "Crazy Cavindish is becoming a detective? Your nephew is rubbing off on you." He hooted. "I can't wait to tell my friends."

"Edgar!" Lord Richford rose slowly, as though he wore a weighted yoke. "I apologize Lady Mary. The grief, you know. It makes us all say things we don't mean."

It had been a while since I'd been called that name, at least to my face. I repressed a smile. I'd been born The Lady Mary Griffin. Upon my marriage I'd become The Lady Mary Cavindish. My nephew and his closest friends had given me the pet name Aunt May. By far, the title I'd derived the most amusement from, however, had been Crazy Cavindish. Having money and being thought eccentric had given me more freedom than I'd ever known.

"Of course, Richford." I stepped forward and took his hand. "Again, my deepest sympathies. And with a Runner and myself looking into matters, we'll find an answer in no time, I'm sure."

He patted my hand before sinking back into his chair. "Thank you. I have a speech I'm to give in next week's session of Parliament. I have to write that."

And taking that as the dismissal it was, I strode from the room, Mr. Rollins hot on my heels.

Once outside the house, Mr. Rollins turned on me. "Lady Mary, as commendable as your zeal for justice may be, your services are not required. I have things well in hand." He settled his hat on his unruly auburn hair and nodded at me smartly, as though the issue were resolved.

I signaled to my driver to open my carriage door and looked back at the house. The servants were just finishing hanging black crepe in the windows. "It's sweet that you think my services are yours to decline." I took my driver's proffered hand and climbed inside. I lowered the window after he closed the door and leaned out. "I assume you'll wish to see where her body was found. Come to the club at tea time. It is usually less frequented then, and you'll be less of an intrusion."

I sat back on my maroon crushed velvet seat. By the look on the man's face, I could tell I'd shocked him, either by my dismissal or the confidence I showed in my abilities to detect.

I only hoped my skills merited the boldness of my mouth.

Chapter Three

Frederick

THE MINERVA CLUB lived up to its storied reputation. It had only been in operation for a year or so, and the sentiment of London society had been mixed: anger at the impertinence of a club for women, amusement, and practiced indifference. Frederick Rollins's own colleagues regarded it with a sort of horrified fascination, and he knew more than a few of his fellow officers were jealous that his latest investigation brought him within its fabled doors.

Frederick opted not to remain in the waiting room where the footman had left him to fetch Lady Mary, but wandered amongst the club, blinking at the sights that met his eyes.

An archery range, with more holes in the surrounding walls than in the targets.

A hallway cleared for lawn bowling, without the lawn.

A room that had been designed to recreate a country pub, complete with some wisps of hay on the floor. Two women sat at the weathered bar, cheroots clasped between their fingers, large mugs of ale before them.

Frederick turned his hat in his hands. No evidence of orgies or Satan worship. The lads would be disappointed.

A furtive movement caught his attention. He followed the

flounce of lavender fabric as it disappeared into a room down the hall. There was a window high in the back wall, allowing enough sunlight to stream in to show the young woman's actions. She pulled the pillows off a crimson settee and dug her fingers along the back of the upholstered seat cushion before moving to the next piece of furniture. This room was obviously situated for conversation, with plump chairs, settees, and even a divan or two arranged throughout. Low tables held a smattering of newspapers and one abandoned glass. When the woman had finished examining each piece of furniture, she planted her hands on her hips and heaved a sigh.

Frederick leaned against the door jamb, curiosity spiking. Something about the woman seemed familiar. Her hair, an average brown, was swept up in some sort of twisting knot, a few soft tendrils framing her face. Her features were even, attractive, and from what he could see beneath the gown and pelisse she wore, her body was pleasing without being striking. He couldn't see the color of her eyes, but they seemed as agreeable as the rest of her, neither too beautiful nor unpleasant.

Her mouth, however, was designed to give a man certain ideas.

The lips were pressed together in pique at the moment, as she tapped one boot-clad toe. Her gaze narrowed on a deep purple settee pushed against the far wall, half-hidden in shadow, and she made straight for it. Dropping to her knees, she stuck her head beneath, leaving her arse tipped up in a most indecent fashion.

Frederick made his way over to her, making sure to stick to the rugs scattered about the hardwood floor so he made no sound. He stood behind her, trying not to notice how her hips swayed enticingly as she swept her hand along the baseboards.

"Looking for something?"

She stilled. "Yes?"

"Perhaps I can assist." Though if she wanted to continue poking about on her own and providing him with the delightful view, he didn't want to seem churlish by complaining.

"I thank you, but that's not necessary." Her words were only slightly muffled from coming from under the settee.

His duty got the better of him. "But I insist." What could she be looking for so intently? She'd been looking over her shoulder as she'd entered the room, a sure sign she didn't want others to know what she was up to. With a murder in this club to solve, no aberrant behavior could be overlooked. "A lady should not be on her hands and knees when there is an able-bodied man available to help."

She sighed, then started making her way out. This process included much wriggling, and the hem of her gown shifted up to her knees.

Frederick drew his brows together. He was certain he'd seen this woman before, but where?

"Well?" She sat with her gloved hand raised to him for assistance.

He pulled her to her feet. More hair had escaped her knot, and a line of dust crossed her pelisse where her bosom must have pressed into the floor. "What is it you're looking for, Miss….?"

"Lynton." She made a half-hearted attempt at brushing herself off. "And I lost a pin the last time I was here. Square. Gold. About so big." She held her thumb and forefinger about an inch apart. Her voice was sure, brisk, but her gaze didn't meet his eyes.

"Are you certain you lost it in this room?" He didn't recognize her name, and if she were a member of this club it was unlikely they ran in the same social circles. Had she been a part of a previous investigation?

"Yes." She gave up on the dust. "I think so. It is of no great import, however." She looked him up and down. "Who are you? Not one of the club's workers."

As the servants were all in livery and he was not, it was an easy deduction. "Mr. Frederick Rollins, an officer of the Bow Street magistrates."

Her eyelid twitched. "I wish you luck in finding whoever

killed that poor woman. We are all most distraught."

From what he'd seen, distraught wasn't the word he would have used. There was an excitement among the club's patrons, an energy not uncommon among the casual acquaintances of a murder victim. Everyone wanted to discuss the tragedy, chew over each horrifying detail until nothing was left, not even bones.

It was an escape from a typically dull life. It also helped to make the survivors feel safe. If they could examine every detail, they could see why it would be impossible for such an event to befall them or their loved ones.

"Since I have you here, I'd like to ask you a few questions," he said.

"Of course." Miss Lynton went to a mirror on the wall and began to fix her hair. "But I hardly knew the woman. I'm sure nothing I can tell you would be of interest."

"Mr. Rollins!" Lady Mary Cavindish stomped into the room, jabbing the floor with her walking stick more in anger than as any sort of support. "I have been looking all over for you."

He held his arms out. "And you've found me." He wasn't sure what to make of the woman yet. She'd created this outlandish club and had a reputation for eccentricity, but surely she hadn't been in earnest about aiding in his investigation. He felt like he had fallen in her disfavor when they'd met, and her declaration had most likely been an attempt to provoke him.

"I would like a space to interview your workers, if I may." Frederick tapped his hat against his thigh. "And the club's members who had any relationship to the victim."

"You can use my office." Lady Mary nodded at Miss Lynton. "And I see you've made a good start. I know you'll want to interview both of us who found the body, so I will make myself available to you at your convenience."

Frederick blinked, then slowly turned to the young woman. "You discovered the body?"

Miss Lynton refocused her attentions on her dusty pelisse. "Hmm? Oh, yes. Did I not mention it?"

"You did not." He tilted his head. "I find that of much *interest.* I'll start my interviews with you."

She gave him a smile that was all politeness but no warmth. "Of course."

Lady Mary examined the woman. "Bernard didn't take your coat and gloves? You must be quite warm."

The girl flushed, and he didn't think it was from the alleged warmth. "I only came in to try to find my pin. I didn't mean to stay long. I'll give him my coat now and meet you in Lady Mary's office."

He watched her go with even more suspicion than when he'd first seen her. "Before we go to your office, if you would show me where you found Lady Richford?" He held his arm out to the door.

Lady Mary did so, pausing several times to greet members. Frederick was a great object of interest, and he foresaw no issue in getting the ladies here to speak with him. An interview by an officer of Bow Street would likely feed their *on dit* for a month.

He was led down a central hall with rooms opening on both the right and the left. It ended at a pair of double doors, thrown open to a cavernous room, mostly empty, with a low stage tucked against the far wall. Lady Mary showed him where the victim had been lying, and he was pleased her account accorded with the sketches the magistrate's assistant had made of the crime scene. After examining the space and testing the door to the alley, he nodded to Lady Mary and followed her out of the room and back down the hall.

Lady Mary's office was in the corner of the club. It was a well-lit room with windows on two sides, which seemed primarily designed to aid the copious plant life. Ferns hung from the ceiling. Exotic agave crowded the window sills, their spiky leaves a deterrent to anyone who'd presume to climb through the casements. What looked like a banana tree in a wide oak tub commandeered one corner of the room.

Her desk was tidy, just one lone ledger resting upon it. A

high-backed chair that wouldn't have looked out of place in a throne room sat behind it, with two much smaller, but just as finely upholstered, guest chairs across.

Frederick brushed a fern frond from his face as he made his way to the desk. "This will do nicely. Thank you."

"You're welcome." His stride was long, but Lady Mary's was faster. She rounded the desk before he reached the corner and took her seat.

He narrowed his eyes. "My interviews require only the presence of me and the person with whom I'm speaking. Your presence—"

"You will be interviewing my workers, my members. I have already spoken with most of them, but I am curious to see how they answer a Runner."

He inhaled sharply. "Lady Mary—"

"Or you can try to speak with everyone after they've left this club." She leaned her walking stick against the desk. "Traveling to over fifty homes, hoping that they'll be available, why it could take days."

He considered his options. Throttling an older woman wasn't one of them. Nor could he lock her up, not with the influence she wielded, not with the nephew she had. But to have an ordinary citizen, and one who was a potential suspect in the murder, sitting in on his interviews just wasn't done.

"Lord Richford hired you," she added, "and he will not object. The more eyes, and all that," she reminded him.

He was coming to loathe that phrase.

His shoulders sagged in defeat, but his mother had taught him it was always better to make the most of a situation rather than complain.

Frederick looked hopefully at her desk chair. "All right, I'll allow you to remain, but I should sit—"

"My office. My chair." She laced her fingers together and leaned back, looking as comfortable as a queen. The cushion was so thick her feet most likely barely reached the floor.

Biting back an oath, Frederick took one of the small chairs and dragged it from across the desk to the side end. He pulled out his notepad and piece of lead, smacking them to the desk with a bit more force than necessary before wedging himself into his seat.

"Would you like some goose fat?" Miss Lynton stood in the doorway, one eyebrow arched. "You might be able to slide your way into that chair more easily."

Frederick scowled. "Please, have a seat." He indicated the remaining chair, trying not to feel resentful that she dropped into it as though it had been formed for her body. This was a women's club. The furniture was probably more proportioned to their smaller statures.

"Should I call for tea?" Lady Mary asked, her light blue eyes bright. "I've never sat in on a Runner's interview. I'm quite unsure of the etiquette."

He flipped open his notebook to a fresh page. "No tea."

"Just as well." Lady Mary crossed one ankle over the other. "With over fifty people at the club now, it could be a challenge keeping enough water boiling."

He turned to Miss Lynton. "How long have you been a member of this club?"

"Almost since its inception." She glanced at Lady Mary. "About eighteen months now?"

"That sounds about right," Lady Mary said.

"And how long have you known the victim?" Frederick held his lead just above the paper.

Miss Lynton folded her hands neatly in her lap. "The Rich-fords have been a part of my family's social set ever since I can remember, although I likely didn't have any true conversation with the woman until we were both members of this club, and even then, we spoke of nothing of significance."

Frederick scratched some notes down. Miss Lynton seemed most eager to downplay any association with the viscountess, whether from a natural inclination to avoid a connection with a murder victim or for more sinister reasons he didn't yet know.

And she was circumspect enough throughout the rest of the interview to keep him in ignorance. She hadn't seen Lady Richford enter the club, nor move through it. She'd only remained after closing to speak to Lady Mary about her family's financial difficulties. She didn't know anyone who would want to harm the viscountess. No matter from which direction he pressed, Miss Lynton remained stalwart in her claim that she had no useful knowledge of the murder.

The rest of his interviews were similarly unfruitful. He was able to establish an approximate time for the murder, sometime after the doorman Bernard Lox had made his parting rounds around midnight and had seen nothing in the Great Room, and twelve twenty-three, when Lady Mary and Miss Lynton had found the body.

"It was twelve twenty-three exactly," Lady Mary said. "There's a longcase clock in the Great Room, and immediately after I sent Miss Lynton to find help, I went and checked the time."

Bobby Carhart confirmed that time frame. The footman was probably in his mid-twenties, with sandy-colored hair and a permanent smirk that made Frederick's hand twitch. "I'd made it to Haymarket, about five minutes away, when St. Martin's bell tolled the half hour. The watch-box was only a few minutes farther."

Frederick made notes in his book. Twenty-three minutes was a small window for someone to come into the club, strangle the victim, and escape. "And no men, excepting the workers, are allowed on the premises?"

"There are a few exceptions made, such as yourself, lecturers, that sort of thing." Lady Mary shook her head. "But none on that night."

"And you didn't know Lady Richford was still at the club?"

Lady Mary stared at the ceiling. "I'd seen her earlier in the night, probably around ten or so. But I'd thought she'd left when we closed our doors at eleven."

Frederick pinned Bobby with a stare. "Did you see her leave?"

"No." The footman lifted one shoulder. "But I didn't see her not leave, if you take my meaning."

None of the other footmen had seen Lady Richford during their nightly rounds, either. The woman had hidden herself in the club, or she'd come back after closing. "And the exterior doors remain locked?"

"Always, except for the front door, of course." Lady Mary nodded at Bobby. "The workers have keys. There's a door from the Great Room that exits into the back alley, and a door next to this office that leads outside. Unless we're accepting a delivery or taking out the garbage, those doors remained closed and locked."

Frederick closed his notebook. "Thank you, Bobby. That will be all, for now."

The footman rose. "Can I bring you a snifter of liquid excitement?" he asked Lady Mary. He bobbed his head at Frederick. "This must be monstrously dull for you."

Frederick folded his hands over his abdomen. He could only hope that Lady Mary found this investigation dull. It would solve at least one problem for him.

"No, thank you," Lady Mary said. "You were the last? No one else to send in?"

Bobby winked as he went to the door. "You finished with the best." And then he was gone.

"Quite full of himself, isn't he?" Frederick removed his handkerchief and wiped the lead dust from his fingers.

"At that age, aren't most men?" She planted her elbows on the desk and rested her chin on her interlaced hands. "That seemed like a singular waste of time. No one had anything bad to say about Lady Richford which could indicate why she was killed."

Frederick frowned. He wasn't much older than the footman, and he'd never acted so cocksure. "Or no one dared." He pushed out of the chair and started to pace. "What do you know of the woman?"

She blew out a breath. "Not as much as I should. She didn't seem like a bad sort, but she was one of those people whom I met that I realized instantly would not become a bosom-friend. She did seem to be close with Miss Abbott. At least she spoke with her more than the others."

Frederick nodded. He'd already made a note to speak with the woman. "No arguments you heard about? No disputes?"

"Not to my knowledge, but I'm not the grand confessor here. There are many members like Miss Abbott who were not here today and who might know more."

Frederick turned, and a fern leaf batted against his face. He frowned. "Your workers all seem to have a standard uniform. Are there any exceptions?"

"No." She gave him a shrewd look. "That cravat wasn't worn by one of my footmen."

She wasn't stupid, he'd give her that. He'd examined the murder weapon when he'd gone to the Bow Street offices. It was made of a fine linen in a shade of cream. There had been no manufacturer's mark, no distinguishing feature of any kind. "Perhaps Lady Richford brought it with her," he murmured. "I'll have to ask her husband if he recognizes it."

Lady Mary leaned back. "You seemed to have a previous acquaintance with the viscount."

As she hadn't asked a question, he refrained from replying. His previous relationships were none of Lady Mary's business. And after all, what good could come from revealing how he and the Richfords had first met?

"Thank you for the use of your office." He slid his notebook and lead back in his pocket and nodded. "I'll notify you if I need any further assistance."

He took his leave, ignoring the twittering of the ladies as he passed. He thought of the Richfords again and reaffirmed his decision to remain silent on how he'd first met them.

The woman was dead. There was no need to tarnish her reputation.

Chapter Four

Eleanor

ELEANOR LYNTON WATCHED from a curtain-draped nook in the Tea Room as the Runner left The Minerva Club. Through the window, she saw him tug his top hat over his thick, wavy hair and give it a quarter-twist. He gave a speculative look at the club's front doors before turning and walking away, his legs eating up the pavement.

Eleanor scraped her teeth over her bottom lip. That one could be dangerous. His eyes had been much too sharp for her liking, his questions much too piercing. Hopefully, they would never meet again.

Before she left the windowseat, she ran her fingers behind the pillows, not holding out much hope. Her mother had been quite specific as to which room she'd left it in.

"There you are." Lady Mary's voice made Eleanor jump. The older woman stood before her, her hands resting on the onyx falcon that made up the handle for her walking stick *du jour.* "You were in such a hurry to leave before, I thought I might have missed you."

Eleanor made a show of plumping up her pillow before rising. "I had more free time this afternoon than I'd thought."

Lady Mary's eyes were a pale blue, like dried lavender that

had seen too many years, but the intelligence in them was as sharp as ever. She held Eleanor's stare until Eleanor was shifting on her feet, then turned and started across the room. "Come on, then," she called over her shoulder. "Keep up."

Disobeying didn't even cross Eleanor's mind. She hurried to Lady Mary's side.

"This financial business with your mother," Lady Mary began.

"I hope I didn't overstate the case the other night." Eleanor forced a light laugh. "I had seen a bill that made me worried, but it was a mistake. Our circumstances are not so dire that mother can't remain a member." No, the true obstacle to her mother attending this club was now gone.

"Is that so?" Lady Mary detoured to the side wall and pulled a fichu from a picture frame it had been snagged on. She folded it neatly before continuing on her path. "I spoke to your mother a fortnight ago. She had indulged a bit too much in our special tea. She seemed…agitated."

"Whiskey does that to her." Eleanor followed Lady Mary into her office, the light-filled room seeming much cheerier than when Mr. Rollins had occupied it. "She's promised to stick to sherry from now on."

Lady Mary tossed the fichu on her desk, then leaned back against it, facing Eleanor. "I know you and your mother are out of mourning for Mr. Lynton, but grief doesn't follow a schedule. If she is having a hard time, I'd like to help."

Eleanor pressed her palms to her thighs, hoping the muslin fabric would absorb the sweat that dampened them. "That is kind, but we're making do."

Lady Mary traced the falcon's head on her walking stick with her thumb. "I, also, have lost a husband. Next time your mother comes to the club, perhaps talking to someone else who has experienced the same pain will help her."

The last thing Eleanor needed was Lady Mary speaking to her mother. In fact, any interest on Lady Mary's part was something to be avoided. "I'm sure my mother would appreciate that." Her mother wouldn't be coming back to the club, not if Eleanor could help it.

Eleanor went to the window and ran her finger down the spiny leaf of some type of succulent. "But when I think about my mother, I think about poor Edgar Bannister, and how he must be feeling having lost his mother. And in such a way. I hope they were able to resolve their differences before Lady Richford died."

It was despicable. The contents in her stomach curdled. She was despicable. But turning Lady Mary's curious mind to someone other than her mother seemed the only way. Her mother was in a fragile state of mind, and Lady Mary's prying could break her.

"There was trouble between Bannister and Lady Richford?" Lady Mary narrowed her eyes. "I didn't know."

"Well, it isn't the sort of thing a family would advertise." Eleanor strolled to the next window, examining the small pink bud on another plant. "Affections always seemed strained between mother and son." At Lady Mary's questioning look, Eleanor explained, "I grew up in the same social circle as them, went to many parties as a child with Edgar. But last year, at the Hardcastle's garden party, Bannister told me he was expecting a large sum of money from his father. He'd cornered me behind the folly. I believe he was trying to seduce me."

Eleanor's skin crawled remembering it. He had been free as to where he'd put his hands, and his oily smile assumed she would delight to fall into his arms. She kept her voice light. "I heard later that Lady Richford forbade her husband from giving Edgar the funds and that there was a great row."

She gave Lady Mary a tremulous smile. "Which is why I pray they made amends before her death, for Edgar's sake."

Lady Mary sniffed. "How…benevolent of you." She laid her walking stick on the desk, then crossed the room. She opened the door to the closet nestled in the corner and dragged out a box.

"Put this on the desk, will you?"

Eleanor hurried to do as she'd asked, hoping any further questions about her mother were forestalled. "What is this?" The box had no lid, and was weighed down with an assortment of items, from a silk reticule to a fist-sized agate to a stained stocking.

"The Minerva Club's box of lost items." Lady Mary tipped the box on its side, letting the contents spill out. She crossed her arms over her chest. "I thought you might look for your pin."

"Oh." The pin that she'd invented. "Of course, how thoughtful." Eleanor dug through the pile, trying to look as though she cared that she found it.

She pulled out a cup-and-ball toy, a broken gold chain. She prayed there wasn't a pin that matched her description in here. That would be difficult to ex—

Eleanor jerked her hand back, a soft cry escaping her lips. Underneath a black-and-white checked turban, a mother-of-pearl handled flintlock pistol lay.

Her mother's gun. The one she had taken to kill Lady Richford.

"Lovely piece, isn't it?" Lady Mary picked it up and sighted one of her hanging ferns. "Whoever lost this must be missing it. I do tell the members to come to my office to check for lost items, but hardly anyone ever does."

Eleanor nodded, though she knew the truth. Her mother didn't miss it. She never wanted to see it again. Because as she'd held it in her hand, intending to hunt Lady Richford down, she'd become horrified of her desire to kill. She'd shoved the gun down behind a cushion in the club and fled.

At least that was what her mother had told Eleanor. Finding the gun in the box of lost items was some proof of that. But if anyone discovered what her mother had planned, they wouldn't hesitate to believe she had only changed her mind as to the manner of execution and had strangled Lady Richford instead.

And Eleanor had to protect her mother at all costs. She'd already lost one parent. She wouldn't lose another.

Chapter Five

Lady Mary

"LADY MARY?" BERNARD stood in her office doorway. "A man is here to see you."

I laid my fountain pen next to the ledger I was going over. "Who?"

Bernard crossed the room and handed me a card.

Enoch Ryder, Esq.

I inhaled sharply. It took some nerve to show his face here. "Show him in, please. Oh, and bring us some tea, if you would."

"Of course, milady."

I closed my ledger and put it and my pen in a drawer. I made sure that nothing was out of place, nothing would catch the eye of a moral ninny. Then I rested my elbows on my desk, steepled my fingers, and waited.

I didn't wait long. Bernard stepped through, followed by Mr. Enoch Ryder.

"Mr. Ryder, milady," Bernard announced, then slipped out the door.

I examined the man. He was about my age, his hair a muddle of what I assumed was his original golden-brown mixed with silver and just a touch of white at his temples. He had a nice square jaw, his chin just beginning to go soft. He'd had to lower his head as he'd crossed the threshold of my door, his height even more accentuated by his lean musculature. He carried a nondescript cane capped with a thick silver knob, though by the surety of his stride it appeared he carried it more for effect.

I sniffed. If the man couldn't afford an eye-pleasing walking stick, then why bother carrying one at all?

I pointed to a guest chair. "Please, have a seat."

"Thank you," he said, his voice a pleasant baritone, and sat. "I'm pleased you'd see me. I was hoping to find you a reasonable woman."

Even though I considered myself quite reasonable, it wasn't an adjective that had ever been applied to me. I didn't think Mr. Ryder would leave here thinking such, either. "A reasonable man might have come to speak with me before writing lies about my club in *The Times*. Or at least a decent man."

His shoulders stiffened. Apparently he didn't like his decency challenged.

Well, neither did I. I might have started The Minerva Club to allow women to let their hair down when society preferred they keep it tightly pinned up, but there was nothing indecent about that.

He crossed one leg over the other and leaned back, giving me a tight smile. "Perhaps you're right, but I am here now. It sounds as though you're familiar with the London Society for Morality and Decency? Our purpose is to encourage healthful activities and wholesome living."

I gave him a smile as sweet as my cook's iced cakes. "I also would encourage wholesome living. I fear that our ideas of wholesome are not in accord, sadly."

He inclined his head. "That would be concerning, but I find it best to look for common ground instead of focusing on our differences."

I muffled a snort. Nothing irritated me more than someone

sounding reasonable when they made unreasonable demands. "I see no common ground in *me* closing my club because *you* wish it."

"A woman was killed in these walls. Has that no call on your conscience?"

My chest burned. I wanted to make a vicious remark in turn, but Bernard returned just then with the tea. He set the tray on my desk and poured two cups. I waited for him to leave before answering. "Thomas Becket was assassinated in Canterbury Cathedral. I assume you don't use that as an indictment against the church's morality, but only as against his killers."

Mr. Ryder inclined his head. "Before Lady Richford's unfortunate death, I still had concerns. If you could be shown that a club that beguiles women away from their proper duties is harmful, what would be your response?" He cocked his head and gave me an assessing look. There was judgment in his gaze, but also a hint of sympathy. Like I was a sinner to be pitied rather than shunned.

My spine went as straight as an iron bar. "And if you could be shown that your opinion on a woman's proper duties is as dunderheaded as the Cato Street Conspiracy plot to murder the cabinet ministers? What then would you do?"

He reached for a cup of tea, his lips twitching. "Apologize, of course, and retract my piece in *The Times*. I hardly think it likely, however."

I stood, irritation putting starch in my voice. "Perhaps a tour is in order. Then you can see that your vile insinuations are baseless."

He looked at his tea sadly before placing the cup back down. He rose, as well. "I would love a tour, Lady Mary." He extended his arm toward the door. "After you."

I stalked past him, chin held high. The scent of fresh soap clung to his pressed dark suit. "The Minerva Club is similar in nature to White's or Boodle's. A place for women to gather to be themselves instead of the person your *wholesome* expectations demands of them."

"And is anyone allowed entry?" He peered around a doorway into the archery room, where Mrs. Stewart had set a portrait of Lord Byron up as a target and was taking aim. For some reason I had yet to discover, the woman loathed the poet. "Or do you have ethical standards your members must maintain?"

I didn't have a set of rules for members. It had never been an issue before. "The same standards as White's. It would take roguish intrigue of the worst kind to be booted out of that club, would it not? Why should my women be held to a stricter standard? My members are fine, upstanding individuals, who only need a bit of space to be themselves."

I showed him the Great Room where we heard lectures, the Tea Room where a group of women were clustered around the fireplace conversing, even the library.

I did not show him my replication of the tavern I'd once visited with my husband, the Old Ram. It wasn't his concern.

We met Timothy, another one of my footmen, in the hallway used for lawn bowling. He was carrying a gold-painted chair. "I got it fixed, right as rain, milady. Took some doing finding the right color paint after replacing the leg, but I got it."

"Thank you, Timothy." I frowned. I didn't remember the chair being broken, but then, many things constantly needed to be fixed in the club. Or walls needed to be patched. The women didn't have the best of aim. Did White's have similar repair bills?

"I think you should ask Mrs. Massey to cover the repair costs." Timothy shifted the chair to his other arm. "She had no cause to smash it like that."

"Smashing chairs?" Mr. Ryder arched a silver eyebrow. "Another fine, upstanding individual in your club?"

I raised my chin. "I'm certain Mrs. Massey was trying to demonstrate something and it got away from her. Perhaps the pounds per square inch necessary to demolish a structure. We did have an engineer in here last month to describe the new building processes involved in the construction of the Egyptian Hall."

Timothy chuckled. "No ma'am. Mrs. Massey was in a right nettle. Arguing and yelling at Lady Richford something fierce. She picked up this chair and threw it right at the lady's head. It smashed against the wall. I understand when damage happens from the bad aim of a thrown axe or something accidentally catches fire, but this was uncalled for."

My mind whirred. I didn't even care that Timothy had just given Mr. Ryder a feast of bad behavior for him to chew on. "When did this happen?"

"'Bout a fortnight ago." He held up the chair. "But it's all fixed now."

"Why didn't you tell Mr. Rollins this when he interviewed you?"

His eyes widened. "He only asked me about the day Lady Richford was killed. I didn't think there was any connection. Do you—"

"I don't think anything right now." I tapped my boot. How had I not known of a fight within my walls? I needed to speak with my workers. Incidents like that needed to be reported. "Thank you, Timothy."

He nodded, shooting a look at Mr. Ryder. "I'll just go put the chair back in the Greek Room."

"Thank you." I stepped aside to let him pass.

Amelia Massey was one of the club's original members. Married, with two children around twenty years of age, she and I had volunteered on several committees together. While I wouldn't say that we were close, I knew her well enough to know that throwing chairs was decidedly out of character.

What had Lady Richford done to anger the woman so much?

Mr. Ryder tapped his walking stick against the wood floor. "Are arguments that lead to physical assaults common at The Minerva Club?"

"They are not." I sniffed, trying to make his question sound as ridiculous as it was. "Timothy might have gotten his facts wrong."

"And he might not."

I ground my jaw. "Am I to expect this gossip to make its way into your next opinion piece? It isn't only my reputation you are taking aim at, but it will also be that of a woman now deceased. I hope you will think of her family."

He seemed to choose his words carefully. "It is not my habit to intentionally injure anyone, not unless by so doing I am affecting change for the greater good. I see no good that would come from gossiping about the fight between Lady Richford and your other member. So long as the proper authorities are notified, of course."

"Of course." I turned, heading for the front of the club. I would have to inform Mr. Rollins of this. Next time I might see him. I'd investigate further before making a trip down to Bow Street. "Now. As you can see, my club isn't a den of iniquity. No pagan rituals…" I quickly closed the door to the Greek Room where the painting the Birth of Venus by Botticelli was being recreated by my members in person, large clam shell and all. "…no bacchanalian revels."

"I've not been here a half hour," he said mildly. "I've heard your members become more boisterous after dark."

I exhaled sharply. "Mr. Ryder, you are determined to think the worst of my club regardless of the truth."

"On the contrary. I hold the truth in the highest esteem." Two women emerged from the Tea Room, one walking backwards and gesticulating wildly with her hands. Mr. Ryder took my elbow and guided me out of their path. He stopped me when I would have pulled away. "And the truth is The Minerva Club is a degrading institution. It cheapens the women who are members, cheapens London society, and I fear, it cheapens you, as well. I entreat you to do what is right: close your club."

His hand on my arm burned, or perhaps that was just my conscience.

A woman had died under my roof. In the club that I had created. Was he right that I emboldened bad behavior? Was I responsible for Lady Richford's death?

I kept my expression even. "Even if what you say is true, there are many clubs in London whose sole purpose is depravity. You know the clubs of which I speak, the one gentlemen go to after their glass of port at White's. There are also the gambling hells and opium dens. I find it curious that of all the wickedness in London, you spend your time trying to shut the doors of The Minerva Club, a place where women can come to have a bit of harmless fun."

He tilted his head. "You question my priorities?"

"I question your intent. Do you truly want to better London society, or do you only want to keep women in their place?" I didn't wait for him to answer. I slid my arm from his grasp and stalked to the entrance.

Bernard pulled a coat and hat from the closet and handed them to Mr. Ryder.

The head of the morality committee laid his coat over his arm and turned his hat in his hands thoughtfully. "Perhaps those other sins you speak of, those other clubs, wouldn't hold such temptation if the women in those men's lives attended to their families more instead of joining a club like yours."

Well, that was too much. I nodded to Bernard to open the door. "I have enough of my own sins to worry about. I won't take responsibility for your sex, as well. If men engage in licentiousness, that is no one's fault but their own."

"Sin and licentiousness?" A man stepped through the door, his startling blue eyes twinkling. He was a little under six feet, had the solid build of a dock worker, and thick, steel-grey hair. His eyebrows were dark as a raven's wing, giving him a devilish look. He wore a Pomona green waistcoat, the only bit of color among his black jacket and trousers. Even his cravat was dyed onyx. A gold lion's head was pinned through its center. "It appears that I've entered this conversation at precisely the right moment."

Chapter Six

Lady Mary

MR. RYDER STIFFENED noticeably as the new man stepped into the club. He inclined his head. "Cooke."

The man named Cooke gave his coat to Bernard. "Mr. Ryder. The man trying to save the world with one small pen."

"I would rather try and fail than give up and succumb to the devil's temptation." Ryder nodded to me, his face carefully blank. "I'll leave you to your guest, Lady Mary. Have a nice day." And he strode out the door.

"I do hope I didn't chase him away," Cooke said sounding anything but sincere.

I examined the newcomer more fully. His face was lined, worn, the deep grooves in his cheeks and forehead speaking to a man who'd lived a hard life. The confident manner in which he held his body said that he'd risen to the challenge. He was handsome, almost devastatingly so, but his looks were not for the faint of heart. A woman would have to have a spine of steel to want to capture this man's attention.

He gave me and the club brief assessments. He had the air of a man who had no patience for trivialities, and my curiosity spiked wondering what had brought him to my doorstep.

"Mr. Ryder had been leaving in any case." I nodded reassuringly to Bernard, who was looking decidedly discomposed at having yet another man enter the club. Or perhaps it was this man in particular. "And you are?"

"Edric Cooke." He hooked his thumbs in his waistcoat pockets. "I have some business to discuss with you."

Bernard had gone still as a mouse when Mr. Cooke had said his name. My curiosity increased. I tapped my finger against my lips. "All right. Come to my office."

I led him through the club, our path the subject of more curious glances. There had been more men traipsing through The Minerva Club in the past week than there had been in the last six months.

Based on the appraising looks my new guest was receiving, the women didn't seem to mind.

I entered my office and went behind my desk. The tea service was still on the desk. "Tea? I can order a fresh pot."

"No, thank you." He lowered himself into my guest chair.

I sat across from him. "So, Mr. Cooke." I spread my hands. "The floor is yours."

He crossed one leg over the other and leaned back. "I've heard so much about your club, I'm glad to finally see it. It is…charming," he finally decided upon.

I inclined my head. It was charming, nothing like the tawdry picture painted by Mr. Ryder. Just because Lady Richford happened to get herself killed here didn't diminish that fact.

"It's unfortunate that it has come under attack in recent days." Cooke stared directly into my eyes, making my body hum with awareness. His eyes were those of a predator, and a powerful one at that. I wasn't one to normally watch my step, but I also wasn't one to run foolhardily into danger. And something told me this man was dangerous.

"We will survive," I said evenly. I always survived.

He dipped his chin. "I know something about attacks on one's business. I thought perhaps I could be of assistance?"

"And what is your business, Mr. Cooke?"

He lifted one shoulder. "I am fairly diversified. Entertainment, security services, deliveries. If there's a way to make money, I'll find it."

I sat back. It was rare for a man to speak to me about base profit endeavors, let alone sound proud about it. The *ton* acted as though business was uncouth to speak of, let alone engage in. And to converse with a woman about it was nigh on unheard of.

I found his frankness refreshing.

"What does a man of such varied interests think he can offer to me by way of aid?" I tilted my head. "And why would he want to?"

"For purely mercenary reasons, I can assure you," he said, the barest hint of Ireland in his voice. "Your club's reputation has taken a hit in recent days. Has membership declined?"

The day after the murder, the halls had been packed, but the curious onlookers had dwindled. I wouldn't know until the start of the new month whether members would pay their monthly dues. "We're doing fine."

"But you can always do better." Mr. Cooke leaned forward and rested his elbows on his knees. "It would be helpful if those articles in *The Times* were put to an end, yes? Perhaps a favorable opinion piece instead?"

I matched his pose, planting my elbows on my desk. "How would you accomplish such a task?"

"I have my ways."

"And what would you require in return for such a service?"

He pursed his lips. "Some guarantees. An agreement not to compete with my business and a percentage off the top."

My eyebrows slammed together. "You're starting a women's club?"

He exhaled heavily through his nose. "Let's not play games, Lady Mary. I've tolerated some of your side ventures because they have been on such a small scale. There is potential here, however. Potential I want a part of."

"What side ventures?"

He dipped his head and arched one dark eyebrow, giving me a knowing look. A look that only managed to irritate me because at the moment I wasn't in the know. I also wasn't in control, not of the conversation or the situation, and my irritation grew.

"How much of a cut do you take off the top for your members'… trades?" he asked. "Whatever profit you're making, I can double it."

My mind raced, trying to make his words make sense. I failed. "You said you don't like games, and I agree. Tell me plainly what you want."

"I want to help both of us maximize our profits." He gave me a smile, all teeth. "I can set you up with competitive vendors to supply your club and I can eliminate the morality committee as one of your obstacles."

A chill shivered down my spine. I feared the method he might use to eliminate said obstacle. And something warned me not to remain too long in this predator's cross-hairs. I stood. "Mr. Cooke, I fear we are speaking at cross purposes, but I can assure you I need no assistance to manage my club. And as to Mr. Ryder, I will handle him myself." I went to the wall and rang for a footman.

He slowly uncoiled, rising to his feet. His bulk suddenly made my office feel small and much too isolated. "Perhaps you should take some time to think this through. Refusing my services isn't a decision to be made lightly."

I was a fool. This was no simple man of business. Mr. Cooke was something else altogether.

"I don't make any decisions lightly." Bobby appeared at the doorway, his livery a welcome sight. "Bobby here will show you out."

With one last piercing look, Mr. Cooke swept from the room.

I sank into my chair, my knees uncomfortably wobbly. I didn't like not being in the know, and there were undercurrents to Mr. Cooke's conversation I most definitely did not understand.

My club was threatened, Mr. Cooke had implied something

disreputable was going on within these walls, and a woman was dead.

There was too much I didn't understand. I pressed my palms flat against the cool oak of my desk. And it was time to get savvy.

Chapter Seven

Frederick

FREDERICK WAS TEMPTED to remain in his position beneath the chestnut tree. Lady Mary's attempts to gain entry to White's were diverting, his amusement increasing in proportion to her rising aggravation. But as he also had a job to do, and as he also understood the frustration of being excluded from a place based on no more than a happenstance of birth, he stepped from the shade and climbed the steps of the gentlemen's club.

"Rollins, officer of the Bow Street magistrate." He handed the doorman his card. "Is Mr. Bannister within?"

"Of course he is." Lady Mary stabbed her walking stick into the ground, perilously close to the doorman's foot. "And as I've informed Mr. Blodgett here, he will want to see me. His family has asked for my assistance in discovering his mother's killer."

Frederick lifted his eyebrows. That seemed like an excessive bit of truth-stretching.

"And as I've informed the lady, only men can enter White's." Blodgett clasped his hands behind his back, his face a deep ruddy shade.

Lady Mary practically vibrated from indignation.

Frederick sighed. "There are exceptions to every rule." It would be easier this way. Let Lady Mary observe his interview rather than have her harangue him for all the details later. "I'm certain your members would understand the small breach in custom under these circumstances. After all, they are smart enough to understand that they wouldn't want White's or its members to come under the scrutiny of Bow Street."

Blodgett still hesitated.

"I do know the tax authorities have been interested in examining the finances of London's clubs after that fraudulent scheme Warwick's was caught out in last year." Frederick kept his expression even, the threat friendly. "I would hate to give them any cause to refocus their suspicions on clubs such as this one."

Blodgett blotted his forehead with a handkerchief. "Well, perhaps just this one time…."

Lady Mary wisely remained silent, but her smile was triumphant as the doorman showed them inside and quickly led them to a small room off the main hallway. Bookshelves lined the walls from floor to ceiling, and oil lamps were stationed on small tables beside each chair. A cigar lay in an ashtray on one of the tables, smoke slowly coiling up from its end. The room had been recently occupied, but was currently empty.

"I'll ask Mr. Bannister to see you here," Blodgett said, quietly closing the door behind them.

Lady Mary found a high-backed leather wingchair and settled herself, smoothing her skirts. "That was well done." She pushed her spectacles up her nose and gave him an appraising look. "You've surprised me."

She made it sound as though that didn't happen often. "I'm glad to have met your approval," he said dryly. He strolled around the room, reading some of the titles. The selection was better than his circulating library's. It confirmed what he'd always thought. Money equaled access: to information, to people of power, to leisure.

The door opened, and Lord and Lady Richford's son shambled in.

But money couldn't protect you from tragedy. Death came

for all.

Edgar Bannister was holding up well. His light-brown hair was neatly combed, the barrel knot in his cravat formed by a steady hand, though Bannister probably had a man to do all that. He dropped into a chair across from Lady Mary and gave them both an insolent look. "What did you want to talk to me about?"

"The root causes of the French Revolution." Lady Mary huffed. "What do you think we wish to speak with you about? Your mother's death, of course."

Bannister slouched in his seat. "What do I know of it?"

Frederick moved a chair so it sat to the right of Bannister and to the left of Lady Mary. He settled into it and leaned forward, resting his forearms on his thighs. "You might know more than you're aware of. Even the most seemingly innocuous detail could be of help."

Bannister shrugged. "Fine."

"As well as being a member of my club, your mother was involved in many charitable committees," Lady Mary began. "Can you tell us all the extra activities she was involved in?"

"Charitable committees." Bannister snorted. "Yes, she was all for feeding the poor, trying to raise money for London's orphanages. She loved to be seen doing good."

Frederick slid his notepad from his pocket. "It is fashionable to be on those public works committees," he said diplomatically.

Lady Mary seemed to have no talent for diplomacy. "You show little respect for your mother. Typically when someone dies, those close to her at least try to pretend they're upset."

"And why should I?" Bannister cracked the knuckles on his right hand. "Did she respect me? Wasn't she always speaking ill of me to my father? My mother was no saint."

Frederick tried to regain control of the interview. "Which is why we're speaking with you. Have you thought more of who might want to harm your mother?"

"The list is long." Bannister slid a case from his inside pocket and removed a cheroot. He picked up the smoking cigar and lit his cheroot from the hot end.

"And it includes you?" Lady Mary asked.

Frederick shot her an annoyed look. Her provoking remarks could insult Bannister into leaving.

Bannister remained silent.

"I've been told that you and your mother exchanged many cutting remarks." She patted the lace cap over her ivory hair. "That you were expecting some blunt from your father, which your mother put a stop to."

The charcoal in Frederick's hand almost snapped. He didn't know if he was more annoyed at her brash questions or the fact that he hadn't been privy to that information.

"It's no secret my mother kept a tight fist on my father's purse." Bannister's nostrils flared. "She was a greedy, petty woman. She said I didn't deserve it. *Me.* What did she ever do to deserve her wealth but spread her legs?"

Frederick had seen and heard much in his time at Bow Street, but even that managed to shock him. "There is a lady present," he reminded the younger man sternly. "Watch your language."

"I am a widow of a certain age," Lady Mary said dryly. "There isn't much about human nature I don't know about." She turned back to Bannister. "Including the disrespect of children, even though I had none of my own."

"What was there to respect? It wasn't only me my mother insulted." Bannister gripped the arms of his chair. "She insulted my father in the worst way a woman can. Do you think she joined your club to take tea with her friends? It was an easy answer to where she was going when she left the house. Even when that wasn't her intended destination."

"An affair?" Lady Mary pursed her lips. "With whom?"

Bannister looked toward the door. "I don't know. I don't care. But if you're looking for her killer, look in that direction. A man will only take such nonsense from a mistress for so long."

Frederick turned to a new page in his notebook. Bannister might not have intended it, but if he spoke the truth, he'd just given his father a motive for the murder, as well.

Once again, Lady Mary's thoughts were in line with his. "Did your father know?"

"No." Bannister dropped his chin in his palm. "He was oblivious, as usual."

"And now that your mother is gone?" Frederick cocked his head. "Will your father give you the money he'd earlier promised?"

Bannister's eyes briefly gleamed before returning to their sullen set. "Who knows? Who cares? I'm well taken care of either way."

Lady Mary gripped the handle of her walking stick, the veins in her hands showing faintly blue through her thin skin. "But Miss Lynton said—"

"Miss Lynton? Ellie?" Bannister jerked upright. "Has that mouse been telling tales? What does she know? Nothing."

The back of Frederick's neck heated. Just how well did Edgar Bannister know *Ellie*? And why hadn't she told him of Bannister's poor relationship with his mother when he'd questioned her?

Lady Mary patted her white lace cap. "She knows enough. You didn't deny that your mother put a stop to you getting money, and Miss Lynton is familiar with financial difficulties."

Bannister smirked. "Her father's windmill did dwindle to a nutshell. She lost several seasons of prime husband hunting when her family lost their money. Probably why no one wants her now, even if she is flush."

Frederick wished his notebook pages were larger. Or his handwriting was smaller. He was going through his book at an alarming rate. Wealthy or not, he found it difficult to believe that Miss Lynton didn't have lots of men vying for her attention. Not with her large, taffy-colored eyes and appealing curves.

"I'd heard," Lady Mary said carefully, "that the Lyntons had fallen on difficult times once more."

"The Lyntons? Rolled-up?" Bannister snorted. "Not again in this lifetime. When Mr. Lynton gained back his fortune, it was the only time I ever saw my mother feel regret. She'd given Mrs. Lynton the cut direct when they'd first lost their money, and she'd burned that bridge but good. When the Lyntons came back into society, they wanted nothing to do with Lady Richford." A sincere smile stretched across his face, making the man look happy for the first time since Frederick had met him.

A knock sounded on the door before it opened. A gangly man with a shock of red hair poked his head inside. "Are you done yet, Eddie? The rest of the lads are leaving for the theater."

Bannister popped to his feet. "I'm coming. I think I've said all I need to these two." And without even a by-your-leave, he trotted from the room.

"Well." Lady Mary arched her eyebrows. "Perhaps being childless isn't such a tragedy if they turn out like that. There was no love lost between him and his mother. He's just gone to the top of my list of suspects."

Frederick put away his notebook and stood. "No. It doesn't mean he killed her, however."

Lady Mary rose, as well. "It doesn't mean he didn't, either."

"How would he get into your club unobserved?" Frederick nodded as Blodgett flapped his hands at them, in a hurry to show them out. A man must have gained entry to The Minerva Club. He had a hard time envisioning a woman committing such a crime, or even having the strength to accomplish it. He was curious what Lady Mary's thoughts were on the holes in her club's security.

"I don't know. Yet." She shaded her eyes as they stepped outside, the door seeming to close unnaturally quickly behind them. "But if a man did sneak into my club, I will find out how."

Frederick gave her an appraising look. For a woman, Lady Mary was made of unusually stern stuff. Perhaps she would discover how a man got into her club. He hailed a hackney and waited for the carriage to pull in front of White's. Feeling benevolent, he offered, "I'm going to the Lyntons to question them. Do you want to come?"

Lady Mary nodded to her own carriage. The driver had hopped down to open the door. "No, I thank you. I have somewhere else to be."

Just as well. He saw her inside, and nodded as her carriage drew off. He had some very pointed questions to ask Miss Eleanor Lynton, and he didn't need Lady Mary there to run interference.

Chapter Eight

Eleanor

ELEANOR DECIDED TO make him wait. Mr. Rollins had been shown into their afternoon parlor, offered a beverage by the Lynton's ever proper footman, and then left to stare at his navel for all Eleanor cared while she went to consult with her mother.

"You don't have to speak with him," Eleanor insisted, pacing her mother's pale peach bedroom. Martha Lynton sat at her dressing table, brushing a bit of powder on her already pale face. "I can tell him you're not feeling well."

"But I feel fine." Her mother looked at her through the mirror, her eyes sad. "I am sorry, Eleanor. You don't deserve any of this."

Eleanor's heart pounded behind her breastbone. She knew her mother couldn't have hurt Lady Richford. Not her mother. Not the woman who had kissed her scraped knees, untangled the curls in her hair.

The woman of the past eight years, the one who'd become bitter and angry, however, the one who'd raged as her daughter had to go out to earn a living, who'd sat stony-eyed at her husband's funeral, well, Eleanor wasn't quite as certain about that woman. What did her mother mean she didn't deserve this? Didn't deserve a troubled parent whom Eleanor needed to care for, or didn't deserve a murderess for a mother?

"This Mr. Rollins is a tricky character." Eleanor grabbed her elbow. "You need to—"

"It will be fine." Her mother took one last look at the mirror, then rose. She gave Eleanor a wobbly smile. "I will tell the truth and all will be well."

"Not all the truth." She followed her to the top of the stairs. "He doesn't need to know *everything*." Didn't need to know her mother had brought a gun to the club planning on killing Lady Richford. Didn't need to know her mother had spent nearly the past decade hating the dead woman. There were some things that were common knowledge and he could learn elsewhere, but all the rest should remain private.

Eleanor took her mother's arm as they made their way down the steps and to the parlor. At the open door, she paused, sucked in a deep breath, wiped all worry from her expression, then entered.

"Mr. Rollins." She inclined her head as the man rose to his feet. "This is my mother, Mrs. Martha Lynton. Mother, Mr. Rollins."

Her mother settled herself on a rose damask settee, smoothing her skirts. "I understand you wish to ask me questions about this terrible business. You may proceed."

Eleanor's lips tilted up as she settled beside her. Her mother might be fragile, but she still had pluck.

Mr. Rollins sat across from them. His jacket fell open as he reached into an inside pocket for his notebook and lead. His dark waistcoat was as conservative as the rest of his clothes and pulled snugly against a flat abdomen and broad chest.

She snapped her gaze back to his face, ignoring the slight curl of heat that coiled in her belly. The devil could take many forms, even attractive ones.

"I understand you have been acquainted with the victim for many years," Mr. Rollins began. "Can you describe that relationship?"

"We had our first season together." Martha arched an eyebrow at Mr. Rollins. "I will not admit to how many years ago that was, but Lady Richford and I have been acquainted for some time."

"And you were friendly?"

Her mother swallowed. "For the most part. We've had some disagreements through the years."

"Regarding?" He looked at her mother expectantly.

"She…well, we just…."

Eleanor squeezed her mother's hand. "Shortly after my father discovered he'd lost his fortune in a bad investment, Lady Richford gave my mother the cut direct at a society function. It was petty, and cruel, and happened almost ten years ago. It is all forgotten about now."

"Especially as Lady Richford is dead." His eyes, a dark mossy green, she realized, held a hint of censure. He scribbled down a note. "Your daughter was at The Minerva Club at the time of the murder. Where were you?"

Both Eleanor and her mother hissed in a breath.

"Lady Mary and Bobby both saw me in the Tea Room when Lady Richford was killed," Eleanor burst out. Mr. Rollins might have stated only a fact, but his tone certainly insinuated her guilt.

"My daughter had nothing to do with this," her mother said in a wavering voice.

A lock of auburn hair fell over Mr. Rollins's brow. "But what about you? Again, where were you when Lady Richford was killed?"

Her mother pressed her fingers to her temple. "I was here." Her voice was faint, her face growing even paler. "In bed."

"Where you should be now." Eleanor gripped her mother's hand and stood, bringing her up to her feet. "You know you should rest when you have your headaches. I can answer any more of Mr. Rollins's questions." She shot the man a narrow look, daring him to object.

He quickly rose, his courtesy merely a formality as his tightened lips showed his displeasure. But no gentleman could object to an unwell woman seeking her chamber. "Of course. I can call again when you feel better, Mrs. Lynton."

Eleanor ushered her to the door, watching as her mother slowly ascended the stairs and disappeared down the hall. She spun around, clenching her hands. "My mother was here. Our servants can confirm that. Unless you have anything further to ask, please leave."

He settled himself back in the chair and picked up his cup of tea. "I'm not done with you, Miss Lynton. Please." He gestured to the settee. "Have a seat." Like it was his parlor they were sitting in, like he was lord of the bloody manor.

Gritting her teeth, Eleanor stalked back to the settee and sat, her spine ramrod straight. "Your questioning is bordering on abuse. The Lyntons are not without friends. If you persist in harassing us, we will have no choice but to complain to your superiors."

He swiped a drop of tea off his bottom lip with his thumb. "If you believe necessary questions are harassment, you must spend much of your life feeling persecuted. Of course, the alternative is that you balk at my questions not from a general objection, but because you fear me learning the answers to them."

As Eleanor had no response to that which wouldn't reflect poorly on her breeding, she settled on a steely-eyed glare. Even as her ire rose, she recognized she was being unreasonable. In her time in service as a lady's companion and later as a tutor, she'd learned that the deference the *ton* expected was irrational. Wealth and status didn't give a man or woman any more virtue than a common Cit. If the situation had been different, she could almost respect the Runner for questioning members of society so doggedly. He seemed an honest, reliable sort of a man, and for someone whose life had become a series of ground-shaking ordeals, that constancy could be very appealing.

But as it was her mother the Runner now challenged, her admiration was somewhat dimmed.

"How many servants do you have?"

She knotted her fingers together and rested them on her knees. "Seven. Cook, Mr. Grosse, our butler, three maids, a footman, and our coachman."

"And how long have they been with you?" He made another damnable note in his book.

"Almost all less than two years."

"Almost all? And the others?" He looked up, his green eyes glinting.

Eleanor's knuckles whitened. She cleared her throat. "Miss Olive, my mother's abigail, has been with us since I was young. But they are all very honest. They wouldn't lie."

But apparently she would. Deception wasn't in her nature, but she seemed to be taking to it quite easily. It wasn't only Miss Olive who had been with them for a long time. Cook, Mr. Grosse, and Ned Coachman had, too. And Eleanor knew just how loyal those servants were. She'd grown up with them all. When the hard times came, almost everyone had needed to be released. They'd barely been able to keep Miss Olive.

When Eleanor's father had recovered his fortune, he'd found the servants who had been like family and offered them a high price for their return. He'd wanted everything to go back to normal. Although technically everyone but Miss Olive had been a recent hire, the circumstances of the situation made her words a lie.

"How long since your father passed?" he asked.

Eleanor gritted her teeth. That fact was public knowledge. Mr. Rollins likely only asked it to unsettle her. "A year and two months."

He focused on her face as he asked his next question. "And what was done with his clothes?"

She knew he was gauging her reaction, yet she couldn't still her expression. She popped to her feet. "My mother did not use my father's cravat to strangle Lady Richford."

His rise to his feet was more languid. It seemed to take forever as he unfolded his body and rose to his full height, forcing her eyes to meet his. "So she used another man's cravat to do it?"

Heat crawled up her torso, clawing its way up her neck to her face. She was too angry to even form words. She grabbed an embroidered pillow from the settee and threw it at his head.

Since he too easily batted it away, she grasped another. Before she could get her throw off, he was there, looming in front of her, gripping her wrist, halting her motion.

"Let go of me." She pulled, but he held fast, his long fingers easily encircling her wrist. She pulled harder and only managed to yank herself against him.

The heat of his body crept behind her bodice and stays. He smelled earthy, masculine, and her anger only rose when she realized how appealing it was. "Unhand me."

"Not until you calm yourself." Mr. Rollins held her waist with his other hand, holding her steady. His hip pressed into her belly, and her muscles there tightened.

She inhaled sharply, his nearness disconcerting. He was infuriating. Dangerous. And if she was forced to admit it, just a little bit exciting. She'd avoided the advances of the well-muscled groom at the house she'd tutored in. Felt nothing when the son of the baroness she'd been a companion for had flirted shamelessly with her. She wasn't about to let a man turn her head now, not when the stakes were so high.

"I am calm," she bit out. "Release me."

He studied her, his scrutiny making her squirm. Finally, he stepped back, but not before removing the pillow from her hand and tossing it onto his chair. "Assaulting an officer of Bow Street wasn't a wise decision."

She huffed. "It was a pillow, not an assault. And you suspect my mother!" As far as she was concerned, people who went around suspecting mothers of horrific acts deserved having objects thrown at their heads.

He picked up his notepad and slid it away in his pocket. "Don't worry." He turned at the door, looking down his nose at her. "With your temper, I suspect you, as well."

❖

Chapter Nine

Lady Mary

AMELIA MASSEY WAS not at home when I called. I shoved down my irritation, along with my suspicion that she was, in fact, at home, just not receiving callers, more specifically, my call, and gave directions to my driver for our next stop. It was but ten minutes before Ernest leapt down from his perch and held open my door. "We're here, Lady Mary."

Lord Anglia was at home, and the alacrity with which he had me shown to his study did a little bit toward soothing my pride. "To what do I owe the pleasure, Lady Mary? I believe I haven't seen you since that little soiree your nephew and his wife held last season."

The Duke and Duchess of Montague had held a ball of over five hundred guests, but Anglia was correct as to that being the last time we'd spoken. He was a handsome man, in his third decade, but with the air of someone who had lived twice that long. He cultivated a mood of *ennui*, as though there was nothing under the sun that could possibly surprise him. He wore his buckskins a bit too tight, and his waistcoat was a shade too bright. He was a man who wanted the world's attention, but didn't want anyone to realize that he wanted it.

I settled myself in the chair across from him. "I wished to

speak with you about opinion pieces in *The Times*. I noticed you had written one in Tuesday's paper. You might have seen the one directed against my club right above it."

The same butler who had shown me in returned with a tea tray. The ends of his shockingly long white mustache curled onto his cheeks and quivered when he spoke. "Lemon or milk, milady?"

"Lemon, thank you." I waited for the cups to be distributed, the napkins to be laid across laps, and for the butler to leave the room. I peered at Lord Anglia over the rim of my cup. "So, did you see it?"

"I did." One edge of his mouth curled up. "Mr. Ryder seems to have set his cap at you, in the most unfortunate of ways. Though he's not the only one who thinks your club was a most distasteful venture."

"Heaven forbid that women have a place to congregate and seek relaxation in the same manner as men." The tartness of the lemon mirrored my mood. The very resistance against the idea proved the need for such an institution.

He raised one shoulder, looking bored once again. "What do you wish to know about opinion pieces?"

I placed my cup on the low table in front of me. In my irritation, I'd almost forgotten I had an ulterior motive. "Do you have to know the editor in order for your article to be published? Pay a certain amount?"

"No payment necessary." He crossed one trim leg over the other. "The paper only seeks increased circulation."

"So the more provoking the article, the more likely it is to be published?"

"Of course." He shifted, and a sunbeam caught the onyx stud pinned to his cravat. The pin stuck through the center of an embroidered *A*, the threads of the letter only a shade darker than the cream of the cloth. "Such is the nature of publishing."

Indeed. "So when you wrote your piece, did you embellish the facts in order to heighten the likelihood of publication?"

He snorted. "I'm an earl, a high-ranking member of Parliament. *The Times* will publish whatever I write."

"Even if it isn't true?" I'd reread Anglia's piece several times since Lady Richford's death. He never explicitly stated it, but he'd heavily implied that the lady used deviant sexual favors in order to control her husband. Even specifying that Lord Richford's *No* vote on a public funding bill to remodel and restore the Palace of Westminster was a direct result of a weekend spent at an isolated house in the country under Lady Richford's skilled tutelage.

Unless Anglia had spies in the Richford's homes, there was no way he could have known such information.

"What are you insinuating, Lady Mary?" He smirked. "That I would tell Canterbury tales in order to have my way?" He tutted. "I hope you don't start spreading stories about me. We do have libel laws in this country."

I stopped just short of rolling my eyes. The man could insinuate filthy things about Lady Richford. He'd be lucky if the Viscount of Richford didn't drag him before the courts. There was no way someone questioning his lies could be held accountable for libel. "You are correct. Truth is important. Which makes me wonder how you could know what went on in the Richford's bedroom. What was the basis for your accusations?"

"Have you met Lord Richford?" He arched a slim brow. "I knew merely by the viscount's manner that his wife had him by the boll—" He cleared his throat. "Held the reins in the marriage, let's just say." He cocked his head. "Why all the questions about the Richfords?"

I pushed my spectacles up the bridge of my nose. "Perhaps I want to know the limits of libel laws to know what possible courses of action I have against Mr. Ryder and his morality committee. I won't deny that since Lady Richford was killed in my club that my interest in her has been piqued. I've heard such varied things since her death. I would like to better understand her character."

"It isn't a difficult study to take." Anglia picked up a biscuit and took a bite, a few crumbs dusting his coat. "She was a woman who thought restraint didn't apply to her. A woman who thought only of her own pleasures without regard to others. A materialist. Altogether a wife unsuitable for a member of the House of Lords."

Even though Anglia was an odious man, his assessment wasn't far from my own. I had also observed the woman's selfish manner on more than one occasion. Lady Richford had sought enjoyment out of every moment, even when it came at the expense of others' feelings. "Then you believe the rumors of her infidelity?"

Anglia paused before dabbing his mouth with his napkin. "I hadn't heard that particular rumor, but it would hardly be surprising. Lady Richford considered herself a modern woman. Believing in the free love movement would be in keeping with that." He leveled me with an impertinent stare. "I'm certain Lady Richford isn't the only member of your club who would agree with her sentiment. Part of the allure of your club is for ladies to have a place to go out from under the watchful eyes of their husbands."

My spine straightened. "Are you saying my members use my club for assignations? I can assure you that I would know if men were being secreted in for any purpose, much less an illicit one." The nerve. Unlike some gentlemen's clubs, I have no guest chambers for overnight stays. Where would such liaisons occur? On a divan in full view of the other members drinking tea or playing faro?

"So you say." He stood. "But if you are to continue your insinuations—"

"Insinuations? I made none."

He gave me a hard smile. "Don't insult my intelligence. It was most unfortunate that Lady Richford got herself killed the day my opinion piece was printed." His face tightened. "I might have to put up with a visit from Bow Street, but I don't have to tolerate your gauche questions."

I sniffed. I was the daughter of an earl. The aunt to a bloody duke. I was never gauche. And if Anglia had noticed that I might have another reason for my inquiries, a proper, civic-minded reason, well, it was tasteless *of him* to point it out.

"Instead of poking around in other people's business, you'd best be more mindful of what goes on inside your own walls." He indicated the door. "You might find that you have more opponents than just Mr. Ryder."

Because he so clearly desired our interview to be over, I settled myself more firmly into the chair. "Is that a threat, my lord? I hardly think the goings-on of one club would be of interest to Parliamentarians."

"You have no idea how determined, and petty, some of my colleagues can be." He jabbed his hand toward the door and the butler who now stood in the threshold. "I have an appointment shortly. I thank you for your visit."

Short of tying myself to the chair, I could think of no excuse to extend my call. I stood and gave him a short curtsy. "Thank you for your time." I met the butler at the door and paused. "One last question. Now that Lady Richford is dead, do you think her husband will be more in line with your way of thinking when it comes to how he votes?"

"As my piece said, the viscount is a very persuadable man." He smoothed his hand down his cravat, his customary smirk back in place. "Without his wife whispering nonsense in his ear, I would bet he can be made to see reason."

I nodded and took my leave. And with the viscount in a distraught state after the death of his wife, I would bet the chances of Anglia's success would be even higher.

Which gave the earl a very good motive for murder.

Chapter Ten

Lady Mary

Amelia Massey was still not at home, at least according to her tight-lipped doorman. He had no knowledge as to her whereabouts or the time of her expected return.

With an irritated sniff, I gave my driver the direction to my next quarry. The information requested on the application to join The Minerva Club was most helpful when it came to a murder investigation.

Miss Lydia Abbott was also not at home, But the sour-faced woman who owned the lodging house where Miss Abbott rented a room was much more helpful. At this time in the afternoon, Miss Abbott could usually be found at Hyde Park, riding.

It didn't take me long to find her. Lydia Abbott was one of the few women seated on the back of a horse instead of enjoying the park in a conveyance, and the only woman riding astride. Tan trousers peeked out beneath her Navy blue riding habit, with a man's top hot placed rakishly atop her raven curls. She was what I considered a young woman, though no longer in her first flush, her face and body composed of angles rather than curves. Her eyes were dark, and tilted up at the edges, giving her a slightly exotic appearance.

My carriage being too large for the crowded paths, I hurried toward the woman on foot, ignoring any greetings tossed my way. "Ahoy, there." I waved at her as she galloped past me on the lawn. "Miss Abbott!"

She slowed her horse and pulled up next to a life-sized bronze statue of a stag.

I double-backed and bustled up to her before she could take off again. "Miss Abbott," I said again, only slightly out of breath. "How do you do?"

"Lady Mary?" Miss Abbott used her crop to swat at a fly. "What a surprise to see you here."

I shaded my eyes as I looked up at her. "Indeed, but the fine weather has lured even me out of doors. I wanted to give you my condolences on the death of Lady Richford. I understand that you and she were particular friends."

Miss Abbott pressed her lips tight, blinking. She cleared her throat. "Thank you. Her death is a great loss."

The back of my neck started to ache. "Yes, and so shocking, too. As it happened in my club, the authorities have pressed me for answers to several questions. I was hoping you might be able to assist me with some of them."

Her horse shifted, tossing his head. Tugging off one glove, she stroked its neck and spoke to it quietly before turning back to me. "I don't see how I can help. And besides, I've already spoken with that Runner. A Mr. Rollins, I believe."

My muscles tensed. Interesting. Mr. Rollins had failed to mention that interview. But no matter. "Sometimes a different perspective is necessary." I rubbed the crick in my neck. "When was the last time you saw Lady Richford?"

"Earlier that day. I took tea at her house." Miss Abbott looked down at her hands, gripping the reins. "She was so happy. I just can't believe...." Sunlight glinted off a slender wrought gold band on the middle finger of the woman's right hand, the flash catching me right in the eye.

I frowned. I was tired of the woman towering above me. I pointed at a young man walking nearby who seemed robust enough. "Excuse me, young man. Can I get an assist?" I patted the back of the stag statue.

"Uh." The man stepped forward and scratched his chin. "Assist with what exactly?"

"Putting me atop the beast." I tapped my walking stick against the stag's back, a dull clank sounding. "Surely, you're strong enough to lift me."

Well, that comment got him moving. His hands were around my waist and I was seated on the bronze statue within seconds, the sun-blasted metal warming my behind. I adjusted my seat. "Thank you, young man." I turned to Miss Abbott. She was still higher than me, but at least my neck no longer ached.

"Now," I said, "what can you tell me about any troubles your friend was having? Did she have any enemies that you know of? Problems that were worrying her?"

Miss Abbott stopped gawking at my new chair long enough to frown. "Of course not. What type of woman do you think she was to have enemies?"

I wrapped my gloved hand around the stag's antler and tried not to raise my eyes heavenward. Not many people, male or female, got through this life without getting on someone's bad side. It was naïve to think good people didn't have enemies. Sometimes it was the best people who were most hated.

"So she hadn't fought with anyone recently?" I prodded. "Not even a minor argument?"

Miss Abbott tugged on the cuff of her riding jacket. "Well, everyone has arguments. I know she and Lord Richford had several disagreements, usually about that son of theirs. But much as I dislike Lord Richford, I hardly think family squabbles would lead to...." She trailed off, as though the word 'murder' was too distasteful to even say.

I wasn't used to mincing my words, but this seemed a sound occasion for delicacy. "I had heard," I began gently, "that relations between Lord and Lady Richford were strained. That perhaps Lady Richford had sought companionship from another man."

Miss Abbott huffed. "That hardly seems likely. Sue found relations with her husband demeaning enough; she wouldn't seek out another man to lie with."

I considered that. Lady Richford and Miss Abbott had been close friends, but even so, it wasn't likely that a woman would confess her infidelity.

Though confession was appealing at times. I should know. A lick of nausea rolled through my stomach.

My glum musings were interrupted by hoots of laughter. A group of fine, young dandies were pointing at me atop the stag and laughing, while the women on their arms hid smiles behind their parasols.

I ignored them. The young could never truly appreciate the value of comfort.

But the commotion sent Miss Abbott's nervous horse to stamping in place. It made a couple of half-hearted attempts at bucking, but slender as Miss Abbott's arms were, she seemed easily able to control the beast with a few sharp tugs on the reins.

When the animal was once more still, I asked, "Do you know what your friend was doing at my club that night? Why she would have stayed past closing?" It was uncharitable of me, but I wished Lady Richford could have been killed somewhere else.

"No." Her horse stamped his foot, and Miss Abbott petted his tawny neck. "I didn't know she was intending to go to The Minerva Club that night. I'd thought she was attending a burletta at Cogburn's Theatre." She smirked as she nodded to a passing equestrian. "She doted on her son, despite his lavish spending and ill humors."

I sensed she was as impatient to leave as her horse was. My next question was perhaps too direct. "Where were you that night?"

Miss Abbott didn't seem offended by the question though she must have understood the implication. "I was attending a salon at Oswald Poole's house on Wells Street. Godwin spoke, mainly about his late wife Wollstonecraft. It was quite stimulating." She waved at another rider, rising in her saddle.

"And the red ribbon found on the stage near Lady Richford?" From the description from the constable it hadn't been that near the victim, but Miss Abbott didn't know that. "It was yours, wasn't it?"

"Yes." Her jaw tightened. "Again, as I told that Runner, I don't recall losing it, but I also don't remember seeing it after I led that discussion group. It must have fallen off then."

I nodded. "So you can't think of anyone who would wish to harm your friend?"

Miss Abbott slid her hand back into her glove with a tug. "She must have been in the wrong place at the wrong time. The only people she had conflict with were her son and husband, and they wouldn't have done something so dreadful. Now if you'll excuse me, my horse has more energy he needs to run off." And with a tip of her hat, she was gone. She quickly brought her mount up to a gallop, her hair coming loose from its low knot and streaming out behind her.

I watched her path. She was a fine horsewoman. Her back was flat, her thighs absorbing any impact. She looked like an untamed thing, and I felt a moment of envy. I thought about the conversation. I hadn't learned much. In fact, my first attempts at investigation were quite disappointing. All I had were questions, no answers.

I looked at the ground several feet below me. I also had no answer as to how to descend from the statue without injury either to my person or my pride. I had enjoyed not having Miss Abbott looking down at me, but I hadn't thought ahead to this moment.

If something caught my fancy, I tended to act quickly, without much consideration as to the pros and cons. Rash, some called me. Eccentric, others. My husband used to call my impetuousness my 'spirit of adventure.' I smiled at the memory. But I'd always been able to figure a way out of any troubles that came from my actions.

This time would be no different.
I settled in to wait for the next robust young man to pass by.

Chapter Eleven

Frederick

"WHAT AM I doing at this play?" Frederick looked around the Cogburn Theatre. It was filled with a hodgepodge of London, from working class men and women to tradesmen and professionals with maybe the occasional toff or two thrown in for good measure. It was the sort of place he would attend, if he liked theatrical productions, but not the sort of theatre an unattended woman of Lady Mary's stature should. "And do you not have an abigail to accompany you?"

The woman in question gave the man seated on the other side of her a solid jab with her elbow when he tried to take over the armrest. She turned back to Frederick. "Three things. First, this is a burletta, not a play. This is a non-patent theatre and isn't licensed for performing plays. Second, my maid Jane doesn't like going out after dark. She's not overly fond of daytime excursions, either. Her bones ache." She gave him a withering look. "And I'm too old to care about keeping up appearances."

Frederick could hardly argue with that. With everything he'd learned about Lady Mary, her reputation would hardly be affected from attending a *burletta* alone. "And the third thing?"

"Hmm?" She frowned at the man seated in front of her. He was being abominably rude keeping his top hat on inside. "Oh, yes. Third, I already told you why we're here. According to Miss Abbott, Lady Richford had plans to come here the night she died." Lady Mary picked up her walking stick, a sleek black one tonight, that had what looked like a small, curving tusk at the top instead of a knob. With the precision of an expert billiards player, she took aim and poked the hat in front of her. It flew off the man's head and spiraled down several rows. "Oh, how clumsy of me," she said when the man turned, eyes bulging. "I do hope you'll be able to retrieve it after the show."

When the man looked like he might cross words with Lady Mary, Frederick leaned forward and clapped his hand on his shoulder. "It's not worth it." He squeezed his fingers, feeling the collarbone shift slightly, hoping to convey just how little Frederick wished for any further engagement.

The man took the hint, nodded quickly, and turned back to face front, jerking his shoulder from Frederick's grasp.

Frederick sat back. "I don't see the relevance. Even if Lady Richford had attended, I can just as easily account for her movements with lead and paper. I don't need to follow in her footsteps."

Lady Mary peered at him over her spectacles. "There was something in Miss Abbott's voice when she mentioned it. Something significant. And *I* am sharing what information I get with *you*."

Did he detect a note of censure in her voice? Sighing, he faced front. Lady Mary had provided the ticket. He was out nothing but several hours from his evening. He eyed the pamphlet an usher had shoved into his hand as they'd made their way to their seats. *The Country Wife* – a modern retelling. Scenes would be interspersed with comedic skits from some bloke named Gervis, with a special aria performed by Lucia Amato.

Perhaps the performance would be entertaining.

When the curtain rose, however, his hopes were dashed. The acting was overly melodramatic, the *modern* twists trite and reductive. The comedy fell flat and Lucia was sorely off-key. The play wasn't even acted out in whole. Only about half the scenes were portrayed, and not even in chronological order. He flipped open the lid of his pocket watch and wondered how soon he could make his escape.

Lady Mary applied her pointy elbow to his side. "Pay attention," she whispered.

"Why? Is there going to be an examination later?"

The glare she gave him was probably well earned. "No, but I think I understand why Miss Abbott was smirking. Look at Alithea." She handed him a pair of opera glasses from her reticule and pointed.

He directed the glasses to the left side of the stage. Alithea was in the middle of a deep swoon, her acting as overwrought as everyone else's. He lowered the glasses and shrugged.

"That is the reason Lady Richford was to attend." Lady Mary pursed her lips. "She wanted to see her son perform."

Her son? Frederick examined the stage once more but didn't see Edgar Bannister. "Where?"

She pointed again, back at Alithea.

"What?" His raised voice earned a disapproving look from the woman in front of him. "That woman there?" he asked in a lower tone.

"He is quite skilled, at least in appearing as a woman." Lady Mary tapped her thumb against her lips. "His acting still needs improving."

Frederick looked through the glasses once more, this time noticing the shoulders were a bit broader than the typical woman's, the hands and feet too large. He lowered the glasses, tipping his head to the side. It was quite common for men to perform female parts, but he'd never seen it so skillfully done. Mr. Bannister had a talent for it.

Like mother, like son, he supposed.

Lady Mary stood. "Let's go."

Frederick was happy to acquiesce. When they reached her carriage, he held the door for her. "It would be easier for a man to roam your club if he were disguised as a woman."

"My thought exactly." Lady Mary took his proffered hand and climbed into the carriage. "Will you return to the club with me? I believe we have more to discuss."

As he had no other plans for the evening, he joined her in the coach. He checked his watch again. Eight thirty-four. "The performance ends around ten in the evening." At least according to that pamphlet. "Lady Richford wasn't killed until after midnight. There would have been plenty of time for Bannister to get to The Minerva Club to do it."

Lady Mary sat back, her chin dropping onto her clasped hands. "Yes."

"You don't like that theory?"

She stared out the carriage window. "A murder is awful regardless, but a child killing his parent? It's unnatural."

Frederick had been with the Runners too long to feel surprise over any act. "Many things are unnatural, yet they happen just the same."

She didn't respond to that. They drove to her club in silence, each pondering their own thoughts. The doorman took their overcoats, greeting Lady Mary cheerfully.

"Good evening, Bernard." Lady Mary shook out her skirts. "You were on the door the night Lady Richford died until we closed, is that right?"

The man nodded, his jowls jiggling. "I left twenty minutes to midnight, milady."

She nodded. "I know neither you nor the other workers saw any men in the club, but did you notice anything at all strange? An unusually tall woman, perhaps?"

He slowly shook his head. "No, milady. Nothing that caught my attention." He hesitated. "But I think you would want to know that you're not the only one asking questions tonight. Miss Lynton has been here several hours talking to the other members about that night."

Frederick ground his jaw. What was that woman up to? "Do

you know where she is now?"

Bernard blinked at his gruff tone. "The Tea Room, I believe."

Frederick nodded, then turned on his heel to find Miss Lynton. At the very least she was interfering with his investigation. At worst, she was attempting to muddle it for her own nefarious purposes.

Lady Mary maintained a surprisingly brisk pace in order to keep up with him. "She has been concerned about her mother."

"Yes." They reached the open double doors of the room. Miss Lynton was indeed within, seated with two matrons, each nursing a glass of amber-colored liquid.

She wore a lavender gown fitted at the bosom, and it irritated Frederick that he noticed just how fine a bosom it was. But even murderers could have fine figures, he thought dourly. He circled until he was behind her seat. She didn't notice his approach, so engrossed in her conversation, and that only increased his irritation. A woman needed to be more aware of her surroundings.

Unless she was accustomed to being the predator and not the prey. Unless she knew she had nothing to fear from the person who'd committed murder in this club.

Frederick cleared his throat. The women who sat across from Miss Lynton looked at him, curiosity flickering across their faces.

Miss Lynton flicked her fingers at him, not turning. "We don't need new drinks yet."

"That's good," he said, planting his hands on his hips, "because you're not getting one."

The start she gave was gratifying, and went a little way to improving his mood. "Mr. Rollins. Lady Mary." She nodded to the woman at his side. "How nice to see you."

She wasn't a good liar, a fact that should speak to her character. She looked anything but pleased to see them.

He turned his professional smile on the other women. He remembered their faces from their interviews with him, but not their names. "If you will excuse us, ladies. Miss Lynton and I have some business to discuss."

That only stoked their interest higher. They gave Miss Lynton a new, inspecting look. "Of course," one of them said. "Anything to help a Bow Street Runner."

Frederick didn't bother to correct them about his title. He stepped to the side of the chair, grasped Miss Lynton's elbow, and helped her rise. "May we use your office?" he asked Lady Mary.

"Of course." She turned and started walking. Over her shoulder, she said, "I was just heading there myself."

Stifling a sigh, he and Miss Lynton followed. Miss Lynton gave gentle, discreet tugs to her elbow, but he didn't relinquish it. The woman seemed like just the type to pull a scarper, and he didn't relish the idea of chasing her through The Minerva Club.

"What is it you wished to speak to me about?" she asked as soon as the door to Lady Mary's office had shut, enclosing the three inside.

Frederick guided her to one of the guest chairs. He wasn't quick enough to acquire Lady Mary's desk chair, the woman herself sliding into it with surprising speed, so he took the other guest chair and positioned it at the side of the desk, as he had when he'd conducted his interviews.

He wasted no time getting to the point. "Why are you questioning the members of this club?"

She lifted her chin. "I am eager to see a resolution to this matter. And as your suspicions are obviously pointed in an absurd direction, it's clear I need to look into it myself."

"So now there's three of us." Lady Mary drummed her fingers on the desk. "We'll soon be tripping over each other."

"We already are," he snapped. He turned his frown on Miss Lynton. "You're investigating because you're worried your mother is guilty. You wish to implicate someone else to keep her from going to prison."

"My mother didn't do this," she said hotly, her knuckles going white on the armrests of her chair. "If I have to discover who the true killer is in order to protect her, I will."

"A noble sentiment." Lady Mary steepled her fingers.

"She didn't do this," Miss Lynton repeated, her gaze beseeching Lady Mary.

Frederick's chest tightened. The woman's big, brown eyes pleaded to be believed. Her concern for her mother seemed real. In a different situation, he would have felt sympathy for her.

"You don't have to convince me, girl," Lady Mary said. "I believe you. I've known your mother too long." She lowered her head and studied Miss Lynton. "It's you whom I'm unsure of."

Miss Lynton stilled. "You suspect me?"

Lady Mary arched a white eyebrow. "Your family isn't having financial problems. You lied to me, and you wanted your mother removed from the club. Was it because you knew she and Lady Richford were at odds? You were worried about what might happen? How far would you go to protect your mother, my dear?"

Frederick sat back. Lady Mary was doing a surprisingly decent job of questioning his suspect. He felt no need to intervene, as yet.

"But..." Miss Lynton blinked. "You saw me. In the Tea Room. We found her body together."

"You came in a couple minutes after midnight." Lady Mary sniffed. "I know because I checked the clock when Bobby wasn't around to top up my drink. It wouldn't have given you much time, but it is possible."

A red stain flushed across Miss Lynton's cheeks. She stared at a point between Lady Mary and him. "Yes, well, you see, the truth is, Bobby and I were delayed for the same reason." She delicately cleared her throat. "We were together, you see."

Silence followed that pronouncement. After a moment, Lady Mary pushed her chair back and rang the servants' bell. As fortune would have it, Bobby himself knocked on the door to answer the summons.

Lady Mary laced her fingers together on the desk and leaned forward. "Bobby, you told me that on the night of the murder, you left your restocking of the bar to check that all the windows of the club were locked before rejoining me at twelve oh eight."

He looked at the three occupants of the room and rubbed the back of his neck. "Well, I don't rightly remember the exact minute when I returned, but yes."

"Miss Lynton has just stated that she was with you from…?"

Miss Lynton's voice was low. "We were together for about fifteen minutes before we joined you in the Tea Room."

Frederick forced his fist to unclench. This was good information gathering. He might finally be getting somewhere in the investigation. Anger was an inappropriate emotion.

"Is it true?" Lady Mary asked.

"Lud, I didn't want to hurt her reputation none, but yes, milady." Bobby rubbed his palms on his trousers. "She wanted me to come to you with a story, something about her mother causing trouble, and she…." He shrugged, a small smile curling his lips. "Well, she asked me *very* nicely."

Frederick's hand was fisted once more, and he felt the inexplicable urge to plant it right in the smug bastard's face. He didn't like men who preyed on scared and vulnerable women.

"And you were together for about fifteen minutes, as she said?" Lady Mary's voice was sharp.

"Yes milady. Timothy almost caught us in the Greek Room when he was making his rounds, making sure everyone was gone." Bobby shifted his weight. "What she was offering was sweet, but I had to get back to work." He turned a pleading look on Lady Mary. "I take my duties seriously, you know."

"Yes, Bobby. You may go." The sound of the door closing behind him was loud in the ensuing silence.

Lady Mary sniffed. "You used my club for your seduction? Truly?"

Miss Lynton slumped in her chair. "Nothing of import happened. It was a failed seduction." Her blush deepened. "He didn't want to risk his employment, not even for…." She chewed on her bottom lip. "Are you angry?"

"I am, but not at you." Lady Mary pressed her palms to the desk and stood. "I should have put together the connection of your arrivals happening within a minute of each other. That was sloppy on my part." She began pacing. "It appears we all have an interest in finding Lady Richford's killer."

Frederick dragged his gaze away from Miss Lynton's rounded shoulders. "Other parties may be interested, but only I have the authority to look into the matter."

"You're investigating because it's your job and you get paid," Lady Mary said archly. "Miss Lynton and I want to uncover the truth because the matter is near to our hearts. I think our motives are superior to yours."

Miss Lynton nodded, slowly sitting up straight. "That's right. The outcome of this investigation won't affect you, Mr. Rollins, but it has the capacity to hurt us deeply."

"Correct." Lady Mary stopped at the end of her desk and stared at them. She took a deep breath. "And I have a proposal. One some of us won't like."

"And that is?" Frederick's body tensed slightly, as though preparing for a fight.

"That we should work together." Lady Mary nodded decisively. "The three of us will discover who killed Lady Richford."

Chapter Twelve

Eleanor

ELEANOR SUCKED IN a breath. The proposition was outlandish. She glanced at Mr. Rollins. Working with that self-righteous prig would most likely be impossible. But whatever she thought about it obviously didn't compare to how absurd the Runner thought the idea. His face was the very expression of horror.

Lady Mary continued. "That means sharing information with the others." She gave Mr. Rollins a pointed look. "Discussing our theories together."

Mr. Rollins jumped to his feet. "That is impossible. I am an agent—"

"For the magistrates of Bow Street, yes, yes, we know." Lady Mary flapped her hand at him dismissively, and Eleanor fell a little bit in love with the woman. "And we are two women of society. We have access to places you do not. And people will talk to us more freely than they would with you."

Mr. Rollins began to pace, batting the frond of a fern from his face when he passed underneath it. "People will speak with me or face a writ for obstruction of justice."

"As terrifying as that prospect may be to some," Lady Mary said dryly, "those with money and connections have no such fear. In a case such as this, you need someone on the inside. We can help."

He stopped and crossed his arms over his chest, the fabric pulling tight around his biceps. "You have a nephew who is part owner of an inquiry agency. The Bond Agency for Discreet Inquiries, I believe it is called. If you don't trust Bow Street to handle this investigation, why aren't you asking your nephew for help?"

Eleanor had wondered that, too. It had been quite a sensation when five noblemen, chief amongst them the Duke of Montague, Lady Mary's nephew, had opened the detective agency. If it wasn't for the wealth and political power of the five friends, chances were they would have been shunned from polite society for engaging in such a trade. They did hire investigators to work the cases and were nominally only investors in the enterprise, but there were rumors that the noblemen dabbled in an investigation or two.

Lady Mary grimaced. "The boys would help, no doubt, but they are all busy men. They all have their own wives and families to look after now. And this, well, this happened at my club. My business. I'm responsible, and I don't want to merely hand the task off to someone else. Besides," she said, sniffing, "who would hire an inquiry agency when there's already a Runner on the case?"

"An officer of the Bow Street magistrates." Rollins rubbed the back of his neck.

Eleanor waited for his next objection, certain Lady Mary would be able to aptly counter whatever it was. To her surprise, Mr. Rollins halted by the window, his black jacket melting into the inky darkness framed behind him.

He sighed, his broad shoulders rounding. "You may be right. My usual cases don't bring me into high society and insiders would be helpful. However, it would be unconscionable for me to involve women in this matter."

"My mother is a suspect." Eleanor pressed her hands into her thighs. "The reputation of Lady Mary's club is suffering. We are involved whether you wish it or not."

Lady Mary nodded. "I fear you misapprehend me, Mr. Rollins. I am not asking your permission. I, and I assume Miss Lynton, will continue asking questions whether you agree or not. I am only suggesting that it would be to everyone's benefit to work together."

Mr. Rollins shoved an aloe plant to the side and plopped down on the wide window sill. "I can't convince you otherwise?"

"Certainly not." Eleanor leaped to her feet and stood next to Lady Mary. She had been feeling directionless these past days, knowing she needed to help her mother but lacking in the skills necessary to conduct an investigation herself. Forming a partnership seemed the perfect solution. Yes, it would mean working with the ninny from Bow Street, but even that would give her the opportunity to convince him of her mother's innocence.

He stretched out his long legs and hooked his thumbs in his waistcoat pockets. After a moment, he sighed. "Then I concede defeat. I am not wholly unaccustomed to working with others." He gave them an assessing look. "I guess you will have to do."

Eleanor and Lady Mary shared a look of their own.

"How gracious," Lady Mary said. She went back behind the desk and retook her seat. "Now, since we are partners—"

"Working together," Mr. Rollins corrected.

"—then perhaps you would tell us how it was that Lord Richford came to call upon you to investigate, Mr. Rollins." The older woman leaned back and steepled her fingers. "It did not escape my notice that he requested your assistance from Bow Street specifically."

Mr. Rollins stared at the hanging fern for a moment before nodding. "You correctly surmise I was acquainted with the family. I had a previous encounter with Lady Richford." He scraped his palm across his jaw. "I have kept quiet some information because it doesn't seem relevant to this investigation and, if released, would only hurt the family. I trust you will honor that discretion."

Eleanor nodded.

Lady Mary inclined her head.

Though Mr. Rollins didn't look completely satisfied, he continued. "I met the woman nigh on three years now, when I was a member of the Bow Street Foot Patrol. It was late at night, and a pickpocket attempted to rob Lady Richford. A small scuffle ensued, and I intervened." He flicked his finger at the tip of the aloe plant, the thick leaf quivering.

"And she and her husband were grateful enough for that intervention for the viscount to remember your name years later?" Eleanor cocked her head. That hardly seemed likely.

Mr. Rollins narrowed his eyes. "The story is not yet finished. And the earl wasn't with her when the theft attempt occurred."

"Ah." Lady Mary pursed her lips. "She *was* having relationships with other men then."

"No." Rollins poked at the aloe again, seemingly fascinated with the small spikes that ran along the succulent's leaf. "At least, not to my knowledge. The lady was alone that night."

Eleanor stomped forward and rescued the plant from his prodding. She held the pot to her abdomen. "You mean to say that a viscountess was out roaming the streets of London unattended at night? That would be madness." And madness was a quality she feared she was becoming all too familiar with lately.

Mr. Rollins cleared his throat. "It wasn't as dangerous as you might suppose. Lady Richford was dressed as a man. And a fairly convincing one, too, if one didn't look too closely."

Lady Mary must have been as shocked as Eleanor, for neither woman spoke for some moments. Finally, the older woman said, "Was she in a play like her son, and performing a male's role?"

"She was not." Mr. Rollins crossed his ankles. "She said she liked the freedom pretending to be a man gave her, the ability to travel without an escort. When I took her home, her husband was clearly surprised at her activities, but didn't seem overly shocked that his wife would do such a thing, if that makes sense."

"He knows what her temperament makes her capable of, even if not the exact form of her actions." Lady Mary nodded. "Well. That changes matters. Could the cravat that she was strangled with have been her own?" She waved her hand and dismissed that almost instantly. "She was dressed in a gown when we found her. If she was still dressing as a man, it wasn't on that night."

Eleanor leaned back against the desk. She absently stroked one of the succulent's fat leaves. "I wonder what it would be like to walk about as a man."

"Keep wondering." Mr. Rollins glowered. "Even dressed as a man, it isn't safe. If some scoundrel had looked closely enough, Lady Richford could have been in real trouble."

"I'd say she found enough trouble wearing a gown, as well." But his point was well made. It wasn't just raiment that made a man. There was increased height, generally, strength, and the body—

"A man's jacket hid…?" Eleanor blushed, gesturing to her bosom.

Mr. Rollins's lips twitched. "I believe the lady wore a wrap of some sort, to minimize her curves."

"Ingenious." Lady Mary stared at the ceiling. "And so the Richfords became indebted to you for your discretion, and when trouble found them again, the viscount called you."

Mr. Rollins drew his shoulders back. "Yes."

"And how much do you wish to remain in Lord Richford's favor?" Lady Mary asked.

"I feel as though you are insinuating something." Rollins narrowed his eyes. "Ask what you want directly, please."

Lady Mary dropped her head to give him a frank stare. "The Home Office gives Bow Street some funds each year, but you are essentially hired by the victim's family. You will receive the bulk of your fee from Richford. In consequence of that, are you considering Lady Richford's family as potential suspects? If the evidence leads to the husband or son, will you have him arrested or will you conceal his guilt?"

The pointed questions weren't even directed at her, but Eleanor still swallowed. The silence in the room grew uncomfortable. She hugged the plant closer and waited for the Runner's answer.

Mr. Rollins slowly unfolded, rising to his feet. "I didn't take payment from Lord Richford when he offered it to me for my discretion on Lady Richford's eccentricity. I followed my conscience and my duty. Even though the viscount has retained me now, I will still follow my conscience, and follow the facts no matter where they lead."

Eleanor pursed her lips. Mr. Rollins was still too arrogant and irritating for her liking, but she was forced to admit he might have some good qualities, too. She had learned what it was to no longer have the protections of wealth and social standing. Without them, the morals of the men she encountered became that much more important. She might not like Mr. Rollins, but he was earning her respect.

A knock sounded at the door. "Enter," Lady Mary called.

Bobby poked his head inside. "Milady, the liquor distributor is here. He says there's a problem with your latest order."

Lady Mary blew out a breath. "Send him back, please." She opened her desk drawer and pulled out a file. "I have to deal with this. Let me know if either of you need any assistance from me on this matter. Perhaps we should meet up again in a couple of days?"

Both Eleanor and Mr. Rollins nodded and turned to leave. Eleanor passed by Bobby, heat infusing her face at his smirk, as she hurried from the room.

Mr. Rollins took her arm, pulling her aside in the hallway for the footman to pass. He waited until Bobby's back disappeared around a bend. "Show me where you and Bobby had your *rendezvous*."

"Why?" She shook her arm free, tipping up her chin. Even though she felt shame for her actions, she wasn't going to let Mr. Rollins see it.

"I need to know where everyone was at the time of the murder. Were you in a position to see or hear anything, even if you didn't notice it at the time? Was Bobby?"

Eleanor frowned. "I saw nothing."

"Show me in any case." There was a steely determination in his voice, and Eleanor knew she couldn't avoid this without a fight, one she would probably lose.

"Fine," she said crossly. She led him down one hall and up another, passing Bobby and the man who must be the liquor distributor. She bent and picked up an arrow that had been left on the ground. She placed it on a side table then stumbled over the bow that peeked out from beneath the same table. She gasped as the floor came rushing up to meet her.

A strong arm banded around her middle, stopping her fall and pulling her upright. "Why are there bows and arrows lying about on the floor?" Mr. Rollins asked. His tone was scornful, whether over the general untidiness of the club or over the fact that women would be engaged in such a sport, Eleanor didn't know. Either way, it put her back up.

"It was only one bow and one arrow." She turned in his arm, her chest brushing against his. The tips of her breasts tingled, but she ignored it. She raised her chin. "I suppose if I went to your rooms I would find your floors spotless?" Actually, now that she thought about it, the Runner's floors probably were spotless. He didn't seem like a man who would abide clutter.

His eyes glittered. "If you were in my rooms, the state of my floors would be the last thing you would be thinking of."

"And what would be the first?" A lock of his dark auburn hair twisted upward, and she felt the oddest urge to smooth it back down.

"You wouldn't be thinking at all." He frowned. "Just as I am not now." He released her and stepped back. "I trust you are uninjured after your misadventure with the bow. Shall we continue?"

Something in Eleanor's chest pinched, but she shook out her

skirts and set her shoulders. "Let's." Without giving him another look, she started on her way. When they reached the double doors of the Tea Room, she turned left, down the long hall that led to the Great Room at the back of the club. The room where Lady Richford was found. Eleanor turned into a room on the left, three doors down from it.

"Here." She swept her hand over the sitting room decorated in cool blues and stark whites. It was supposed to feel like one had stepped into ancient times, and the Greek and Roman busts that sat in small alcoves that were carved into the walls helped with that immersion. Scattered tables held historic games like *tabula*, *terni lapilli*, and *tali*. Golden thronelike chairs were interspersed with low-slung chaises.

Eleanor led him to one such chaise longue that was angled across one corner of the room. "We sat here and talked." Her eyes dared him to disagree with her description of events.

Mr. Rollins fingered a screen made up of large palm fronds sewn together which partially hid the seat. He moved the screen a foot, and the door was obscured from sight. "You thought it out. Didn't want anyone to observe you if they happened into the room."

"Nothing untoward happened," she said stiffly.

"You were trying to seduce him," he reminded her.

"I wanted his help." She crossed her arms under her chest. "There might have been a kiss"—or two—"but we didn't...I didn't know how...." She stopped herself just short from stomping her foot. As a proper, youngish miss, it was humiliating admitting to such impropriety. As a woman, it was even more shameful admitting that she'd failed. "Nothing happened."

"Was the door open or closed while you were *speaking* with Bobby?"

Eleanor kept her voice even, but she could do nothing about the color that rose to her cheeks. She was not, by nature, a blusher, yet she spent half her time around Mr. Rollins with her cheeks burning. It was most infuriating. "It was closed."

To his credit, Mr. Rollins didn't focus on the implication of the closed door. "So you and Bobby wouldn't have seen anyone walking past. Are you sure you didn't hear anything? No cry? Not even footsteps?"

"Nothing." Her heart had been pounding so hard at the time, it would have been difficult to hear anything over it. She'd never tried to seduce a man before, and Bobby had seemed quite aware of her lack of experience. It had been embarrassing. An unmarried woman of her station should be inexperienced, but she had seen much more of the world than was typical of her station. Going from a pampered young miss to a pauper when her family had lost their money had been devastating. Having to find employment to keep a roof over her head had been eye-opening.

She knew the trouble a woman could get into. Had seen it happen to more than one daughter of the tradesmen she had become friends with in that life. Had even had hushed conversations where the act was described in full, shocking detail. She should have been more worldly. Should have been able to persuade a footman to help her by using her feminine wiles. She'd witnessed the flirting among the servants whom she'd worked with. Fended off enough advances of her own.

The fact that relations happened outside of marriage no longer surprised her. Perhaps that was why she had been willing to give up her virtue in order to save her mother.

And perhaps because, deep in her heart, she'd felt her actions to be wrong was why her attempt to seduce Bobby had failed.

"Wait here." Mr. Rollins exited from the room, closing the door behind him.

Eleanor stood for a few moments, unsure of his purpose. When she had just decided to sit, a muffled sound came through the door. She hesitated. Was that a shout? Had something fallen?

He came back before she could investigate, crossing the room to her. "Did you hear me call?"

"I heard something, but I didn't know it was you calling. Was I supposed to go to you? You told me to wait here."

"No need for petulance." He absently rubbed his jaw. "I went to where Lady Richford was found and shouted for you. Fairly loudly. That door is thick and heavy, but you still heard something."

"What does that prove? I didn't hear anything that night." Showing that she could have heard a noise but hadn't didn't seem to add anything to their understanding.

He proved her wrong. "It suggests that Lady Richford didn't scream as she was being attacked. Either she was taken completely unawares, or she knew her killer."

Eleanor paused. She hadn't really thought about it before, but as she'd sat here and fumbled with the footman, a woman was having the life choked out of her. A chill shivered down her back. Her head went light. If she had left the room a minute earlier, would she have run into a killer?

Mr. Rollins gripped her upper arms. "All you all right? You've gone quite pale." His eyes narrowed on her face.

She inhaled slowly, trying to calm her nerves. His clean, woodsy scent helped. He was standing quite close to her. It only made sense, as he appeared worried she was on the verge of toppling over. For once, she didn't find his presence irritating. It was oddly comforting, instead.

A fact she would never admit to him. She locked her knees and stepped back. "I am well." Any strong, capable man would have felt just as comforting. It was nothing special to Mr. Rollins.

He must have noted her cool tone, because his expression changed to match it. "Did you know we've met before?" he said casually. "I knew I recognized you, but it took several hours looking through past files to remember from where."

Eleanor cocked her head. "I don't remember."

"It was several years ago. I was still in uniform on patrol." He rubbed his chest. "A grocer had been hurt during a robbery. You were shopping at his store at the time. When I arrived, you were comforting his young daughter."

She snapped her mouth shut. She did remember now. The

obscene amount of blood the grocer's head wound had produced. The fear of his child. And the man in the navy blue coat and red waistcoat of the Bow Street Patrol who'd taken her brief statement. "That was you?"

He nodded. "It was my first year in service. I probably asked you all the wrong questions. But I remember how kind you were to that girl. A fine lady like you wiping a stranger's tears away."

Eleanor's throat went thick. "I wasn't a fine lady then. I'd barely had money to purchase the apples I was there for that day."

"Money doesn't make a lady." His green eyes darkened. He cleared his throat and pulled out his pocket watch, checking the time before sliding it back into his waistcoat. "I must be going. If you intend to ask questions outside this club, inform me beforehand so I can keep you out of trouble."

Eleanor's shoulders drew back. "I am quite accomplished at keeping myself out of trouble, thank you very much." Just when she thought he had a heart, he had to open his mouth again and show his insufferable self.

"You haven't seen this sort of trouble before." He stepped forward, stopping a scant inch from her body. "And Miss Lynton...." His gaze dropped to her mouth before flitting back to her eyes, holding her gaze. "Trying to seduce information or favors from a target is a skill, one best not attempted by amateurs. Don't try anything like that again."

And with a tip of his head, he was gone. Leaving before she could find a pillow to chuck at his head.

Chapter Thirteen

Lady Mary

ALTHOUGH SHE MADE a merry chase, I finally tracked down my quarry on The Strand at Twinings. Mrs. Amelia Massey had her arm hooked loosely with her daughter's as they browsed the aisles of tea leaves, the girl out just this season. Mrs. Massey graciously nodded her head to the other patrons, the green feather in her turban fluttering with the motion.

I cut across the store, ignoring the enticing scents coming from the bins, and joined the two Massey women. "I have been trying to speak with you for many days."

Mrs. Massey turned to me. "Lady Mary." She slowly inclined her head, the action almost unwilling. "I must have missed seeing your card among my callers."

My card was near impossible to miss. It was printed on a thick, ivory cardstock, with my name in a bold font that took up almost all the space of the card. "How fortunate, then, to find you here." I eyed her daughter. "This is a conversation best kept between us, I believe."

"Mother?" Miss Massey asked.

Her mother sighed. "If Lady Mary wishes to speak privately, I am happy to accommodate her. We passed Miss Smythe at the haberdashers next door. Why don't you go speak with her? I know you wish to discuss your gowns for the upcoming Vauxhall gala."

"All right." The girl hurried away, seeming eager to chat with her friend.

"Now." Mrs. Massey lowered her voice. "What is it you wish to say?"

Seeing no reason to dither, I asked her directly. "Your fight with Lady Richford at my club. What was its cause?"

Mrs. Massey pressed her lips tight, her cheeks flushing nearly as dark as the puce of her muslin gown. After several moments of silence, she said, "It was private."

"You threw a chair at her in my club." I pushed my spectacles up my nose. "If you wanted it to remain private, you did a very poor job of it."

She shot me a glare from the corner of her eye. "A broken chair is hardly the worst damage that occurs at your club. With the arrow holes, that catapult accident, and the lawn bowling dents, I'm surprised you even noticed a broken chair."

A gentleman jostled my elbow as he reached for a sack of assam tea. Tired of blocking the shoppers, I herded Mrs. Massey out of the way and into a shadowed nook. "Come, come. You cannot be unaware that with the death of Lady Richford your actions would come under scrutiny. If the officer from Bow Street hasn't been to question you, he soon will."

"There is nothing to say." She shifted her wrapper higher up her shoulder. "You know how Lady Richford was. Always trying to win a point when she spoke with you. Looking for any weakness to exploit. I lost my temper, but it was nothing to kill her over."

"You threw a chair." And my chairs were made out of solid oak. It wouldn't have been easy. "You weren't angry over just a cruel word. It was something more."

Mrs. Massey slid her gaze to the left and frowned. "It was a personal matter."

I waited. People tended to abhor silence. Mrs. Massey was no exception. She spoke to fill the void, her voice unnaturally airy.

"Lady Richford was a bit too free with her attention to members of the opposite sex." She fussed with the feather in her turban, adjusting it so it stood more upright. "When she turned that attention on Mr. Massey, I objected. The attention was one-sided, of course, but she was interfering with my family."

Mrs. Massey lowered her hands and gave me a hard stare. "I won't let anyone harm my family. A set-down was required."

The only portion of the woman's statement I knew to be true was that last one, that she wouldn't let anyone harm her family. The other bit, about Lady Richford's roaming eye landing on Mr. Massey, rang untrue. It would support Edgar Bannister's assertion that his mother looked outside her marriage for companionship, however, so perhaps Mrs. Massey was merely uncomfortable telling me, or anyone, about it. Perhaps Mr. Massey had returned the attention.

How far would Mrs. Massey go to protect her marriage? Could the prim woman in front of her commit murder? And if Lady Richford and Mr. Massey were having an affair, would Mr. Massey have killed the woman to hide it?

I rubbed my forehead. I'd come for answers but only came away with more questions.

We said our farewells, mine a bit annoyed, hers frosty, and I had my driver return me home. I loved my club, but with all the problems surrounding it, my house was my only refuge.

Mr. Stavers greeted me at the door and took my cloak and walking stick. "Your nephew called on you, milady. He said to tell you that he's available if you need any assistance with The Minerva Club."

My chest tightened. Dear Marcus. As the Duke of Montague and one of the wealthiest men in England, I could only imagine in what form his assistance might come. His inquiry agency, of course, but with his money he might also offer to buy *The Times* to ensure no more filth was printed about me.

But Marcus was a new father. He'd had enough trials in his

life without taking on his dotty aunt's problems, too. Unless facing the direst need, I wanted to handle my club's problems myself.

Mr. Stavers held up a silver platter, his nose close to touching it because of his stoop. "The correspondence that arrived today, milady."

"Thank you, Stavers." The man had been in service to my husband's father. It was past time for him to retire, but whenever the offer was made, he flatly refused. And if I was being honest, I didn't want to lose him, either. He was a connection to my husband, and there weren't many of those left.

I took the four missives. Two were from friends, one was a bill. The other only had my name scrawled across the front with no indication of whom it was from. I started walking to my sitting room and opened that one first.

When I read the first line, my feet froze. "Who delivered this?" I asked Stavers.

He seemed taken aback by my tone. "A young lad. He seemed impressed upon receiving a shilling on delivery as well as pick-up."

"Not one of our usual couriers then?"

"No milady." He ran his needlelike fingers through his thinning hair. "I'd never seen him before."

I nodded and changed my course from the parlor to my library. I kept brandy in the library. After I'd settled myself in my favorite wide upholstered chair with a tumbler of liquor on the table next to me, I reread the note.

Those that inquire into an area often become the subject matter.

It didn't have to be a threat. It could be someone's idea of a joke. Or merely a warning from a concerned party.

I took another sip of brandy, letting the sweet heat from the alcohol warm my chilled body.

It didn't have to be a threat. But it certainly felt like one.

Chapter Fourteen

Lady Mary

I DIDN'T THINK I'd ever seen a black as dark as Lord Richford's mourning garb. It seemed to suck in all the light around it, even making the white of his cravat seem dull in comparison.

The day of Lady Richford's funeral would have been warm except for the constant blowing of the wind. Without a cleansing rain in weeks, the sky was sepia-tinted, making even the heavens look as dirty as this whole sordid affair was.

The funeral was well attended, the section of St. James's cemetery where the viscountess was buried a veritable crush of somber greys and deep blues and purples. The back rows of mourners had little chance of actually seeing Lady Richford's casket lowered into the grave, or hearing the minister's sonorous words as the wind whipped them away.

Being a white-haired society matron had its benefits. Most people gave way to me out of politeness, and when they didn't, a well-placed strike to the shin with my walking stick did the trick. I had a front-row view of the funeral.

It wasn't long. A chapter from Psalms was read. A few prayers. A creed. But for Lord Richford, it wasn't over soon enough. As the gravediggers lowered the coffin into the earth, the viscount seemed to go down with it, his shoulders drooping, his knees sagging, until finally they hit the ground. The viscount let out an undignified wail as he knelt before his wife's grave.

Bannister frowned down at his father. He rested his hand on the viscount's shoulder and squeezed.

It could have been a squeeze of sympathy, I supposed, but it looked more like one of rebuke.

The minister rushed over his last blessings. Lord Richford's grief was painful to witness. Shifting in my low-heeled boots, I looked over the crowd. Mr. Rollins was easy to spot, his auburn hair and top hat rising a foot above the women who seemed to have congregated around him. I suppose I couldn't blame the women. He was a good-looking man, and his job as a Bow Street Runner lent him an air of intrigue.

I didn't see Miss Lynton, but she could have been hidden amongst the throngs.

I did, however, see one Mr. Enoch Ryder. He tipped his head when our gazes met. A woman next to him touched his arm, seeking his attention. He broke our connection to smile down at her.

I rubbed the seam where my fichu met my neckline. Mr. Ryder appeared untroubled, serene even, an irritating quality for someone who was trying to destroy my business. And, I reminded myself, for someone at the funeral of a woman who was violently murdered. It was downright indecent to look so at peace.

Bannister raised his father to his feet and started guiding him out of the cemetery, an arm around the broken man's shaking shoulders. A small form in a charcoal grey gown stepped in front of them.

Bannister's eyebrows slammed together.

I tried to edge closer, threading my way between the departing mourners, to see who had brought such displeasure to Lady Richford's son. "Pardon me," I said as I pushed past the minister, ignoring his pained expression when I accidentally stepped on his foot. I skirted the open grave, found myself blocked by a group who had decided to chat instead of move out of my way, and marched up the slight incline on my right to circumvent them.

I heard Bannister's sharp voice, his father's appeasing one, but couldn't make out their words.

"Lady Mary." A man stepped into my path, blocking my way. "How lovely to see you again."

I flicked my gaze to Mr. Cooke. He looked as piratical as ever, his finely-tailored swallowtail jacket a navy so dark it was almost indistinguishable from all the blacks around him. He'd even managed to procure a rosebud of the same shade for the buttonhole in his lapel. His silk breeches ended at the top of leather boots so finely crafted I knew even my nephew would be envious of them.

Crime paid well, and Mr. Cooke seemed to be enjoying the fruits of his sins.

I clutched at my hat as a strong gust of wind whipped through the cemetery. "Mr. Cooke." Angling my body, I put Bannister, Lord Richford, and the woman in my sights. "What can I do for you?" If she would only turn her head. I could only see a slice of her cheek, the hint of her jaw.

"I wanted to apologize for my previous behavior." He pressed his large, brown hand to his chest. "I was operating under a misapprehension."

"Is that so?" I said, straining to see past him.

The woman turned, her eyes narrow as she spoke in a low voice to Bannister. Miss Abbott looked as though she'd been crying, the skin around her eyes swollen, the tip of her nose red. With a last remark, cutting if her expression was anything to go by, she spun on her heel and marched out of the cemetery.

In my conversations with both Miss Abbott and Bannister, I knew there was no love lost between the two, but what could have caused an argument by the side of Lady Richford's grave? And in front of poor Lord Richford?

When I returned my attention to Mr. Cooke, he was glaring at me, chin lowered and eyebrow arched. He probably wasn't used to being ignored.

I faced him fully. "What misapprehension was that?"

He gazed around the cemetery. The crowd was thinning, and we were garnering some curious glances, including one from Mr. Ryder. There appeared to be a crack in his serenity now, a fact I found most interesting. "Perhaps this is a conversation best held somewhere private," Mr. Cooke said. "Will you accompany me to the office at my club?"

I must admit I was curious what the office of such a man would look like. After he'd threatened me in *my* office, I'd done a bit of research on Mr. Cooke. Only a certain type of person had knowledge of Cooke, and those people spoke of him in hushed tones.

A criminal, Mr. Cooke had his finger in all the seedy pies of London's underworld. Gambling was his legitimate business, but I also heard tell of smuggling, robberies, and prostitution. He didn't engage in any of those activities personally, of course, but he directed the illicit activities like a foreman managed his factory workers.

I could hardly countenance that such a man was now within my realm of acquaintances. Life took such interesting turns. But with the reminder of violent death just next to me, I couldn't find it in myself to be so reckless as to disappear into his office. I also didn't want the man at my club again.

"Do you know Button's Coffeehouse? If not, your driver can follow my carriage there."

He nodded. "Privacy amongst the many." He offered his arm, and seeing no polite way to object, I took it and let him lead me to my carriage. As he handed me in, I felt a disapproving gaze on my back, but that could have been my own conscience.

Fifteen minutes later, I was seated across from the man, two steaming cups of coffee before the both of us, mine heavily laden with cream and sugar, his, the devil's black. The coffeehouse was only half full, but the conversations were loud, bouncing off the uncovered wooden floors and walls, making it necessary to lean over the table to hear my companion.

"So, Mr. Cooke, what was it you wished to speak with me about?" I added one more lump of sugar to my brew before lifting it to my lips. Coffee wasn't my normal beverage of choice. It was too bitter, too matter-of-fact. But there were some situations where the civility of tea seemed inappropriate, and the sweetness of chocolate, childish.

He watched all my motions with interest, his gaze assessing, curious. It would have been flattering if I didn't have the impression that he was looking for weaknesses, a wedge to give him leverage. I'd seen a stuffed shark once at a naturalist exhibit, its black eyes and sharp teeth the thing of nightmares. I had a feeling that Mr. Edric Cooke would have felt right at home in the ocean.

He rested his forearms on the table and laced his fingers together. "I want to start with an apology, Lady Mary. When last we spoke, I had made some assumptions that I now believe to be false. They led me to speak to you in an unforgivable manner."

I did enjoy being apologized to. "Go on."

The edges of his lips twitched. "It had come to my attention that for some months there were members of your club who were engaged in what might be termed a business competitive to mine. On a very small scale, of course, but I do like to keep track of such things in case…."

"The scale becomes larger?" And a potential threat.

"Just so."

I tapped my thumb against my cup. "Your business interests are quite varied. Which type are we speaking of?"

He chuckled. "Very diplomatically asked. Let me just say that when I heard that a woman met with a fence in your club, I became curious. I reached out."

A sudden chill iced my core. "Members are using my club to meet with a dealer in stolen goods?" I thought I ran a tight ship. I had a doorman, footmen who kept an eye out for trouble. It hardly seemed likely that clandestine meetings with criminals were occurring in the Tea Room.

He nodded. "And I assumed you knew and were taking a cut of the proceeds."

I fear I gaped like a fish. I had been accused of many things in my lifetime, but never criminal behavior. "That's absurd," I finally managed to splutter out. "I would never."

Mr. Cooke's mouth broke into a full-out grin. "Wouldn't you? What a pity."

I ignored how handsome his face was when he smiled. I was too old to feel any sort of fluttering just because a rakehell decided to be charming. "Do you know who the woman was? The fence's name?"

"I won't tell you his name. He is not the sort of man with whom a woman like you should become acquainted." His eyes went dark. "But the woman is one you know. We both attended her funeral today."

I sat back in my chair. Lady Richford had been a viscountess, for heaven's sake. Her husband a prominent member of the House of Lords. I knew virtue and vice were equally distributed among the classes, but if she had been caught, her and her family's lives would have been ruined.

And it wasn't as though she needed the money. I didn't have a wealth requirement for my club, but my fees weren't cheap. If one was a member, one had the means to pay. It didn't make sense.

"Why?" I rubbed my temple, which showed the faintest beginnings of a megrim. "Was she a gambler? Was she in debt?" I looked to Mr. Cooke. He, after all, did run several gambling hells.

But he merely shrugged. "If she was playing cards, it wasn't at my clubs."

That was a thoroughly unsatisfactory answer. I frowned at the man. He'd opened up a Pandora's box of motives and new suspects but without giving me any names to attach to the motives.

His eyes twinkled, expressing no guilt over his neglect. "If you are ever interested in going into business together, I can assure you it would be highly profitable. I hadn't thought of using women before for some of my…activities, but they do have access to some things and places men do not. And who would suspect them? Your club would make a useful location for certain meetings."

"Absolutely not." I gathered my reticule and my walking stick from the seat next to me, my back stiff. Certain people already thought I and my club were immoral; I wasn't going to prove them right. "Are you sure that you won't give me the name of the person Lady Richford met with?"

"Positive." He stood and cupped his palm under my elbow, helping me to rise.

I didn't need the assistance, but I had to admit the gesture was appreciated. I had servants, friends, family, but the common courtesies of a man helping a woman in intimate little ways were almost forgotten to me. I had been a widow now for longer than I'd been married. The realization depressed me.

He guided me toward the door and out onto the street. "And are you sure you won't change your mind about a business association?"

"I won't." I lifted my chin to let him know my seriousness.

"I believe you." He held onto my arm until I was settled in my carriage. He slid the window down before closing the door, then rested his elbow on the sill. He tipped up the brim to his hat, setting it at a jaunty angle. "Though I must admit, Lady Mary, it would be most amusing to try to get you to change your mind."

And with one last nod, a smack to the side of the carriage, he strolled out of sight.

I called to my driver to be underway. Leaning back, I forced myself to look straight ahead, not seek out his form as we passed. Mr. Cooke was a devilishly irritating man.

He was also a dangerous one, a fact I shouldn't forget. I felt in my reticule for the note I had decided to carry with me on a whim. The paper it was written on was thick, expensive, and to my fanciful mind, held a tinge of malice.

In Mr. Cooke's line of work, he must be quite accustomed to making threats. A man didn't get to be as feared and powerful as he was by being considerate. But I didn't believe he had sent me this threat. I couldn't see Mr. Cooke writing the note, much less sending it anonymously. He was much more direct, in both words and action. His threats would come at the end of a pistol, no doubt.

Or would they come at the end of a cravat? If Cooke thought Lady Richford was encroaching on his business somehow, could he have sent someone to kill her?

I pressed a hand to my throat. I didn't want to believe it of the man. I knew his reputation, but there was still something about him I liked.

But I'd been wrong before.

Chapter Fifteen

Frederick

FREDERICK SAW EDGAR Bannister in the same room at White's as he had before. Entry into the club went much more smoothly this time, however, without Lady Mary at his side.

"This is becoming a bad habit, you showing up here." Bannister lit a pipe, looking for all the world like a child playing grown-up. He tossed the burning spill into the fireplace and took a seat, puffing away on the onyx stem. "What more could you possibly want to ask me?"

Frederick settled across from him, pulling out his notepad and bit of lead. "New questions are always arising in an investigation. I know you and your father would want me to persist until I find the person who killed your mother."

The victim's son merely looked bored. He made a circle in the air with his index finger. "Proceed."

Frederick unclenched his jaw. A man should have more interest in getting justice for his mother's killer. Unless the man were somehow involved. "I wish to go over your movements on the night of the murder again. I've learned that your mother intended to see you that evening."

"I find that unlikely." He lifted his head, trying to blow a smoke ring. It came out more an amorphous blob.

"Were you not performing at the Cogburn's Theatre?" Frederick examined Bannister for a reaction. As he hadn't mentioned his performance at his earlier interviews, Frederick assumed it was something he didn't care for many people to know.

Aside from a long pause, Bannister remained unaffected. "I was. You're not saying that Mother intended to see the burletta?"

"We learned from one of her friends that she was intending to. You didn't know?" Frederick thought about what his mother's reaction would be to finding her son on the stage. It most likely wouldn't be one of approval. Unless one reached the pinnacle of fame, acting wasn't a well-respected profession. Especially if a man was donning a gown and affecting a high falsetto.

But the upper classes were different. Bannister obviously thought of it as a bit of a lark; Lady Richford perhaps would have felt the same.

Bannister blinked rapidly. "I had no idea she knew I was in that performance, much less that she would come to see it." He rested his pipe on his thigh.

Frederick gave him a moment, concentrating on writing down some notes. When he looked up, he asked, "Would she have been upset at your taking part in a stage performance?"

"As long as it didn't cost her money, Mother was broadminded. If she liked my performance, she might have even bragged to her friends about it."

Frederick leaned forward, resting his forearms on his thighs. "Why do you do it?"

"Perform?" At Frederick's nod, Bannister shrugged. "Why not? It's a spot of fun. It relieves the tedium. Also, the bit of blunt I get pays for drinks."

Frederick sat back. The tedium. Never once had he thought of his life as tedious. He was too busy working, spending time with his family and friends, to suffer *ennui*. He had an acquaintance with the *ton*, but didn't truly understand them. Bannister, like Lady Mary and Miss Lynton, were members of the leisure class. Had servants to take care of all their needs. It was difficult to imagine Edgar Bannister having the fortitude to actually pick up a cravat and do the dirty work of murder himself.

He bit back a frown. "So you didn't see your mother that night? She didn't go backstage?"

Bannister shook his head.

"And what time did you leave the theatre?"

That question sharpened Bannister's gaze. "The play ended around ten. I didn't leave the theatre until about eleven. Some of the other performers and I went to Carpenter's after that. We didn't leave until early in the morning."

Frederick noted the name of the popular coffeehouse that also served spirits long after other pubs had closed. "The names of your companions?"

Bannister listed them, his face reddening. "When my father asked you to investigate, he did not intend for you to include me in said investigation. He will not be pleased when I inform him."

Frederick arched an eyebrow. "I'm looking for the truth, not playing favorites. But as you've named four actors who can corroborate your location at the time of the murder, you have nothing to worry about."

Bannister looked down at his hands. "Yes. Of course." He shifted uneasily, and Frederick made a note to find these friends of his as soon as possible to confirm, or deny, his alibi.

He decided to change tack. "I was at your mother's funeral yesterday. How is your father?"

Bannister huffed. "He depended upon her too much. He's having a rough go of it, but he'll survive." The dismissal in his voice put Frederick's back up. As someone who had a good relationship with his parents, the lack of respect from Bannister to his own was difficult to understand. Frederick would never be so dismissive of his mother's or father's pain, or their opinions.

"Miss Abbott," Frederick said. "I noticed the dispute between you and her at your mother's graveside. What was it concerning?"

Bannister scowled. "That has to be the most irritating woman of my acquaintance. After all the times she counseled my mother to cut off my funds, she had the nerve to approach father and me and...." His knuckles whitened around the pipe's stem. "She wanted to express her availability should we need a consoling bosom. I told her I would rather find comfort in a porcupine."

"And that was the extent of it?" Frederick stared at the man, unblinking. "The raised voices were all because she offered unwanted sympathy?"

"No, it was because of her impertinence." Bannister sucked on his pipe. "She wanted to come to our house. Help us sort through Mother's belongings. Make sure we ate and rested properly." He glared at the ceiling. "Not only did she act as though she thought us incompetent to manage, she assumed her presence in our home would be wanted. It is not."

"I see." But Frederick didn't quite. Miss Abbott's attentions might have been irritating, but surely they were well-intentioned. One would think Bannister would have the breeding to excuse himself from conversation with her without insulting the woman. Or having the matter degrade into a public fight feet away from his mother's coffin.

Frederick rubbed his jaw. But perhaps the improper time and place was the reason. Perhaps Bannister was more affected by his mother's death than he let on. Grief could make tempers snap where before they'd only bent.

And perhaps Bannister still held a grudge against Miss Abbott for counseling frugality in Lady Richford's dealings with her son and had never had the breeding instilled within him to hold his tongue.

Suddenly disgusted with Bannister, with the supple leather of the wingchair he sat upon, the brandy in the Bohemia crystal decanter on the sideboard that he was sure cost more than his month's salary, Frederick stood and stowed his notebook and lead away. "Thank you for your time, Mr. Bannister. I will be in touch." And with a nod, he strode from the room and from the club.

He ignored the hansom cabs rolling down the street and walked to his offices. The afternoon London air, while he wouldn't exactly call it clean, held a freshness after the sterility of White's. The odor of horses, the sweat of the man tugging a brewer's wagon as he stumbled past, the smell of coal smoke, were real, scents of the world he knew and lived in. When he spent too much time with the upper class he sometimes forgot the true world. For a few select, it was expensive liquor and irresponsible gaming and carefree liaisons.

For the majority of the populace, it was back-breaking work, scraping to get by, hunger pangs in the dead of night. Frederick was one of the fortunate ones. He had a good job, steady pay.

But he would never be one of the elite.

He hung his coat and hat in the small cloakroom of the Bow Street office. Crossing to his desk, he nodded at the other men. This was his world. Runners shouting smutty jokes across the room, the drudgery of writing up reports for the magistrates, working long hours. He excelled in this world. Felt comfortable in it.

It was a world where young misses of gentle breeding and wealth beyond his imaginings didn't belong, no matter how impertinent their mouths or kind-hearted they might be.

And for the first time in his life, he longed for more.

$$\sim\!\!\infty\!\!\sim$$

Chapter Sixteen

Eleanor

ELEANOR KEPT HER focus on the fern as the door behind her opened and closed. Several of the leafy strands were turning brown, and she plucked those dying bits from the plant. She felt his gaze on her back like a magnet, tugging at her to turn around and face him, but she kept her focus on the poor fern.

Lady Mary's desk chair squeaked as she nudged it forward. "You got my note," she said to Mr. Rollins. "Good. I received one of my own."

Finally, Eleanor turned. She could avoid it no longer without appearing churlish. And besides, she was curious about why Lady Mary had brought all of them here. It had only been three days since they'd agreed to investigate together, hardly enough time to come to any conclusions.

At least it hadn't been for her. To be fair, Eleanor hadn't asked many questions the last few days. She rubbed her sore wrist. Her mother had taken all of her attention.

Lady Mary pushed a piece of parchment across the desk, and Mr. Rollins picked it up. He raised one eyebrow and darted a glance at the older woman. "Where and when did you get this?"

"It was delivered by a child to my home two days past." Her lips pressed flat. "My butler didn't know to question the boy as to who gave him the note."

"What does it say?" Eleanor asked.

"*Those that inquire into an area often become the subject matter.*" Rollins flipped the paper over, running his thumb along the grain. "Quality paper. The print neatly written."

Lady Mary steepled her fingers. "Yes, and very indeterminate. I cannot tell if a man or woman wrote the letters, though it is someone who has the means to purchase expensive paper. Or steal it."

Mr. Rollins shifted his gaze to Eleanor, and a shiver raced down her spine. She didn't know if his look was one of suspicion or want. Either one sat uncomfortably. "That could mean many things. Why send such a strange message?"

He looked back at Lady Mary. "I only see one interpretation of the note. It is a pointed warning. It would be wise for both you and Miss Lynton to heed it."

"Not that nonsense again." Lady Mary pressed her palms on her desk and stood. "If you two would follow me, I would like to return to where Lady Richford was found."

Mr. Rollins waited for Eleanor to pass before falling into step behind her. Watching her. Walking used to be a natural action, one she didn't even think about while doing. But each step now needed concentration. She felt every press of her sole on the ground, each sway of her hip.

It was silly. Mr. Rollins most likely took no note of her, but his presence behind her was all her mind knew.

"All right." Lady Mary strode into the middle of the Great Room, eyeing the space. "Let's go through this logically."

There had been no events in the room since the murder, so the floor was empty, the chairs and benches stacked along the walls. Late afternoon sunlight filtered in from the high windows on the east wall, dancing motes of dust caught in their beams.

Eleanor skittered toward the stage, putting space between her and the Runner. "Go through what?"

"The murder." Lady Mary frowned at her, and a flush of

embarrassment heated Eleanor's cheeks. "We know that Lady Richford was found dead at twenty-three minutes after midnight six nights ago. Timothy came through this room around midnight, checking the doors and windows, and finding nothing amiss. Neither he nor Bobby saw Lady Richford, nor anyone else but me and Miss Lynton in the club while closing. So, were Lady Richford and her killer still in the club, or did they gain entrance somehow right before her death?"

"It wouldn't be difficult to remain unnoticed after closing." As two sets of eyes turned on Eleanor, one curious, one slightly accusing, she gripped her elbow and lifted her chin. "If I'm hiding, say in the music room, I would merely wait as Timothy checked the Quiet Room across the hall. When he was finished, he would move on to either the library or the Art Room next door, and I would slip into the Quiet Room when his back was turned."

"You've thought about this a lot, have you?" Lady Mary eyed her shrewdly, but the edges of her mouth twitched.

Unfortunately, Eleanor *had* thought about it. She knew she needed to watch over her mother, but there had been nights when all she'd thought about had been escape. There were several chaises and sofas that made a decent bed for an uninterrupted night's sleep. Unconsciously, she rubbed her forearm, letting the dull ache she found there remind her of her purpose.

It was only natural her mother would be unsettled, first with thoughts of revenge and then with the worry of being a suspect in a murder. Once the real killer was found, she would once again become the kind, gentle woman who had raised Eleanor.

Mr. Rollins's gaze was heavy on her once more. His eyes seemed to search for something she couldn't let anyone find. Eleanor cleared her throat. "It would be easier for Lady Richford to remain unnoticed by staying in the club rather than trying to gain entry after closing. She could have let her killer in the door there after Timothy made his rounds." She nodded to the door beside the stage that led into a back alley.

"If the killer entered that way, how did he leave?" Mr. Rollins widened his stance. "He couldn't have locked it after himself. Not without a key."

"Which only I and my staff carry," Lady Mary said.

Eleanor tugged at the cuff of her sleeve and cast a wary glance toward the open door that led back into the club proper. "Are we sure that one of the servants didn't have a reason to kill Lady Richford? As the only men in the club, it would have been easiest for one of them to be the murderer."

"The only men we *know* were in the club. And you're assuming the killer wasn't a woman." Lady Mary tapped the floor with her walking stick for emphasis.

That didn't answer Eleanor's question. "But...."

Lady Mary sighed. "I have my men investigated very thoroughly before I hire them. They weren't involved."

"And I've checked their finances since the murder," Mr. Rollins added. "If one of them was paid to commit the murder, I've found no evidence of it. And, of course, young Bobby does have an alibi." He ignored Eleanor's scowl. "But you've brought up the possibility of a woman committing the crime again. I'm still not sure a woman would have the strength to strangle another."

"Then let's put it to the test." Lady Mary briskly strode to the low stage and plopped her bottom down upon it. Her light blue eyes were lit with some amusement as she looked between Eleanor and the Runner. "Well, go ahead, Miss Lynton. Try to strangle him."

An empty feeling opened in the pit of Eleanor's stomach. "What?"

"Take Mr. Rollins's cravat and see if you can choke the air from him," Lady Mary explained patiently. She turned to Mr. Rollins. "I assume you have no objections to this little experiment. If she starts to hurt you, just raise your hand as a signal for her to stop."

Mr. Rollins dipped his chin. "She will not hurt me."

"Then there can be no objection." Lady Mary stretched her legs out in front of her. "I have no cravat handy. We'll have to use yours."

Mr. Rollins sighed but brought his hands to his throat and began untying the knot. "Let's list our suspects. Edgar Bannister. There was no love lost between him and his mother."

Eleanor's gaze was transfixed on the quick movements of Mr. Rollins's hands. The whisper of linen as one tail of his cravat dragged against the other, exposing the tanned skin of his throat. His shirt gaped, a thatch of dark hair appearing in the vee it made. She had never seen a man perform an action of undress, not even her father.

"What was that?" Lady Mary frowned. "What did you say, Miss Lynton?"

Whatever noise Eleanor had made hadn't been for public consumption. She dragged her gaze away from Mr. Rollins's dishabille. "Only that Bannister could have used his stage costume to gain access here, and escaped out of the club in the tumult after we discovered the body."

"Anyone could have escaped out of the club in the same manner." Lady Mary laced her hands together on top of her walking stick and rested her chin on top of her hands. "I still have a hard time believing a son could kill his mother."

Mr. Rollins held out his cravat. "He says he was with friends, at Carpenter's after the performance, but his friends lost track of him on a few occasions, notably around midnight. He left for some minutes with an unknown woman. He could have abandoned the woman to run here. The timing would have been tight, but not impossible. I have associates questioning jarveys in the area to see if he hailed a ride that night." When Eleanor hadn't moved, he shook his neckcloth, like a matador waving a flag at a bull.

And like the stupid bull, Eleanor moved forward until she stood before the man. Without looking at him, she took his cravat, ignoring the warmth it still held from his skin. "Turn, please."

Mr. Rollins let out a soft grunt, but turned as ordered.

"I spoke with Mrs. Massey." Lady Mary cocked her head.

"You'll have to squat down some. Try to approximate Lady Richford's height." She nodded when Mr. Rollins sank lower. "She says her argument with the viscountess was because Lady Richford had become too friendly with Mr. Massey."

"An affair?" Mr. Rollins dropped to his knees. "I know I am now lower than Lady Richford would be, but maintaining a squat while Miss Lynton tries to figure out how to put a cravat about my neck is untenable."

All hesitation on Eleanor's part evaporated. She grabbed the ends of the cravat in each hand and whipped the cloth over his head and down to his neck. She yanked back, but beside from a slight sway to his body, Mr. Rollins appeared unmoved.

"She says not." Lady Mary leaned to the side. "Can you turn so I can see what Miss Lynton is doing?"

They shuffled their bodies until they faced the windows, giving Lady Mary an excellent view.

"A little flirtation doesn't seem provocation enough to violence," Mr. Rollins said.

"No, but I don't know that I believe her reason for her fight with the viscountess, either." Lady Mary frowned. "Can't you pull any harder, Miss Lynton?"

Eleanor tried, and although Mr. Rollins's breathing became a bit labored, it didn't stop. "Perhaps if I get some leverage." Raising her leg, she pressed her knee into his back.

Mr. Rollins reached back and gripped her hands. He swiveled his head, glaring at her from the corner of one eye. "There was no bruising on Lady Richford's back, and besides, she wouldn't have been as low as I am so the positioning wouldn't have worked."

"No knee?"

"No knee," he confirmed.

"Now that Lord Anglia seems like a nasty piece of work," Lady Mary continued. "I don't know that killing the woman who directed his peer's vote is enough of a reason for murder, but such viciousness from him wouldn't surprise me."

"It would be a large risk for a man in his position," Mr. Rollins said. "I can't see him committing the crime without a very strong reason."

"He also wears monogrammed cravats." Lady Mary tapped her thumb against her bottom lip, squinting. "I've never seen him without one with a large *A* stitched into the fabric."

"That doesn't mean he couldn't obtain one." He twisted again to look back at Eleanor. "Are you even trying?"

Her jaw went tight, an ache forming. The problem was that the damned fabric slid through her hands when she pulled hard. Another problem was that Mr. Rollins was so irritating that she wanted to choke him in earnest.

Winding the ends of the cravat around her palms, she moved in closer. Her breasts brushed his shoulders, the scent of soap and man rising from his skin to tickle her nose. The flutter in her belly only served to increase her irritation, and the next time she pulled on the cravat, it was harder than was wise.

Mr. Rollins fell back against her, his head cradled in her bosom. He muttered an oath. "You might break my neck, but you won't choke me."

She looked at his position, on his knees in front of her yet still speaking to her in such a condescending tone. His russet hair was stark against her lavender bodice, the locks tousled and looking altogether too...pettable. Her stomach clenched. Breaking his neck wasn't as unwelcome an idea as it should have been.

Lady Mary pushed on her walking stick and rose, striding over to them. "You're doing it all wrong. If you want leverage, grasp the right tail of the cravat in your left hand and the left in your right."

Eleanor followed the instruction.

"Now you can pull the cravat tight." Lady Mary showed her, pulling tight on nothing but air but getting her point across nonetheless.

"Oh, that is easier." Eleanor could even press her forearms into his shoulders to really tighten the noose.

Mr. Rollins flapped his hand at her. "Get lower."

Eleanor ground her jaw. Did the man have to critique all her actions?

"He's right," Lady Mary said. "The killer most likely wouldn't have been so much taller than Lady Richford. Try hunkering down and see if that changes the effect."

Eleanor dropped into a slight curtsy, keeping the cravat taut. "No, it feels the same no matter how much higher I am."

Mr. Rollins waved again, and a little growl came out of her mouth. If he couldn't even be bothered to tell her with words what he wanted her to change, just point at her like some—

"Oh." Quickly, she dropped the cravat, and Mr. Rollins fell forward, sucking in deep draughts of air.

Eleanor grimaced and took a solid step back. They had agreed that him waving would be a signal. She'd quite forgotten. "What about that Mr. Cooke?" she said brightly. "You had said that he made some vague threats about you and the club after Lady Richford died. Could he be involved?"

She kept her eyes on Lady Mary, trying to ignore the man beside her as he slowly got to his feet and rose to his full height. Out of the corner of her eye she saw him turn slowly, his fists clenching and unclenching, his chest seeming to test the very limits of the fabric of his shirt and jacket with each breath he took. She took another step away from him.

Lady Mary's snowy eyebrows drew together. "I spoke with him again. He apologized for the threat. He thought I'd allowed illegal activity to take place in my club for a cut of the profit." Her small foot tapped on the floor. "He seemed to think Lady Richford was somehow involved."

"Involved in what, exactly?" Mr. Rollins's voice was rough, low. Angry?

Eleanor snuck a look at his face. He'd asked the question of Lady Mary, but his dark glare was all for her. Definitely angry.

"The selling of stolen goods." Lady Mary sniffed. "I'd assume that would mean she was also stealing said goods. It is hard to believe a viscountess would act so."

"But it would give us another motive as to her death." Eleanor willed her heated cheeks to cool. Mr. Rollins had agreed to the experiment. She didn't need to apologize for its success. She frowned. It had been a success, hadn't it? "Are we agreed that a woman could have been the murderer? That with the right technique, a woman is strong enough to choke the air from a person?"

"From Lady Richford, yes." Mr. Rollins plucked his cravat from the floor and wrapped it around his neck. He paid the knot he tied much attention. "As a man, I could have easily taken you over my shoulder to get you to release me, but it can be assumed that Lady Richford didn't have the skills or strength to do likewise."

The corners of Lady Mary's eyes tipped up. "Of course, Mr. Rollins. I would never have thought otherwise."

Lady Mary and Eleanor watched as he put the final touches on his cravat, smoothed the tails down inside his jacket. The silence in the room turned heavy, tangible. Eleanor waited for someone to bring up her mother as a final suspect and thought of all the ways to defend her.

The reason Eleanor knew her mother was innocent was the one she couldn't voice. Her mother had become angry and bitter and violent over the years, and it had only gotten worse when Eleanor's father had died. But she knew from personal experience that her mother's episodes were spontaneous. Impulsive. Her mother might have tried to throttle Lady Richford in the Tea Room, but nothing so calculating as waiting to find her alone. And if she had come upon her after hours with no one around, after the deed was done, her mother wouldn't have had the self-discipline to sneak out of the club unobserved.

Her spite made her impetuous.

But neither Mr. Rollins nor Lady Mary voiced her mother's name, and Eleanor was grateful for it. "So, have we come to any conclusions?" she asked.

"No conclusions," Lady Mary said grumpily. "Only more questions."

Mr. Rollins tugged at the ends of his cuffs. "That is often the way with investigations. Questions emerge, confusion grows, until finally one bit of information is uncovered that makes all the evidence fall into place and an answer becomes clear. I only need to keep digging."

"We only need to keep digging." Lady Mary shot him a narrow-eyed look.

"That's what I meant." He gave her a charming smile. "And now, ladies, I must return to my office. Let me know if you discover anything else." With a nod, he turned on his heel and strode from the room.

"Did he sound skeptical that we would discover anything else?" Lady Mary asked.

"He did indeed."

Lady Mary sniffed. "That's what I thought."

Chapter Seventeen

Lady Mary

M Y HAND HESITATED only a moment before I knocked on Lord Richford's door. I had a legitimate reason to be here. It was my Christian duty to offer comfort to my neighbor, after all. But I knew that wasn't my true purpose, and a small part of me hated myself for it.

"Lady Mary." The earl's majordomo greeted me when he opened the door. "How nice to see you."

I shuffled inside before he could deny me access. "How is Richford today? I've come to offer whatever aid I can."

He turned a solemn face to me. "My lord is reviewing proposed legislation in his study. I will inform him of your presence."

I waited impatiently in the foyer, hoping Lord Richford would be too polite to turn me away. We were socially acquainted, but didn't know each other well. Pretty soon he might think me as interfering as Miss Abbott.

His man returned, inclining his head. "Follow me, please."

He led me into a richly appointed room, its full-length windows inviting in the western sun and illuminating the stacks of papers on the wide oak desk. A thick Berber carpet muffled my footfalls, and the chair I was shown to cushioned my rump like I was sitting on a cloud.

Lord Richford waited until I was seated before retaking his own chair. "Lady Mary, how kind of you to call."

"I wanted to see how you were faring after the funeral." I shifted. "I have experienced what it is to bury a spouse, and I thought perhaps you'd want to speak with someone who understands what it is you're going through."

His shoulders drooped. "That is kind. I do sometimes feel as though no one knows how I suffer, but of course that isn't true. Many of my peers have faced the death of loved ones."

"Yes, but even when I lost my Cavindish I had some comfort in knowing it was God's will and he was no longer in pain." My stomach twisted, and I wondered that I could be so disingenuous to a grieving widower. But I pressed onward. "Lady Richford was in the prime of her life. And to have someone take her from you must be an exceptional kind of pain."

He swallowed, his Adam's apple bobbing beneath his whiskered throat. "Indeed. I still cannot understand why someone would do that to her. It doesn't make sense."

"The actions of a madman rarely do." I traced my thumb along the lion's head that topped today's walking stick, following the curves of its mane. I needed to phrase my next words delicately. "There has been some talk at the club that your wife was using some of my rooms after hours for her own purposes. Do you know anything about that?"

Richford gripped the edge of his desk, his knuckles going white. "You've been speaking to my son. I can assure you that his insinuations that his mother was…was… enjoying the company of other men are completely unfounded. She was mine and I was hers. And any accusation to the contrary is insulting."

I sat back. I'd never heard Richford speak so forcefully. It made me like him more, especially as it was in defense of his marriage.

She was mine and I was hers.

It was a lovely notion. There had been a time when I'd felt the same way about my husband. When the first notes of marriage had made our days easy, our nights pleasurable. Before other considerations had intruded and added false notes to our song. Until I'd taken that final step that had put a permanent wedge between me and my husband. And he'd become someone who was no longer mine, and I was someone he had a difficult time being in the same room with.

The back of my throat burned. That was the past. It was no use crying over what could never be changed. It was the present that needed my attention.

"I actually hadn't thought that was the reason for your wife using the rooms in my club. It is a women's only club, after all." A one-off assignation perhaps. It appeared that the security at my club wasn't all that I had thought it to be, but conducting a continuing liaison at a place where men were conspicuous would be the height of foolishness. Add to that the fact my club had no beds, only some divans and chaise longues that would be uncomfortable for the task, and I could only conclude there were much more sensible places for Lady Richford to have an affair. "Perhaps she was using if for another purpose? Did she have a hobby she didn't want to bring home? Business that would be easier to conduct at my club?"

Richford's body sagged into his chair. "I apologize. Of course, you wouldn't entertain such vile ideas."

I rubbed my ear. It was sweet he believed that.

Richford sighed. "My son is a good man, but he and his mother often butted heads. They were too much alike, I fear." He gave me a wan smile. "Now Edgar is eager to assist me with my business matters. He wants to help me through my grief. He doesn't realize that I need to keep my mind engaged or else…."

"Your thoughts stay fixed upon your loss." I nodded. That I could understand. I didn't think, however, that Bannister's newfound interest in business was entirely pure of heart. The young man was greedy for money he didn't earn, and it wouldn't surprise me if he had an angle to somehow pad his purse.

"And her staying at my club late?" I probed gently. "Do you

know the reason?"

Richford scratched at a mark on his desk. "We loved each other dearly, but my wife did enjoy time on her own. She sometimes thought her social duties as viscountess tedious. It wouldn't surprise me if she only wanted a few spare moments to rest where she wouldn't be disturbed."

I refrained from looking at my surroundings. The Richford townhouse was quite large. There would be many rooms where the viscountess could find solitude if she so desired. I had come here to prod answers from Richford, but even I couldn't bring myself to strip him of that happy delusion.

But Richford showed no signs of deception. If he knew his wife was a thief, I would think he'd show some signs of guilt or embarrassment. I saw none. He was either an exceptional liar, or he was unaware of his wife's shameful activities.

If she'd engaged in such shameful activities. I only had Mr. Cooke's word on the matter.

He pulled open the top drawer of his desk and pulled out a folded ticket. His eyes brightened. "We were to travel to the Continent, to explore the castles along the Rhine. Susan asked for the trip. She said she wanted to start fresh, recapture the bloom of new love." He blinked rapidly as he gazed at the scrap of paper. "She said she missed me and wanted it to be as it was when we were newly wed, just the two of us."

Richford cleared his throat. "With Edgar out of the house, it sounded like a lovely idea."

I nodded. I could only imagine how a marriage would change when children were brought into it. In many ways, the change would be a blessing, but there would have to be a change in the feelings between husband and wife. You could no longer put the other first. That place of primacy belonged to the child.

I slowly rose, suddenly feeling every year I'd lived in my bones. "I've taken up too much of your time, Lord Richford, but if there is ever anything I can do for you, please send word."

He nodded, but made no move to rise and show me out. His

attention was all on that ticket, and to the reinvigorated marriage that would now never occur.

When I stepped outside, I raised my face to the sun. That visit had made me feel unclean. I should have gone to the viscount with the sole purpose of offering my aid and comfort. Instead that had been merely subterfuge.

Of course, Lady Richford's murderer should be brought to justice. I didn't question my decision to help find the malefactor, only my methods.

I plodded to my carriage, my driver holding the door for me. I also questioned Lady Richford's reasons for that trip to the Continent. Was the distance she'd felt from her husband the natural result of time and motherhood? Or was there something else she felt was coming between her and her husband? Was she going to disclose her misdeeds to Richford and seek forgiveness for her sins?

And if she had been going to confess all, was that the reason for her murder?

Chapter Eighteen

Lady Mary

THE MAN DANGLED some one hundred feet off the ground from a rope that seemed much too thin for the task. He scraped at the dirt that had accumulated on the hour hand of the clock on the left tower of Westminster Abbey. A worker on a scaffold some twenty feet below him shouted a direction and pointed, presumably at a spot that he'd missed.

These past months I had found watching the efforts to ready London for George IV's coronation a satisfying diversion. The scrubbing of our national monuments, the furnishing of Westminster Abbey and Hall with jewels and plate, the construction of a triumphal arch that the new king would likely march through. Even though opinions on the new king ran low, there was still an optimism about the coronation. A revival of national spirit that one couldn't help but enjoy.

Usually. Today I watched the goings-on from my usual seat on the bench across the park from the abbey with a heavy heart.

It was my guilt of course. Lord Richford was a grieving widower, and I'd poked and prodded at his bereavement like a gull tearing at a dead fish on the beach. And had it been because I wanted to see justice for his wife?

Or because I wanted to protect my club?

I nodded to an acquaintance but gave him no encouragement to approach. I feared I didn't have the fortitude for polite conversation at the moment. The six abbey bells rang out the afternoon hour and still I sat.

Another couple of my acquaintance passed by, but there was no friendly nod from them. I would always be tolerated. My status and that of my nephew's would made certain of that. But with the recent events at The Minerva Club, some of that toleration had taken on a freezing air.

A shadow blocked out my sun, and someone sat down on my left. Mr. Ryder leaned back on the stone bench and watched as the Reigate stone and Purbeck marble of the abbey was buffed to a shine, his gaze as admiring as mine. He said nothing, only sat next to me, the silence washing over us. I felt myself relaxing back against the bench.

He had a solid, calming presence, and once I realized that, my ire began to fester. The man was trying to close my club, had insulted my morals, and now he thought he could sit next to me and provide comfort? Not on my watch.

"Did you track me down for a purpose?" I scooted an inch away from him on the bench seat. The sun was becoming hot, and I wished I had thought to bring a parasol.

"This meeting is pure happenstance." Mr. Ryder stretched out his long legs. "At least on my part. Perhaps there is a purpose for this meeting unknown to both of us."

I frowned. In a city of over a million souls, London sometimes felt too small by half.

I stood, my abrupt motion seeming to startle Mr. Ryder out of his meditation. He took up the hat sitting on the bench next to him and rose. "I hope my presence isn't chasing you away. It is a fine day for thoughtful contemplation, is it not?"

"I suppose your idea of thoughtful contemplation entails me realizing the error of my ways and shuttering my club." I pushed past him, turning toward the Houses of Parliament. My jaw tightened as he fell into step beside me.

"Not every comment has an ulterior meaning." He smiled down at me. "I was only making conversation."

"Hmph." We turned down George Street, away from the river. Since Lady Richford's death, my mind had become more and more suspicious. There was a chance, a small one, that I might have misjudged Mr. Ryder. Perhaps his words were innocent.

He took my elbow and guided me out of the way of a young chimney sweep running down the pavement. "But since you bring it up, I would like to speak with you further about The Minerva Club."

And perhaps not.

"I have work to attend to, sir." I tugged my arm free. "Good day."

He nudged his hat to sit farther back on his head. The ends of his hair curled about his collar, looking about a week past its trim date. The sun caught the silver threaded through the golden-brown. "I don't mean to offend you. I'm planning to take a turn through St. James's Park." He bent his arm, holding out his elbow. "Will you walk with me?"

I shifted my weight. I had nothing but some correspondence to catch up on waiting for me at home, but the routine task would be preferable to a lecture.

"Come on." He waggled his elbow, giving me a charming smile. "A walk in the fresh air is beneficial. Unless it would be too painful." His gaze dropped to my walking stick.

My muscles quivered. As should be clear to anyone with a functioning mind, my cane was more a statement than used out of actual need. My hair might be white, but I was far from infirm.

I took Mr. Ryder's elbow and started to walk at a brisk pace.

His laugh was as warm and sweet as hot spiced rum. "You needn't prove anything to me." He covered my gloved hand with his own and slowed. "Lazy afternoons are made for strolling, not racing."

My shoulders lowered an inch. A few clouds gathered in the

sky, giving the hope of rain. A pelican swooped through the air, heading for the lake in St. James. I took it as an endorsement of Mr. Ryder's proposition and decided to follow it. "I am not closing The Minerva Club. It is a necessary space for women to come together and enjoy one another's company without the strictures society places on them. As I'm certain you wouldn't deny men a bit of frivolity at their clubs, nor should women be denied such."

He guided me through a small gate into the park, the pavement under our feet transforming into a pebbled path. "Frivolity is fine, in its place." He raised his face to the sun. "When it leads to something darker, to a weakening of morals and duties, then I'm sure *you* wouldn't deny that it has become an evil."

I looked up at him, frowning. "How, pray tell, does learning how to shoot a bow and arrow, having a drink while playing some games, weaken morals?"

The edges of his eyes crinkled as he smiled down at me. I hadn't noticed the color of them before, the soft brown they were, like chocolate mixed with cream. They were really quite lovely, and my frown deepened.

"Nothing is wrong with a bit of play on its own," he said, nodding to a passing couple. "But when it makes a person forget or become resentful of one's duties, causes a discontent in one's life, an urge to make all of life as meaningless as that bit of play, it can have severe consequences."

He held up his hand as I began to object. "And I say the same applies for men. I will continue to speak out against the hells and illicit clubs that your friend Mr. Cooke provides to the dissolute. Just because men sin won't stop me from warning against immorality in women, as well."

I had some doubts whether he spoke out so vociferously against the male-oriented clubs. I sniffed. "Mr. Cooke is a recent acquaintance. Not a friend."

We walked in silence for a moment before he said, "I'm glad to hear it, but you must also be careful in your acquaintances.

Edric Cooke is not a man one can safely associate with."

My body temperature spiked. I'd had a father. A husband I'd needed to defer to, at least in public. As a widow of means, I no longer needed to heed the wishes of men.

I stopped and pulled my hand from his arm. "I grow weary of your constant censure, Mr. Ryder. As you are someone whose counsel I needn't regard nor respect, I see no need to continue this conversation. Good day."

Turning my back on his surprised face, I stomped toward the park's exit.

Mr. Ryder was most likely correct about the character of Mr. Cooke, but if it came down between the two men, I much preferred Mr. Cooke's frank knavery to Mr. Ryder's softly-spoken moralizing.

I didn't want to examine what that might say about my own character.

⁕ ——— ◦◦◦◦◦ ——— ⁕

Chapter Nineteen

Frederick

FREDERICK HAD GONE into the wrong line of work. The offices in the House of Lords chamber in Parliament were large and airy, the furniture an expensive mahogany, the carpets finely-woven Turkish-Berber blends. It was a far cry from his desk at Bow Street where he needed to wedge a piece of folded paper under one leg to minimize the wobbling, and the wood floors of the office were fortunate to be swept once a month, much less see a mop.

Of course, he was in the section for the nation's peers. Perhaps the offices of the Commons would be different.

Frederick was almost surprised when Lord Anglia agreed to see him. He had come without an appointment, but once he entered his private offices, he knew the reason why.

Charles Addison, Earl of Anglia, eyed Frederick like he was an exhibit at Astley's Amphitheatre, his curiosity dripping from his expression. Frederick was to be an experience for him, one he would most likely chew over with a drink with his friends, the Bow Street Runner who had the temerity to question a nobleman.

"Mister…" Anglia dropped his gaze to Frederick's card. "Rollins." He said Frederick's name as though he were tasting it, determining its quality. His condescending smirk told Frederick he had deemed it wanting. "You have questions to ask me?"

"Indeed." The earl didn't offer him a chair, but Frederick took one anyway, sitting across the desk from him. "It is concerning Lady Richford."

"I had guessed that." Without dropping his gaze, Anglia pulled a lacquered snuffbox from his waistcoat pocket and put a pinch to his nose. "What answers do you think I can provide?"

"I understand you were not an admirer of the lady." Frederick didn't bother trying to ask the question with delicacy. He had a feeling it would be unsuccessful, and that the direct approach would be more appreciated. "You had qualms about her influence over her husband when it came to matters of government."

"That is hardly a secret. My opinion piece in *The Times* made that clear." The earl smoothed a hand down his abdomen, and Frederick's gaze fell to his cravat. The bunch in the fabric made the letter hard to read, but there was definitely something embroidered into the cloth. It was not plain like the murder weapon.

"It was also clear just how vexing you found Lord Richford's opposition to some of the bills you want passed. I understand that two in particular have gone through committee now that Richford has been absent from his duties for the past week and will go to the full chamber for vote soon."

The amused curiosity left Anglia's face. He wasn't many years older than Frederick, his body hale. He would easily have the strength to strangle a woman.

Frederick forced his hands to remain at his sides, not rub at the remembered ache of his throat. If Miss Lynton could figure out how to produce an effective strangulation, then any man, even those not in the prime of their lives, could so do so as well, he supposed.

"Richford will be returning soon." Anglia drummed his fingers on his desk. "A week's respite is hardly enough reason to commit murder. Besides, if I had intended to kill the woman, I would hardly have published my complaints about her in the paper to expose me for a suspect."

That was true, if the murder had been premeditated. Frederick wasn't so certain of that. It took anger to choke the life from someone, and that spoke less to a deliberative action and more to an impetuous crime. But why would Anglia meet with the lady in The Minerva Club in the first place? And would Lady Richford agree to see a man who had printed such awful things about her? Frederick could sooner imagine the viscountess attacking the earl than the other way round.

"The two bills that passed committee, they were a prison reform bill and one concerning the funding of a national hospital, is that correct?" Frederick poised his bit of lead over his notebook.

Anglia nodded.

"We've had several prison reform bills pass in the last decade," Frederick said. "Much money is spent but no real reform ever seems to occur."

Anglia covered his mouth to hide a yawn. A fake yawn if Frederick was any judge. "Was there a question there?"

"I suppose I was wondering why you were so angered by Lady Richford's interference, if she did indeed interfere. There will always be an opposition party, always an adversary to clog the gears. What made her actions so special as to deserve your attention?"

Anglia shrugged, his jacket pulling tightly across his shoulders. "There was nothing special about her. As you say, there will always be obstacles to progress. But I've found if one makes an example of one such hindrance, it deters others who might be of the same mind. She was merely my latest example."

"Of course." Frederick tilted his head to the side. "It is the same in my line of work. The hangman's noose not only punishes the guilty, but scares many others into lawful behavior. At least in theory."

If the mention of a noose bothered Anglia, he didn't show it. "Are we done yet? You are becoming tiresome."

"Just about." Frederick looked down at his notes, as though reading a report. "You own shares in the English Engineering Corporation, do you not? A company that could obtain the contracts to build a new prison or new hospital if those bills pass?"

It was useful being an officer for Sir John Stauncey. As the younger son of a baron, the magistrate was kept abreast of society gossip, including the business ventures of its peers. It had long been whispered that Lord Anglia used his position in the House of Lords to benefit his personal holdings.

Unfortunately, the earl was not alone in his actions. If there was any patriotism among the men in government, it was difficult to find.

Anglia sighed, long and deep, as though he was being tried in a most cruel manner. "I have many business interests. English Engineering is not as profitable as it once was. Now, I must return to work. You may go." And he pulled a ledger in front of him and gave it his full attention, acting as though Frederick never existed.

Frederick put away his notebook and lead and stood. "Thank you for your time." He gave the barest of nods before exiting. Lord Anglia as murderer seemed farfetched. After all, he did have many business interests. A corporation he was invested in not obtaining one or two contracts would hardly bankrupt the man. But if Lady Richford interfered with his plans one too many times....

Using a side door, he exited onto a narrow street next to Westminster and turned for his office.

Lady Richford might have been like a pebble in one's boot. A minor annoyance at first, but if one couldn't remove it? If the annoyance never left, was a constant pinch whenever one turned?

Well, what might a man do to get rid of it?

Chapter Twenty

Eleanor

T HE HUSHED VOICES and angry gesticulations weren't what Eleanor was expecting of the conversation between Edgar Bannister and Miss Lydia Abbott. They looked as though they knew each other much better than a son to his mother's friend should. And hated each other.

A sharp point of bark dug into her hand, even through her glove, and she loosened her hold on the ash tree she hid behind.

The grounds in front of the Queen's House were a good place for a meeting. It was open and innocent, a place where many couples and individuals happened into one another, strolling the paths around the lake in St. James's Park. There was enough space to find one's conversation completely private. Eleanor couldn't hear a word they said.

But they should have had more care with their expressions.

Miss Abbott shook her head, her face pinched in disappointment, and turned to leave. Bannister watched her go, his face red. He took off his hat and slapped it against his thigh before replacing it. He started to leave but was stopped by a man calling his name. This conversation seemed more amicable.

"What are you doing?"

Eleanor jumped, her heart pounding so hard it hurt. Spinning, she pressed a hand to her chest. "Mr. Rollins! You shouldn't sneak up on people."

"What are you looking at?" He crowded into her, resting his forearm above her head on the tree, and peered around the trunk.

His throat was at her eye level, the strip of flesh above his collar so close she could roll up onto her toes and kiss it.

Her cheeks heated. *That* was a very inappropriate direction for her thoughts. "I was looking at nothing. Merely taking my afternoon walk."

He turned his face to look down at her. "And your walk just happened to follow the path of Edgar Bannister?" His arched eyebrow expressed his disbelief even more than his tone.

Eleanor leaned back, pressing her spine to the trunk, trying to make some space. "It would appear so."

"Do you have an assignation with Bannister?" Mr. Rollins narrowed his eyes. "What exactly is the man to you?"

Eleanor sucked in a breath. The Runner's mind was always interpreting her actions in the worst possible light. She pushed on his chest, but he didn't move. "He is an acquaintance, nothing more. And one who is a suspect in the murder we all agreed to investigate. For one whose job is deduction, I would have thought my reasons for being here obvious."

"If you believe he might truly be a killer, you shouldn't be anywhere near the man." He looked around the tree again, his jaw clenching. "Keep your questions to the ladies at The Minerva Club."

Eleanor's chest tightened. She was torn between kicking the buffoon in his shin and curling into his chest. It had been so long since anyone had shown a concern for her safety. So long since she'd felt safe. And for all the vexations Mr. Rollins caused her, she couldn't deny his presence felt like a shelter no danger could penetrate.

She restrained herself from doing either action.

He dropped his arm from above her head to the section of trunk by her waist. When she turned to leave in the other direction, he grabbed the other side of the trunk.

Trapping her between his two arms.

She ignored the frisson of excitement that danced up her spine and gave him her most severe look. "Mr. Rollins, you do not have the authority to direct my behavior. You are not my father, brother, or husband. Stop this foolishness and release me."

He lifted his right hand, brought his palm up the length of her arm, his touch so light she wasn't sure she didn't imagine it. He followed the line of her shoulder, her neck and jaw, before brushing an errant curl off her cheek with the pad of his forefinger. "No, I'm none of those things, and it is a shame you don't have a father or brother to keep your behavior in check. Is it not customary for a lady to at least have a maid accompany her when she travels out of doors?"

"I haven't always been a lady." She shifted her weight, her leg brushing against his boot. "There was a time my family had very little money, certainly not enough for an abigail to traipse about after me as I went out to work." If he was surprised by her admission, he didn't show it. There wasn't the censure in his expression that she saw in so many of her acquaintance if she ever broached the topic of her former employment. "Now that we can afford such luxuries, I find I have neither the desire nor the need to pay someone just to follow me about London."

"It's for your safety."

Eleanor huffed out a laugh. "It's for appearances only. If someone wished to do me harm, I can assure you that Emmy, my maid, would provide no obstacle. I could blow her over with one puff from my fireplace bellows."

He frowned, the skin around his eyes wrinkling. They were exceptionally lovely eyes. A deep green, like moss over old stone, that did funny things to her stomach. The shrewdness in them made her stomach churn for an entirely different reason.

"This isn't a lark," he said sternly. "A woman is dead. You need to take more care. Trailing after a murder suspect is not a task to be taken lightly."

"Am I the murder suspect in question?" a voice said at Eleanor's right side.

Mr. Rollins straightened, putting space between himself and Eleanor. She tensed. She didn't know which was worse: Bannister finding her improperly close to Mr. Rollins or him finding out she had been following him.

She cleared her throat. "Mr. Bannister, how nice to see you."

He smirked. "Come now, Ellie, we know each other better than surnames. I have seen your underdrawers, after all."

Something that sounded very like a growl emanated from Mr. Rollins.

Her cheeks heated. "I was eight!" She smoothed her palms down the abdomen of her gown. "I was climbing a large oak tree," she told the Runner. "And he was a perverse child who stood underneath me to try to steal a glimpse."

"You were more droll as a child." Bannister cocked his shoulder against the tree trunk and crossed his arms. "I fear as you've grown older you've become much duller. It must have been those years you were forced to actually work for your food. That humiliation must be such a burden to overcome. If it ever can be."

It was good that her father had recovered his fortune so that the gloves she wore now were of a fine Italian silk, not the threadbare cotton ones of before. Now, when she dug her nails into her palm, all she felt was a slight pressure, no pinch. "Yes, there was a time I earned my wages. I didn't have to go begging to mummy for a farthing." She'd never been able to enjoy her wages. They had always gone to the family's support. But she wouldn't give the sapskull the pleasure of knowing how hard life had been.

Anger flashed in his eyes but was quickly gone. "Those days are over. Father and I will come to an agreement. He would never let his son face deprivation."

She ignored the assessing glance of Mr. Rollins. He seemed all too content to let one of his suspects argue with the daughter of another, waiting to see if any sensational tidbits were revealed. "Where were you from half past eleven to half past midnight when your mother was killed?" If she'd had any qualms about so directly insulting the man before, they were now gone.

His smirk deepened. "I was with a lady friend. We left Carpenter's and took a stroll across Waterloo Bridge. You do remember what it's like to dally in the moonlight with a man, don't you?"

It had only been a minor annoyance, that evening at Lady Hurst's dinner party, the way Bannister had maneuvered her away from her friends and attempted liberties in the darkened cove of a folly. Now she wished she had raised an alarm, blackened his name. Or at least given him a good whatfor right in the bollocks.

"If I was ever in the company of a man under the moonlight, the attention was most unwanted and very short-lived."

Mr. Rollins crossed his arms over his chest, his disapproving look seeming to encompass both her and Bannister. "Why did you not tell me of this woman when last we spoke? You said you were with your friends all night."

Bannister shrugged. "She was very friendly, and I was back at Carpenter's in under an hour."

"What is the name of this woman?" Rollins asked.

"She didn't give it; I didn't ask."

"A most convenient story." Eleanor tried to imagine this man whom she'd played with as a child strangling his mother. Her mind didn't want to acknowledge the possibility. "Without her, the only people who can attest to your whereabouts are your friends, who lost sight of you for nearly an hour. More than enough time to get to The Minerva Club and back."

The amusement drained from Bannister's face, replaced with fury. "Watch your tongue before somebody cuts it out. Everyone knows my disagreements with my mother, but I will not tolerate the slander that I killed her. Your newfound family wealth won't protect you."

"Protect me from whom?" His switch from calm disdain to rage took only a moment. Now Eleanor's mind could envision him becoming physically violent much more readily. "The man who strangled his own mother?"

Quick as a viper, he struck out, grabbing her arm, his grip bruising. He tugged, and she stumbled into his body. "We tolerate you because your father was respected for regaining his fortune. That doesn't mean we like you. With one word, I can make all of society turn their backs on you and your mother, treat you like the outcasts you should have remained."

Mr. Rollins took the wrist that held her. Bannister yelped and released her arm. Rollins dropped the wrist and grabbed Bannister's throat instead, propelling him around the tree until they were out of sight behind the broad trunk.

Eleanor stepped to the side, rubbing her arm.

"Stay there," Mr. Rollins said, his gaze flicking to hers. It wasn't a request.

She shifted back, putting the tree between them again. There were a few curious glances sent their way, so she leaned against the tree, trying to look unconcerned and hoping to hear whatever Rollins had to say to Bannister. Only a few indistinct murmurs met her ears.

Bannister certainly had the temper to kill. But if he were to sneak into the club, he would have had to leave his friends, the woman he'd left the coffeehouse with, changed back into women's garb, and then raced the ten or so blocks to find his mother. Or raced to the club and then changed in a back alley? Either way, if he were dressed as a woman, where did that cravat come from?

Lady Richford could have let her son into the club through the back door, but that hardly seemed likely. If she'd wanted a private conversation with him, having it at home would have made much more sense.

If Bannister had brought the cravat with him in a reticule or such, that would mean he had planned his actions. Eleanor could believe he would commit an act of violence once his blood had been heated, but she had a hard time believing he could plot to kill his mother.

But she'd been wrong about people before.

The two men rejoined her on her side of the tree. Bannister's face was flushed, his jaw set. He inclined his head. "I apologize for laying my hand on you, Miss Lynton. I can assure you it will not happen again." And without another look at them, he spun on his heel and marched away.

Eleanor blinked. "What did you say to him? I've never heard Edgar Bannister apologize before. And he's had ample reason to."

"What I said isn't important." Mr. Rollins took her hand, his fingers flicking the pearl button open at her wrist. He began to roll her sleeve up her arm.

Her heart picked up its pace. "What are you doing?" She tried to pull away to no avail.

"Checking to see if he left bruises. I made him a promise if he left bruises," he muttered.

"I'm fine." She pushed at her sleeve but it was too late.

His fingers tightened around her wrist, his muscles hardening. "What is this?"

The back of her throat felt thick. She blinked. "You know what it is." The ugly red streaks could only be nail marks. It didn't take a detective to see that.

"Who," he said, the softness of his voice its own special emphasis, "did this?"

"It was an accident." She finally managed to remove her arm from his hold and rolled her sleeve back down. "She becomes agitated at times, especially in the evenings. She didn't mean to hurt me."

"Your mother?"

She nodded, focusing her gaze over his shoulder instead of on his face.

"How often does your mother accidentally hurt you?"

She stifled a sob, willed her breathing to remain even. *Too often.* There were times she didn't even recognize her mother. And then there were times when her mother was all sweet smiles and gentleness.

Those times were almost harder to bear. It made the contrast between her other moods more perverse.

"As I said, I'm fine. We're fine, but I thank you for your concern."

"Look at me."

It was beyond her strength to refuse. She met his gaze, held it. The concern she found there was almost her undoing.

"Do you have no one to help you?" he asked. "No other family of your mother's?"

She shook her head. Taking her mother to the country, away from society, would likely be the best option, but they had never purchased another estate once they had means again. Perhaps it was time to start looking, at least for something to lease.

He cradled her cheek, his palm warm against her skin. He looked up and down her body then angled her head, his gaze assessing as he inspected her, as though he could see beneath her clothes, beneath her skin, straight to her broken heart. "Do you have any other injuries?" he asked.

"No." Nothing recent, nothing but some fading bruises. Besides, most of the hurt her mother caused her was internal. It couldn't be healed with cold compresses and soothing teas.

She closed her eyes and just let the moment wash over her. The warm sun. A delicate breeze. A kind man's gentle touch, his thumb tracing along her cheekbone.

"Miss Lynton." His voice was like crushed velvet, soft yet full of texture.

She opened her eyes, her breath catching in her throat. She saw the same uncertainty in his gaze that she felt. The same want. She swayed closer.

A furrow creased his brow. He blinked once. Twice. Then stepped back, dropping his hand and smoothing his features to a businesslike concern.

He cleared his throat. "If your mother isn't well," Rollins said carefully, "if she is prone to violence—"

"She didn't kill Lady Richford." Her body cooled. How silly of her. In her stupider moments she dreamed of a savior, someone who would come to take away her troubles, to rescue her. And how nice would it be if that savior came in the shape of a man like Mr. Rollins, someone who would not only offer help, but love.

But those were the dreams of a child. She had no protector, no guardian angel. Her mother was her responsibility and hers alone. A part of her still wanted to tell him everything, lay her burdens at his feet. His shoulders seemed broad enough to carry them.

But he was an officer of Bow Street. His primary objective was solving the murder, not giving assistance or sympathy to Miss Eleanor Lynton.

She adjusted her bonnet, slid the pearl button at her wrist back through its loop. "I thank you for your concern, but it isn't needed. Good day, Mr. Rollins."

He didn't try to stop her from leaving.

But she felt his gaze on her back the entire way out of the park.

$$\text{\textasciitilde}\!\!\infty\!\!\text{\textasciitilde}$$

Chapter Twenty-One

Lady Mary

I PRETENDED NOT to look. The moment between Miss Abbott and Mrs. Sanders appeared intimate. Tender. They sat on a high-backed settee in the library, their words low before Mrs. Sanders rested her forehead on Miss Abbott's shoulder and cried. Mrs. Sanders was a more recent member of my club, but she appeared to be taking Lady Richford's death hard.

Finding no reason to continue standing in the doorway, I continued my rounds of the rooms. I didn't used to prowl about my own club, looking for anything amiss, but now I found myself making the rounds several times a day.

I frowned. Were there fewer women enjoying the club today? It was difficult to measure. Bernard recognized the members and allowed them entry when they appeared at the door. He didn't keep a written record of who arrived or when. I contemplated the feasibility of implementing such a system. Bernard certainly wouldn't like the additional work.

I changed direction to speak to him about it. When I arrived at the front door, I caught my doorman reading a paper. When he caught sight of me, he shoved it behind his back.

"You know I don't mind if you occupy your mind while you're stationed at the door, Bernard. No need to hide the paper."

"Of course, milady." But the paper remained behind his back, his arm bent at an uncomfortable angle.

I narrowed my eyes. "Is that *The Times*? I didn't find my usual copy on my desk this morning."

He hemmed and hawed, his jowls jiggling slightly. "There are times, milady, when the paper is not worth reading."

My suspicions grew. If the paper wasn't worth reading today, than why had he been nose-deep in its pages? I held out my hand. "The paper, please."

"I really don't think...."

"Bernard." I kept my voice firm. It was that dratted Ryder. He had written more drivel about my club, I just knew it. I pushed down the hint of betrayal I felt. We'd had what I considered a convivial conversation. He apparently took it as an opportunity for more information gathering for his letter writing campaign.

With a mournful sigh, Bernard handed me the paper.

"Thank you." Forgetting my purpose in seeking the doorman out, I turned from Bernard and marched to my office, paper tucked under my elbow. When I arrived, I cleared everything else off my desk and opened the paper to the opinion section.

It wasn't difficult to understand why Bernard hadn't wanted me to see this.

"Scandal continues to lurk amongst the newest addition to London's gentlemen's, ahem, gentlewomen's, clubs. Instead of acting as an equalizing force, and being promoted as a sanctuary for women to have a moment of freedom from society's strictures, The Minerva Club is instead a haven of corruption, a place designed for illicit assignations, a willing accomplice to its members' depraved inclinations.

This author has learned that the husbands of several of its members have withdrawn their permission for their wayward ladies to frequent such a club. As its monies dries up, thankfully, its doors will soon close.

And is it any surprise that such a club should come to so ignominious an end? It's owner, Lady M—, has long been suspected of mental…fragility, shall I say? That she should have been allowed to open such an establishment in the first place is a judgment on all our heads. From the time she set fire to a skiff on the Serpentine to her most recent misadventure of riding the bronze stag in Hyde Park, it is clear that instead of being allowed free rein to start sinful businesses, the lady should instead be taken in hand, perhaps sent to live out her remaining days on some country estate. We know her nephew has a large one.

If her relations are unwilling to check her behavior, well, there are other institutions that would willingly take up the cause."

I leaned back in my chair and focused on my breathing, sharp inhales through my nose, slow exhales from my mouth. It did little to calm my ire. This opinion piece was anonymous, and much more vicious than the last. I no longer thought Mr. Ryder was its author. He seemed the type to put his name on his opinions, and even though he wanted to shutter my doors, I didn't feel as though he would make his attacks so brutal and personal.

Who knew about my concerns that The Minerva Club had been used for *illicit assignations*? I had told very few people about my concerns. Could this piece have been written by someone in the club, someone who knew about those assignations because he or she had taken part in them?

And what of the comment about dwindling membership? The halls of the club had seemed a bit emptier than usual, but if the husbands of my members were revoking their ladies' memberships, then the author had inside knowledge to which I was not yet privy. Or was this a case of stating something as fact in the hopes of making it come true? Would my members' husbands read this nonsense and think it was their moral duty to also refuse their wives this leisure time?

I pulled my ledgers from a bottom drawer, examining the past numbers. I had been making a profit, and it steadily grew each month, but my margins weren't large. If membership fees started drying up, it wouldn't be long before I ran into trouble.

I slumped back in my chair. I sometimes wondered if The Minerva Club had been a mistake. It had been born from jealousy, and nothing good usually came from that. My nephew and his friends seemed to enjoy their time drinking, relaxing, communing in their gentlemen's clubs, and I had wanted something similar for myself. My home was my haven, but issues domestic did occur. At those times, a woman should be able to escape those pressures for an hour or two, just as a man could.

The insults to myself I could ignore. I had earned a reputation, and it was one I was just a bit proud of. Being thought eccentric had allowed me to act with more freedom. I was the batty Lady Mary. The aunt of a duke who had more daring than sense. The *ton* might roll their eyes at some of my actions, snicker behind my back, but no one had ever tried to stop me from implementing my will.

Until now.

I walked back through my club with fresh eyes. There were definitely more empty seats than usual. There was no game of lawn bowling occupying the hall, no shouts from the archery room.

There *were* some whispered conversations that abruptly cut off when I entered a room. Several pairs of eyes darted my way, some glowing with the natural joy of gossip, some with malicious glee. Even as the owner of a club these women obviously enjoyed, I wasn't exempt from their disdain or mockery. Human nature reveled at seeing others brought low. Perhaps it made us feel safe somehow. That if a tragedy was happening to someone else, we would be spared.

But no one was spared in this life. Lady Richford was a stark reminder of that.

Chapter Twenty-Two

Lady Mary

THE REST OF the day passed quickly. I readjusted my orders in deference to the expected loss of patrons I was to have for the next few weeks at the least. Wrote a few letters asking the recipients to inquire with their contacts as to who the author of that anonymous piece had been. Even started a timeline of everything we knew about the murder and its suspects. That outline spanned several pages of paper, and only a lack of pins kept me from attaching it to my wall.

Tea time had come and gone without me partaking, and when my stomach rumbled for the third time, I decided it was time for supper. Instead of ringing a bell for a servant, I stretched my back as I straightened from behind the bar in the Country Pub room where I'd been taking inventory, and headed for the kitchens next to the Tea Room.

I passed by a sitting room where two women sat on the circular settee, faces close together, red staining their cheeks as I passed.

I lifted my chin and kept marching. My steps paused at the doorway to the Tea Room. My partner in crime-solving sat on one sturdy wooden stool at the bar along the east wall, tracing a pattern on the mahogany bar top with the tip of her finger, a half full sherry glass in her other hand.

Changing course, I made my way over to her. "Miss Lynton, are you all right?" We were the only ones in the room, except for Bobby, who stood slouched behind the bar, looking bored.

"Just lovely." She blew out a breath, a lock of hair lifting from her cheek before slowly drifting back down.

"You don't look lovely." She looked half-sprung, not the appropriate condition for a gently-bred young miss.

Mr. Ryder's voice whispered through my mind, murmuring the barest of 'I told you so's', but I shoved it aside. My club did not encourage licentiousness.

Miss Lynton threw back the rest of her drink, her face twisting into a grimace. "Another please," she asked Bobby.

"Are you certain?" I asked. "You don't look as though you enjoyed that one."

"I detest the taste of sherry, but it is the drink for ladies."

I considered sending her home. Or ordering her coffee instead. I slapped the bar. It had been a trying day for more than just me, apparently, and a stiff drink or three sounded like a good idea. "Try a brandy instead. It's my drink of choice. Make it two," I told Bobby.

He slid the glasses in front of us, taking the sherry glass to clean. I took Miss Lynton's elbow and guided her off the stool before she could drink. "Let's take these to more comfortable seats." Hard wood stools were a trial for my back. I nodded to Bobby. "Our patronage is slim tonight. Why don't you start closing up the other rooms. Anyone who wants a drink can join us in here."

"I don't want to be surrounded by people," Miss Lynton complained.

I sighed. "Don't worry, you won't be."

I led her to the sofa along the wall covered in a lovely lavender brocade. When it was daylight, the large windows across the room let the sun warm this seat. This evening, the airy room was reflected in watery lines on the panes of glass against an ebony backdrop.

Miss Lynton took a large swallow of the brandy. Her face contorted, her tongue pushing against her lips as though trying to push the taste of the liquor out. "This is worse than sherry."

"Sip it, don't quaff it like ale." I took my own sip. My brandy was from the Cognac region of France, aged four years in an oak barrel. It was delicious, and obviously wasted on the youth. "Now, what brings you here tonight seeking answers in the bottom of a drink, Miss Lynton? And you should know, liquor answers no questions." Though it could soften the jagged edges of a day quite nicely.

"You may as well call me Eleanor. We are trying to solve a murder together." She sat back and rested her glass on her abdomen. "I didn't want to be in my house any longer."

"Ah." Some women wanted to escape their husbands when they came here. For Eleanor, it could only be her mother she wished to avoid. "Is Mrs. Lynton fretting about Lady Richford's murder? Does she worry about being a suspect?"

"I don't think she's aware she is a suspect." She took a tiny sip, grimaced. "It wasn't losing our fortune that hurt my mother the most. It was losing her place in society. From being a respected woman of the *ton*, having her opinions and well-wishes sought after, to being cast out and into the ranks of a Cit. Even now, it still weighs on her. She never truly recovered."

"And her company is unpleasant as a result?"

Eleanor averted her gaze, staring at a round table across the room where three ladies had taken up occupancy. "Not unpleasant. Only…difficult."

I was hard-pressed to see the difference. I thought of the woman in question. When she'd petitioned to join the club, her smile had seemed just a little too bright, a little too brittle, but I'd accounted that to her struggle to regain her place in society. She had trod a difficult road, and I respected her resiliency.

Perhaps Mrs. Lynton hadn't been as resilient as I'd thought. "You are always welcome here, but whatever problems you're having with your mother, hiding won't help them."

"Oh, let's speak of something else." Eleanor huffed. "I'm tired of worrying about it." She held up her glass. "I saw that you made the paper again today. Did you really set a boat on fire?"

I grimaced. "I was merely giving my beloved *spitzhund* a Viking funeral. He was from Finland, you understand." The fact that people still remembered that one rankled. It had happened nearly twenty years ago. But Henrik had deserved the grand send off. That dog had the noblest spirit I'd ever known.

"And were you pretending to ride the bronze stag in Hyde Park?" The edges of Eleanor's eyes crinkled. "You do know it can't take you anywhere."

"I was merely seated upon it so I didn't get an ache in my neck when speaking to Miss Abbott. She sat upon a large bay." One would think I'd been shouting tally-ho and waving my chemise about my head for all the fuss it made. At the time I'd been rather impressed with myself, solving a problem creatively, creating a seat where none had existed.

Creativity tended to be frowned upon in my circles, however.

"Were you astride or side-saddle?" she asked, her lips twitching. "I want a clear picture of it in my head."

I narrowed my eyes. "Drink your brandy."

We sat in companionable silence, me enjoying my drink, Eleanor merely tolerating hers. But the muscles in her shoulders seemed to loosen, the tension in her face released. I considered asking about her mother again, but frankly, I had enough problems of my own. I wasn't in the mindset to take on some of her burdens.

"The mood is most somber in here this evening." Mr. Rollins strolled into the room and stopped before us, looking sharp in a navy blue jacket.

Eleanor popped up straight. Apparently, I wasn't the only woman to think so.

"What are you doing here?" she asked, her voice peevish.

The Runner arched an auburn brow. "And a good evening to you, as well."

Eleanor stared down into her now empty glass. "I apologize. You surprised me. I wasn't expecting to see you tonight."

"Not all surprises should be unwelcome." He crossed his arms over his chest.

I thought about scooting over, making room for him between Eleanor and me, but I didn't want to make it too easy for him. A man should put in some effort when he wooed a woman. I had no doubt Mr. Rollins wanted to woo Miss Lynton, though I didn't know if he would allow himself that pleasure.

Or whether Miss Lynton would welcome it.

The group of women across the room stood and drifted to the scattering of wingbacks nearer to us. They kept their gazes averted, but Mr. Rollins's appearance could be the only reason for their change of setting. The Runner was still a curiosity, and a handsome one at that. They wanted to eavesdrop.

As I had nothing of importance to discuss, I would allow it. "Find a seat instead of looming over us," I told him. "And we're not somber. Merely contemplative."

"May I contemplate as well over a drink with you?" He looked toward the bar. Bobby had yet to reappear, and it was currently unmanned.

"Help yourself." If The Minerva Club shuttered its doors, at least I would have an impressive inventory of liquor in which to drown my woes. "The glasses are behind the bar."

Eleanor held up hers. "Can you bring me another brandy?"

Rollins cocked his head, examining the rosiness of her cheeks, the slight glaze to her eyes. "No." He turned on his heel and strode toward the bar.

"Did he just say no?" Eleanor blinked, her expression pinching. "The impudence." She rose to her feet with only the slightest of sways. "The nerve."

One of our listeners tittered behind her hand.

"The waste of time." I jutted my jaw toward where Rollins stood behind the bar. "Instead of complaining, go get one yourself."

"I will." Chin lifted, Eleanor marched across the room. She had just reached the bar when one of the large windows facing the street exploded into a tiny million shards.

Eleanor screamed, turning her back on the flying glass. She dropped to her knees on the floor.

Two streaks of light cascaded in a graceful arc through the broken window and smashed onto the floor. Two separate fires blazed up, stretching toward the ceiling, before reaching for each other, becoming one large conflagration.

My brain tried to catch up with what my eyes were seeing. "Go!" I told the women who had flown to the doorway to huddle in it, eyes wide with horror. "Get out of the club. Get Bernard."

I didn't wait to see if they obeyed. Because as I watched, a lick of flame stretched its fingers toward Eleanor, toying with the hem of her gown. I started to move forward, pulling out my handkerchief but knowing it wouldn't be sufficient to smother out a fire.

Rollins gripped the edge of the bar and leapt over it. Whipping off his jacket, he smacked at the flames as he dragged Eleanor away. With her gown merely charred, he lifted her in his arms and hurried over to me, placing her back on her feet. "Get out of here, both of you." Without sparing us another glance, he went back to the fire, battering it with his jacket, kicking furniture out of its path.

Bobby emerged from the kitchen, his eyes flaring wide before he, too, leapt into action. He hollered for Timothy, and the two of them set to trying to douse the fire with buckets of water they filled from the kitchen.

I pushed Eleanor in front of me, prodding her out the door.

"We can't leave him." She coughed, a tear trickling down her cheek.

"He's not alone. Bobby and Timothy are with him." And the three of them had better know when it was time to get out. I loved my club, but it wasn't worth their lives. "If you want to help, find Bernard. Have him send for a night watchman. And then wait on the street."

"But—"

"Go!" I pushed her lower back, and finally, she went.

Lifting my skirts, I trotted to the Great Room at the back of the club. From there I made my way forward, checking every room, calling loudly. I found a couple of women in the Greek Room, a few more playing darts. Once I was assured that all my members were out, I joined Eleanor on the street and watched as the flames flickered through the windows, praying for a miracle.

I looked at the sky, but it remained cloudless above. There would be no saving rain.

A crowd gathered. The flames continued to crackle.

Eleanor took my hand, gripping it tightly as all the hopes I'd put into my club burned before me.

Chapter Twenty-Three

Frederick

THE TEA ROOM was a disaster. Even as high as it was, the cream coffered ceiling was coated with soot. Two-thirds of the hardwood floor planks were either warped from the heat or eaten right through from the flames. Perhaps a few chairs and settees along the far wall could be salvaged, but the rest were charred, torn, and reeked of smoke.

In a stroke of luck, the antique mahogany bar remained unblemished, along with the many bottles of liquor racked behind it.

"This is only the second time I've seen this. Nasty business," the marshal of the London Fire Brigade said, shaking his head. "And shortsighted. No matter how much someone might not like this establishment, if you and the other boys hadn't stopped this fire, it could have set off the whole block. Damn, the whole neighborhood for that matter."

Frederick thought trying to burn The Minerva Club was bad enough. And anyone rash enough to commit this act wasn't sound enough of mind to consider all the possible consequences.

The Runner toed at a bit of clay by his boot. "What exactly was it? These two clay jugs came flying through the window, and the next thing I knew, flames were everywhere." Including burning Miss Lynton's gown. His stomach curdled. He'd never forget how he'd felt when he'd seen her on the floor, a red-gold flame licking up her skirts. He never wanted to feel such again.

Frederick was never one to avoid the truth. He had feelings for Miss Lynton. He could no longer deny it. He'd almost kissed her in the park, in broad daylight. It had only been the appearance of a young family strolling along the path near them that had brought him to his senses. The thought of what could have happened to her if she'd been closer to the window when it shattered, or closer to the jug that had started the fire....

"We call them burn bottles." The marshal rubbed his pinkened cheek. Frederick didn't know if it was the result of catching the tail end of their fire and getting too near, or if his face had just gotten too much sun earlier in the day. "Mix alcohol with a bit of tar, stop up the bottle with a bit of cloth to use as a fuse, set it alight and throw it at yer target. When the bottle breaks, the alcohol spreads and sets everything near alight. Nasty business," he repeated.

It was nasty. Frederick ground his jaw. Was it targeted at Lady Mary's club because of the moral outrage those two pieces in the paper had raised, or did it have anything to do with Lady Richford's death?

He rubbed his forehead. At the moment, he didn't care. He wanted to throttle the individual responsible, regardless of motive. He looked at the shattered remains of the clay jugs again. Or two someones. The jugs had flown through the window at almost the same moment. It would have been difficult for one man to throw two of them, unless he was very talented with both of his hands.

"You'll send your report to me?" he asked the marshal.

The man grunted. "As soon as you come by and sign your witness statement, you can pick it up."

Frederick nodded, not wanting to get into a pissing duel with the insurance company that ran the fire brigade. He made sure that Timothy and Bobby knew to board up the windows before closing up the club, then stumbled out. All his muscles ached, his lungs burned. He was sore and irritated and out of patience.

The knot around his chest loosened when he caught sight of Miss Lynton standing with her arm entwined with Lady Mary's. A few stragglers lingered, but most of the crowd had wandered off in various degrees of relief that their neighboring homes and businesses were safe and disappointment that a more exciting outcome had been averted.

He crossed the street to the women. "How are you?" he asked Miss Lynton. "Do you need a surgeon?"

She shook her head. Did he imagine the relief that crossed her face when she'd seen him? "Aside from needing a new gown, I'm fine."

Something about her tone alerted him. Her voice was too light. Too airy.

He gripped her waist, walked her two steps back and hefted her onto the waist-high stone wall that fronted the office building across from the club.

"Put me down." She slapped at his hands, but he ignored her.

He squatted and raised the charred edge of her skirts. Her protests ended in a shocked gasp.

The gas street lamp nearby wasn't bright, but it illuminated enough. He traced around the edges of the burn on her calf. "There is a slight reddening of the skin, but there will be no lasting harm."

She flicked her skirts back down to cover her legs, glaring. "As I said, I need no doctor. It does sting like the devil, however."

"I'd recommend whiskey for that kind of hurt." Lady Mary pulled her lace shawl closer about her shoulders. "Brandy and sherry are too civilized for burnt flesh."

His stomach hardened. Miss Lynton needed a safe home to retreat to, someone to provide her care. Instead, she had a mother who needed her own care, a home that was more danger than refuge. Muscles tense, he turned to Lady Mary. "I will see her home. Can I drop you along the way?"

Lady Mary blew out a breath. "I'll send for my carriage after I assess the damage. How far did it spread?"

"The fire was contained in the Tea Room, although the paper lining the walls in the hall next to that room might smell of smoke for a while." He lifted Miss Lynton down. It had been warm enough earlier in the evening for him to leave his greatcoat at home. And his jacket was burned to ashes. He had nothing to offer Miss Lynton to warm her.

A hackney rolled a block up at the cross street. Frederick brought his fingers to his mouth and loosed a piercing whistle. The jarvey looked their way, and Frederick held up his hand. "Let's get you home," he told Miss Lynton, wrapping an arm around her shoulder.

She must have been more shaken than she let on for she didn't utter a protest. Saying their farewells to Lady Mary, they walked down the street to the waiting hackney. Once he'd handed Miss Lynton in, he gave the driver his direction.

She started to poke her head back out. "That's not my home."

He climbed the steps, forcing her back inside. He shut the door tightly before sitting back on his bench. "No," he agreed. "It's mine."

She was silent a moment. Then, "Why?"

The hell he knew. But he had to come up with some reason. "I want to take a better look at your burn." That at least was the truth, but he could have examined her in her own parlor. She seemed to have decent servants, loyal, at least he'd found after his few conversations with them. He wouldn't be leaving her untended there.

But not only did he want to go home, he wanted her in his home, as well.

"Mr. Rollins—"

"Frederick," he growled. They were past formalities. "When we're in private, you'll call me Frederick, Eleanor." He rolled her name over his tongue, like it had substance, like he could taste it. "I don't want you at your house. Not now. You need to be somewhere safe, where you can recover without further threat."

She looked down at her hands clasped tightly in her lap. "She wouldn't hurt me, not truly. She isn't thinking clearly at times."

Whether it was from a disturbed mind or malice made little difference to him. The end result was the same. Eleanor needed relief from her mother. He had yet to determine how best that relief should be obtained.

"Nevertheless, I want to examine your burns somewhere quiet." Somewhere they wouldn't be disturbed. He sank back on the seat, suddenly exhausted. When the hackney pulled to a stop in front of his lodging house, he was almost too tired to climb down. It was only Eleanor's nervous glances, the twisting of her fingers, that had him moving. He didn't want her feeling unsure, not when he'd never been more sure of anything in his life.

He'd known it the moment she'd screamed in terror. Known he'd do anything to prevent her fear in the future.

This woman was his. It didn't matter that he didn't deserve her. That she had her pick of dozens of men better than him in both understanding and status. She was his. He was hers. There was no going back.

He led her up to the first floor, to his rented rooms on the right of the staircase. Settled her on one of his two chairs in his small parlor. Kindled the coal on the fire, more for comfort than for heat. Then dug out a small box he kept in a chest at the foot of his bed.

"Lift up your skirts," he told her when he returned. He knelt in front of her, wishing he had a rug instead of just the hard wood beneath his knees.

Eyes wide, she inched up the burnt cotton. The top edge of her boot came into view, then the cuff of her stocking, the skin of her calf. It would have been sensuous if the skin she exposed hadn't been swollen and reddened.

He swallowed. It could have been so much worse. He knew how precarious life could be; he saw it every day in his job. But this had rattled him.

He pulled a bandage from his box, a container of salve. As he tended to her burn, he wanted to demand she leave off investigating Lady Richford's murder. That she stay locked away at home until he discovered the culprit, but remaining at home wasn't safe for her, either. He examined his options, and liked none of them. Short of kidnapping Eleanor and keeping her in his rooms....

His hands paused.

No, he couldn't do that, no matter how appealing. He finished the knot on the bandage, letting his fingers linger a moment longer on her soft skin before rolling back onto his heels. "All done. You will survive."

"As I said all along." Eleanor pushed her skirts back down, her hands trembling faintly. "It does feel better, though. Thank you."

He took her hand and squeezed. "You're safe now."

A harsh chuckle tore from her throat. "It's hard to feel safe when the ground under your feet is constantly shifting. I just need to get through the next weeks, ensure my mother isn't arrested for something she didn't do"—with that she gave him a pointed look—"then wait for the next hurdle to cross our path. There's always another hurdle."

His leg beginning to cramp, he rose and pulled her up with him. "You don't have to face those difficulties alone." He rubbed at a smudge of ash on her cheek. "Why haven't you married?"

"I..." She raised one shoulder, her gaze fixed at a point on his chest. "I suppose I never met anyone with whom I match. We were struggling when I came of age, but I was raised a gentlewoman. I didn't fit into the lives of the merchants or men of service around me. I suppose I could have found a nice tutor or clergyman, but it never seemed important. Staying with my parents, helping them as much as I could, that was what mattered."

He cupped her chin, raised it until she had no choice but to look in his eyes. "That does matter, but it's all right to let someone help you, as well. Let someone take care of you for once."

Her breath caught. "Are you offering to be that someone?"

Damn right. His mental response came immediately, without hesitation. He didn't let his mind wander to all the reasons this was a bad idea. To all the reasons they shouldn't be together. Eleanor could have died that night. Could have come home with more than a light burn. As much as he needed to reassure her, he needed comfort himself. His blood raced, reminding him they were both alive, and that life was precious and short.

He didn't answer her with words. He pulled her to him, his fingers burrowing into her thick hair, knocking it free from its pins. He clutched her to him for one breathless moment before taking her mouth with his own. Tasting her sweetness. Swallowing her moan.

Eleanor wrapped her arms around his back, fitting her body against his. Banding one hand around her waist and the other under her rump, he lifted and carried her without ceremony or grace to his bedroom.

Their fingers tangled in a rush to remove clothes. Eleanor must have felt the same madness as he, the same driving urge to prove they had cheated death. The weak glow of a half-moon and the remnant of light from the lamp in the other room provided more shadow than illumination. His palms skimming her heated flesh cast an image of her in his mind rather than sight. His lips memorized the swell of her breast, the soft curve of her belly.

Frederick didn't think about his duty to catch Lady Richford's killer, couldn't worry that this woman's mother might be guilty. His only thought was how fortunate he was to be able to hold her in his arms. How a few inches difference in where that burn bottle had landed could have taken this night from him, this woman. And with the backs of his eyes burning with an emotion he couldn't quite place, Frederick eased himself inside of her.

Their breaths heated each other's lips. Their bodies moved as one. And for the first time that he could remember, Frederick felt truly at peace.

"I'M GLAD YOU never found a nice tutor."

Eleanor couldn't contain her snort of laughter. She buried her face in his side. His warm, very naked side. She still couldn't quite believe what they had done. The audacity of the act made her giddy. All the advances she'd rebuffed over the years. The marriage proposals her father's wealth had elicited that she'd turned down. Only to find herself in the arms of a Bow Street Runner.

A Runner who thought her mother might have killed a woman.

Her euphoria waned. She wasn't wont to act irrationally, and she frowned, unsure of her next step. The idea of leaving his bed, his warmth, getting dressed and going home left her cold.

But she couldn't stay here. She had more freedom than most women her age with no male family member to check her movements, but staying out all night was a bridge too far, even for her independent spirit. And what would Frederick expect of her now? What did she want of him? The one predictable part of her life, her status as a single, unmatched, unmated woman, she'd blasted a cannonball through in under one hour.

Her stomach twisted. Would he expect her to change her whole life now?

And how much worse would it be if he wanted nothing to change?

He tugged on a lock of her hair. "What are you thinking about? Your entire body went hard as a rock."

She ran her fingers over his chest, marveling at the hard muscle underneath, the springiness of the hair above. She might never get another chance to explore his body so. "Only that I'd better start home. Maids do talk."

He rolled, pinning her beneath his body. "Then we should give them something worth talking about."

He lowered his mouth just as a loud knocking battered against his front door.

Frederick dropped his forehead to hers, blowing out a breath. "Stay here." He climbed out of bed and found a banyan, shoving his arms through.

Eleanor got out after him, looking for her shift. No matter what he said or how much she might want to stay, it was better to leave now. It would be far too easy to fall asleep curled next to him, and where would that get her?

Her self-restraint wasn't needed. Because she was eavesdropping as Frederick opened his front door, she heard the other man clearly.

"Stauncey wants you. There's been another murder. Edgar Bannister is dead."

Chapter Twenty-Four

Frederick

EDGAR BANNISTER LOOKED surprised that he was dead. His eyes were wide and glassy, his mouth hanging loosely open. The amount of blood that surrounded his body proved all too well, however, that Lord and Lady Richford's son was gone.

Sir John Stauncey's arms were crossed, his hands tucked up under his armpits, a pinched look on his face. "This will devastate Lord Richford. I don't know if the man will recover from losing both his son and his wife."

Frederick breathed through his mouth, the smell of blood giving him a headache. "I will have to question him. There is the possibility he's involved." Lord Richford was family to both victims. It made him an obvious suspect.

Stauncey looked up at him, glaring. "I know Richford. He's not a man capable of this."

"Even if he discovered his son killed his beloved wife?" Frederick was thinking aloud, trying to process all the possibilities. When his employer shook his head and said, "Not even then," Frederick was forced to agree. He would speak with the viscount, of course, but in his heart of hearts Frederick knew the man was innocent.

Stauncey sighed and ran his hand up the back of his head.

"What do you think?"

Frederick examined the scene again. Bannister was in the parlor of his rooms at the Albany, a lodging house to many bachelors of wealth and rank. His body lay a few feet from the fireplace, a hole piercing his throat, his life's blood soaked into the thick carpet underneath. A scrap from a piece of paper lay inches from his head. "The weapon was a small caliber, possibly a thirteen millimeter? Fifteen at the largest." The misshapen wad of lead embedded in the wall might tell them more about the gun.

"A woman's pistol?" Stauncey said.

Frederick nodded. "Or one a man can easily conceal." Pointing at the bullet, he continued. "Bannister was standing before the fire when he was shot, I'm guessing at close range both because of the accuracy of the shot through the center of the neck and because of the velocity needed for the bullet to exit his neck."

Stauncey nodded. "Notice how high the bullet is lodged in the wall? The shooter must have been very small in stature and pointing up at Bannister."

Frederick had noted that, too. He would make the formal calculations based on the victim's height and the height of the bullet in the wall, but the idea of a female killer was looking more and more probable.

"He must have known his killer." Frederick pointed to the nearby chairs, arranged just so around a low table. To the books orderly stacked on the mantel. "There was no struggle. Bannister invited the person in." He looked again, but only saw one glass on a low side table. "He didn't offer his visitor a drink, or hadn't gotten to that point yet."

"The paper?"

Frederick stepped around the pool of blood and squatted by Bannister's head. "A piece of a letter, perhaps? Only a few words are visible. *Shouldn't.* And then the next line, *cannot wait for.* The rest is gone, most likely ashes in the fire."

Stauncey cracked his neck. "A letter from the killer, destroyed to hide his identity?"

Frederick made a noncommittal sound. If Bannister had been holding it when he'd been killed, the remainder torn from his hand and destroyed by the killer, why was this lone piece above his head, on a small section of floor not covered in blood. It seemed almost positioned. But why?

"The neighbors?" Stauncey asked.

"Are being questioned now." Frederick rose, staring down at the body. He hadn't liked Edgar Bannister in life, but he would do his damnedest to serve him in death. There were few people who truly deserved this fate, and Bannister hadn't struck him as one of them. He had been petty, immature, greedy, but none of those faults were worthy of a death sentence. His behavior toward Eleanor deserved a sound throttling, but not death.

Frederick would find out who had killed him, not only because it was his job, but because this killer was beginning to make him bloody angry, not least because the call had taken him from his bed that had been warmed by Eleanor. He'd tried to convince her to stay at his lodgings, to wait for him, but looking at the scene before him he knew she had been right to go home. This would take the rest of the night to work. Dropping her at her home, watching her go inside not knowing if she would be protected, had been more difficult than he'd anticipated.

"We got the safe open," an agent said from the doorway to the bedroom.

Frederick nodded to the two men who stood guard at the front door. "You can take the body to the surgery now." Watching a dissection was his least favorite duty, but useful information could be gleaned. He hoped the coroner would find something to point to their killer.

He and the magistrate went into Bannister's bedroom, through to the dressing room. A rack of dinner jackets had been pushed aside exposing the safe embedded in the wall. The now open safe.

Frederick pulled out his notepad to take inventory. One hundred and twenty-seven pounds. An emerald cravat pin. A gold ring with his family's insignia. A black velvet sack. He directed the agent to take out the sack and remove the contents so Frederick could continue writing the inventory.

The agent upended the bag, and the contents tumbled to the seat of a settee in front of a dressing mirror. Jewelry glittered under the gas lamps. "Mostly ladies' stuff," the agent said, poking through the pile. "Gifts to lady friends?"

That Bannister stockpiled beforehand? That hardly seemed likely. But Frederick dutifully cataloged each item. Three necklaces, one pure gold, the other inset with emeralds, another with rubies. Several bracelets, a set of drop earrings. A man's silver pocket watch, the top of the hour hand inlaid with a cut diamond. And two rings, one plain, the other a wrought gold posey ring with the words *Je t'adore* engraved in script on the surface.

Frederick fingered the ring. Something about it seemed familiar, though for the life of him he couldn't think why.

"Box it all up," Frederick told the agent. "Put it in our safe at Bow Street tagged with the case number."

The man nodded, and Frederick and Stauncey wandered back into the bedroom. The magistrate planted his hands on his hips and surveyed the slight disorder. "Whatever pressure we felt before from Lady Richford's death will now be doubled. We need to make an arrest."

"We need to arrest the murderer."

Stauncey gave him a narrow-eyed look. "There are times when calming a frightened public takes precedence over…"

Frederick's stomach turned. "Truth? Justice?" He agreed that the public deserved the peace of an arrest, but he wouldn't knowingly take in the wrong person. See an innocent person face the gallows.

His rebellion must have shown on his face because Stauncey jabbed his finger at him. "Wrap this up quickly, or I'll assign someone who will."

Someone who'd put politics above due process. Frederick

nodded. He only had a couple of days to resolve the case before it was taken from him. He'd best make the most of them. He strode for the exit, only to be brought up short by one of the agents calling him back.

"We found something else in the back of the safe. It must have fallen out of the sack of other jewelry." He held it up, the piece catching the light of the gas lamps.

It was another ruby necklace, but the stones on this one were larger, the filigree gold chain finer. Frederick took it from the agent, feeling its weight. It was a beautiful piece of jewelry, and worth a small fortune. He turned it over, and a small engraving in the clasp caught his attention. He moved to a wall lamp and held it closer to the light.

The engraving was only two letters: A.M.

The initials were common enough. Frederick wrote down a description of the necklace in his notebook, snapping it shut when he'd finished. Common, but to his investigation, telling.

He needed to have another conversation with Amelia Massey.

Chapter Twenty-Five

Lady Mary

THE NOISE AND tumult in front of my club matched that of my heart. I stared out one of the remaining windows from my Tea Room at the crowd protesting The Minerva Club. The boards across the other window were an ugly reminder of the hate someone had directed my way.

I examined some of the protesters' signs, saw one with my name on it.

They weren't just protesting my club. They were protesting me.

It was a strange feeling, having a mob deride your name. A few even called for my arrest, though I didn't see what law they could claim I'd broken.

"Lady Mary?"

I turned, and saw Bernard standing in the doorway. Behind him, two painters were setting up a small scaffold.

I tried to give him a reassuring smile, like having someone try to burn your place of employment down was just a part of doing business. "Yes?"

"There's a gentleman here to see you. A Mister Ryder." Bernard's sniff told me he knew who my caller was and didn't approve of the man.

I considered turning him from my door. Mr. Ryder deserved a good snubbing if ever anyone did. But with an angry mob outside my club with the ability to destroy it before this room had even been restored, I put my anger aside and let my better sense rule.

"Send him to my office. I'll see him there." The smell of smoke in this room still made my eyes burn, and I wouldn't have him think me so upset my eyes teared.

I passed Timothy in the hallway, a ladder slung over his shoulder. "Would you send a tea service for two to my office? And if we have any of those cakes left over from yesterday, I would appreciate it." I needed something sweet right now when everything else seemed bitter.

In my office, I tipped the cushion I had on my chair for my back to the seat, wanting the extra inch of height for this conversation. A repetitive chant reached my ears from the street, muffled and the words indistinct. I thought I heard my name. I thought the rhyme made of it less than flattering.

Mr. Ryder nodded to Bernard as the doorman showed him inside. "Thank you." He turned, his gaze latching on mine. "Lady Mary."

My eye twitched. He wore a dark brown jacket, the knot of his cravat somehow managing to look both relaxed and pompous at the same time. "Mr. Ryder." I indicated the seat across the desk. "Please. Sit." If I gave the order with a bit more bite than usual, I thought I could be forgiven under the circumstances.

He sat, resting his plain walking stick against the desk.

Timothy entered, and I waited for him to set up the tea between us and leave before speaking again. "What brings you to my door today? And with such a large crowd accompanying you."

He took a cup of tea and sat back, crossing one long leg over the other. "I can take no credit for today's protest. Gathering into a mob and shouting obscenities isn't my idea of an effective tactic to change a person's mind."

My eyebrows shot up. "You expect me to believe that it is mere coincidence that you have set your cap at shutting my doors, and the London public has crowded my street for just the same purpose of their own volition?"

"I hope you will believe me." His soft, chestnut eyes crinkled at the corners. "I have been nothing but upfront with my opposition to your club. I hope you will not think that I've sunk to deception now."

I stirred a lump of sugar into my tea, the spoon tinkling against the rim of the cup. "If you aren't here to discuss terms, then why your visit?"

"Terms?" The man had the audacity to laugh. "We are not at war. I am not your adversary."

I laid my spoon down with a decided clack. "You wish to close my business. You are very much my adversary."

"I am sorry you feel that way." He took a sip of the Darjeeling, then rested his cup on his knee. "I heard about Edgar Bannister's murder. I came to see how you fared."

I swallowed and looked past him to my hanging fern. Several spindly leaves were brown; I should pick them out and water the poor thing. "I was not well acquainted with the boy."

"No, but it must impact the investigation into his mother's death, with which you are intimately involved." He gave her a sad smile. "This latest tragedy must have affected you."

I narrowed my eyes. He must have an ulterior motive. Our relationship was fractious at best. It seemed strange that he would come to offer sympathy. But even suspecting his motives, even knowing he wanted nothing more than to wipe my club off the map, his words still made the backs of my eyes burn. I didn't have many people in my life to offer me sympathy. My nephew and his friends thought me stalwart, an emotional rock who never suffered distress. And for the most part, they were right. I rarely let life bother me.

But a young man had just been murdered. A man who'd had his whole life ahead of him. A man I'd suspected of the most dastardly deed. My emotions were not as rocklike as I might have wanted.

"I'm fine." I inhaled sharply. "No, I take that back. I'm angry. There is little doubt in my mind that the same villain who killed Lady Richford also took the life of her son. Such depravity... offends me."

The smile he gave me was warm, although I didn't think our conversation warranted such a cheerful expression. "My dear Lady Mary, I do so admire your spirit. Even when I think it is misdirected, you are a force to be reckoned with."

I sniffed, pushing my spectacles back up my nose. There was little worse than preparing oneself for a fight and instead finding one's opponent all that is accommodating and flattering. It quite soured the mood.

Ryder finished his tea and set his cup on the desk. "I thought you would accuse me of penning that recent opinion piece in *The Times*. If you did think I was the author, I wanted to assure you that I am not."

I flapped my hand at him. "I know you aren't the author. The manner of writing wasn't your style."

There was that lovely smile again. "And do you know who did write it?"

"Not yet." My fingers dug into the fine china of the teacup. "But I have my suspicions. The writing was in the style of another opinion piece recently in the paper."

His eyebrows drew together. "Which..." His face cleared. "Lord Anglia. The man who wrote the vile piece about Lady Richford."

I raised one shoulder. "As I said, it's only a suspicion."

"You need to take care." Ryder frowned. "That piece was venomous."

"I need to do a great many things." I placed a wedge of apple cake on a plate, offered it to him, then set it in front of myself when he shook his head. "Taking advice from someone who wants to close my business most likely isn't one of those things."

He raked his fingers through his hair. "If you won't take my advice, perhaps you will heed a warning. This Mr. Cooke whom you've associated yourself with—"

"I've hardly done that," I objected.

He continued as if I hadn't spoken. "Cooke has an association with Lord Anglia. He controls the construction guilds that always seem to get the contract for the public construction projects Anglia so likes. Large sums of money are involved. You seem to have caught the eye of both these men, and their attention is best avoided."

I put my fork down, the bite of cake uneaten. "How do you know this?" I knew Cooke was involved in many criminal enterprises; I hadn't realized he was involved with the guilds.

"I like to keep an eye on Cooke's activities." A muscle twitched in his jaw. "Once upon a time, we used to be friends."

I opened my mouth. Shut it. Mr. Ryder couldn't have surprised me more than if he'd declared his undying love for me. "You. And Mr. Cooke. Friends."

One edge of his mouth lifted. "I do have some. Even some with whom I maintain severe disagreements." He sobered. "But I no longer count Edric among them."

"Well." I was confounded. The moralist and the ruffian. I suppose there were odder friendships, but I hadn't yet seen one. I thought again about Mr. Ryder's purpose for coming here today. Perhaps that was his tactic. Befriend the sinner, in his eyes at least, and try to redeem them with kind words and soft cajoling.

My back straightened. That wouldn't be happening here. "Mr. Ryder, I—"

"You would not believe the impudence of some people." Eleanor stormed into my office, gaze fixed on the cuff of her lavender gown as she swiped at it with a handkerchief. A large reticule knocked against her thigh. "I think someone threw a tomato at me. Or perhaps it was at Bernard. Either way, I might need a new pelisse. Bernand's trying to clean it now."

"A tomato?" Anger burbled in my stomach. First her skirts

caught on fire at my club and now attack by nightshade? The protest out front had gone too far. I stood.

"Yes, a very ripe...." Eleanor finally looked up and caught sight of my visitor. "Oh. I didn't mean to interrupt."

Mr. Ryder unfolded to his feet, plucking up his walking stick. "You haven't. I was just about to leave."

I circled my desk. "I'll show you out. And then speak with these protesters." The word tasted foul on my tongue. "I won't tolerate my members being pelted with fruit."

Mr. Ryder held up his hand. "If they have descended to throwing things, you, as the main object of their hatred, need to stay inside. I'll speak with them."

I pursed my lips. He could be an effective spokesman, especially if he was the one who—

"I didn't organize this," he said, as though reading my mind, "but I'll speak with them. Don't leave this club until they have dispersed." And with a nod to Eleanor and myself, he departed.

I suppose his order was kindly given. That he had the sort of generalized concern for my well-being as he would for any human.

That knowledge didn't stop it from vexing me. "Bother! The nerve of the man."

Eleanor folded her handkerchief, giving up on cleaning her sleeve. "What was that?"

"Nothing." I looked at the cake on my desk but decided I needed something more substantial. Anger always seemed to stoke my appetite. "Come on. Let's see if the kitchen can make us anything to go with that tomato."

Chapter Twenty-Six

Lady Mary

THE WORKERS OF The Minerva Club, Eleanor, and myself finished up our snack in the club's kitchens. I'd decided to gather everyone together to eat and discuss the club's security. The mob outside seemed to be dwindling, no doubt due to Mr. Ryder's silver-tongue, but that wasn't to say such a scene couldn't be repeated.

"I know some lads who can watch the streets outside," Timothy said, putting his dish in the sink. "They can't prevent a protest, but they might be able to stop any more bottles being thrown through windows and fires being started."

Another expense, and one the club could ill-afford, not if membership dropped, but I could pay from my personal accounts. I had wanted the club to be self-sustaining, but if watchmen made my members and staff safer, it was a cost I would pay.

I nodded. "Have them come speak with me."

Bobby cut another slice of cake for himself. "I know some lads who can disperse crowds if it's called for, if you don't mind a bit of the rough stuff, that is. If things go sour, they won't peach on you to the magistrates, neither, and I can guarantee none of those protesters will dare come back after they've tussled with my boys."

I blinked. I'd known Bobby had grown up in St. Giles, but he'd always seemed such a sweet boy. "Let's keep that option as the last resort," I finally said.

Bobby tapped his finger against his nose. "Too right."

I turned to the cook and kitchen maid. "I know you like to keep the kitchen window open to the alley for fresh air, but until matters are resolved, I'm going to ask you to keep it shut and locked. That window above the stove isn't large, but it is better to be warm than have your kitchens invaded by tomatoes and flame bottles."

The cook didn't look happy, but she agreed. "Yes, milady."

I looked around. "Right then. I know the times are strange, but all will return to normal soon." I forced more certainty into my voice than I felt. "We will open to our members again tomorrow, although the Tea Room will remain closed until it has been repainted and the window replaced." Hopefully, the stench of smoke would have dispersed by then, as well. "Any other concerns?"

My workers shook their heads.

I clapped my hands together. "Right then. Thank you all for the extra work you have been putting in. It will be reflected in your pay. Bernard, you're responsible for locking up tonight. Miss Lynton and I have to attend to some errands."

Eleanor trotted after me as I left the kitchen and headed for the cloakroom. "We do?"

"Indeed." I tugged on my burgundy-colored spencer, affixed my bonnet, sparing only a quick glance at the mirror by the door. "We still have several threads to pull at, and I've wasted too much time."

And another person had been killed.

I waited impatiently for Eleanor to don her own bonnet. "My pelisse…."

"It is quite warm enough to go without." I pointed at the rack of raiment that had been left behind by inattentive members.

"That shawl there should be sufficient."

With a shrug, she laid it over her shoulders and followed me.

My carriage waited at its usual spot halfway down the block. My driver put down a book when he caught sight of us and hopped down, opening the door. "Where to, milady?"

"The Poole residence on Wells Street." I settled myself inside, lowering the far window.

Eleanor tucked her skirts away, and Ernest closed the door. The carriage jostled as he climbed back to his perch. "We're going to ask about Miss Abbott's alibi."

"To start." We had one less suspect now, and one more time of death for our remaining suspects to account for. But I'd start with Miss Abbott's claim that she was at a salon at the time of Lady Richford's murder. It should be simple enough to confirm.

And it was. Mr. Poole agreed to see us and confirmed that Miss Abbott had been there that night to hear William Godwin. She'd asked a question near the beginning of the lecture and added a comment somewhere near the middle.

Mr. Poole's doorman didn't know Miss Abbott by name or face, but he was certain she hadn't left early. "There were refreshments after the lecture. The attendees didn't leave until about one that morn."

"No one left early?" Eleanor asked, a line wrinkling her brow.

"No single women," the doorman confirmed. He rubbed his jaw. "No women in pairs, neither. A couple men left early, and with the topic, no wonder, but no women came out until the end."

"Any other doors someone could have exited by?" The townhouse was two stories high and wedged between others in the middle of the block. There were no side exits, obviously, but Miss Abbott could have crept out the rear, climbed over several fences to get to the side street.

Not likely, but possible.

The doorman shook his head. "I closed the house that night. The back door was locked. If someone had slipped out of it, there was no way to lock it again behind them."

I sighed. We would have to ask Miss Abbott where she was at the time of Bannister's death, but her whereabouts during Lady Richford's seemed certain.

"What now?" Eleanor asked, looking up and down the street as though expecting inspiration to ride down and greet us.

"Now we part ways." I nodded to Ernest, and after giving the necks of my pair of greys one last rub, he opened the carriage door. "I need to speak with Lord Anglia. It's better if I do so alone."

I wouldn't have Anglia turn his vicious eye on Eleanor. With the problems her mother was having, there was too rich an avenue of attack on the Lynton family. "Perhaps you could seek Mrs. Massey. Determine her whereabouts at the time of Bannister's murder. Subtly, of course."

Eleanor hefted her reticule. "Mr. Rollins gave me sketches of jewelry found at Bannister's home. Jewelry unlikely to belong to him. He asked me to speak with the local jewelers and see if I can find out the ownership of any of the pieces." She blushed. "If I had time."

I tilted my head, examining the girl. "When did you see Mr. Rollins last? Bannister was only killed last night."

Her blush deepened. "We had luncheon together before I came to the club." A small frown crossed her mouth. "He was exhausted. I don't believe he had slept at all since he took me home last night."

I pressed my lips together to suppress my grin. She sounded much too concerned over our Runner's welfare, considering they had been butting heads mere days ago.

My smile turned nostalgic. I remembered some of the fights I'd had with my husband, and how those had ended. Sometimes a passion of one sort transformed into another in the most delightful of ways. "Is there an understanding between you and Mr. Rollins?"

"We haven't...we don't...." Eleanor swung her head left,

then right, then dragged me behind the carriage. "Lady Mary, I need your counsel. How can one be certain?"

"Of a man?"

"Of love." She darted a look over her shoulder, confirming we were still not overheard. "When I am with him, it all seems so clear. But now that we're apart...."

"Doubts creep in." I prodded my walking stick into the ground. I wondered if Eleanor was more or less fortunate than the young women who had no choice in the matter of whom to marry. With her father's death and the inheritance already bestowed upon her, she was in the position to make her own decisions about whom to marry or whether to marry at all. Some women would envy her that freedom.

"My father arranged my marriage," I said. "I suppose if I had vociferously objected, he would have taken my feelings into consideration, but Cavindish seemed virtuous and kind. And he filled out his pantaloons in quite a distracting way."

Eleanor chuckled.

"We found love because we both chose it." I lifted one shoulder. "It doesn't have to be more complicated than that."

She nibbled on her bottom lip. "If one could trust the man to choose it."

I slapped her on the back. "And if he can trust you. Now, if you are going to be scouring all the jewelry shops in London, you should take my carriage and I'll find a hackney."

Ernest popped his head around the side of the carriage, his face pinched. "Milady, you shouldn't be riding alone in a hired coach."

My irritation rose, knowing it was most likely my age that made him worry. Or he thought my wealth made me a target. Or he was worried that if something happened to me, he was out of a position. Perhaps his concern shouldn't annoy me.

Eleanor flushed, seeming to realize our conversation hadn't been as private as she'd intended. She cleared her throat. "He is right. I left my own carriage at your club. I'll find a hackney to take me back there, then have my driver take me around."

Ernest stepped into the street and hollered to the jarvey of an antique looking barouche trundling toward us. "Oy, driver. You free for a fare?"

The gristled jarvey smacked his cap against his thigh, dust billowing. "Sure 'nough."

"This young lady needs to go to 45 Jermyn." Ernest drew back his shoulders, transforming from friendly to threatening in a moment and making me remember why I'd hired him. "Make sure she gets there safe."

The cabbie rolled his eyes, but climbed from his seat and opened the carriage's door readily enough.

Eleanor nodded to Ernest. "Thank you." She brushed a kiss against my cheek. "We should meet again soon to see what each of us has learned about the investigation. I'll ask Mr. Rollins when he is free." And with a fluttering of skirts, she climbed into the barouche and rolled away.

Another meeting of minds was a good idea. I climbed into my own carriage and gave my driver the direction to my next destination.

Now I only had to discover something of value to relate to my fellow investigators.

Chapter Twenty-Seven

Frederick

REDERICK ADDED ANOTHER lump to his already sweet tea, hoping the sugar might erase the sleep from his eyes. He needed his bed. Preferably with Eleanor in it. The only way he would sleep soundly was if he knew Eleanor was safe, and the only way she was safe was when she was within his arms.

But his bed was hours away. Holding Eleanor even further. He could only move forward with his plans once he found the killer. So, he sipped his too-sweet tea and faced his hosts. "Mr. Massey, Mrs. Massey, I am glad you were both able to see me."

Mr. Massey shifted on his chair in his front parlor. He looked around fifty years of age, his hair still dark, with deep grooves cut into his face. He shot a quick look at his wife. "When a man from Bow Street knocks, it makes me curious enough to answer his call. What brings you to my door, Mr. Rollins?"

Frederick set down his mug and reached into his inner pocket. "This." He held up the necklace found in Bannister's boot. The late sun shining through the west windows caught the rubies, making them glint darkly.

He had to hand it to the pair. Neither of them so much as blinked. If Mrs. Massey's smile seemed frozen, only a particularly observant investigator would notice.

Frederick prided himself on his observation skills.

"Your initials are on the back of the clasp, Mrs. Massey. I was wondering how your necklace came to be in the possession of Edgar Bannister."

"My wife's initials aren't unusual," Mr. Massey said. "There must be thousands of individuals with the same initials in London alone."

"Not quite so many with the means to afford such a lovely piece." Frederick laid the necklace on the low table between them. "Don't make me waste the boot leather going around to London's jewelers. Your initials are etched in a very elaborate script. It will not take much for a jeweler to recognize it. And the persons who commissioned it."

Frederick rubbed his jaw. Was Eleanor wearing down her soles as he spoke with the sketches he'd given her? It had seemed the safest way to channel her assistance into the investigation. If he couldn't demand she stop her interference, then at least he could guide her to the most harmless avenue of inquiry.

Mrs. Massey shifted forward. She was plump with lovely red hair that she tended to pat when she was nervous, Frederick noted. "The necklace is mine," she admitted. "I thought I'd lost it."

Frederick didn't say anything, only stared at her, expressing his disbelief in silence.

Mr. Massey took his wife's hand and held it on the armrest between them. "I believe now is the time for truth, my dear. After all, we were the victims."

"Victims of what? Of whom?" Frederick asked. He wanted to pull out his notepad but felt him jotting down every word the Masseys spoke might tighten their jaws.

"Lady Richford," Mrs. Massey spit out. The calm mask she'd worn since they'd first sat down to tea had broken. "She demanded it from me for her silence."

Blackmail. It made a nasty business even nastier. "Silence for what?"

The husband and wife exchanged a look, their lips drawing tight.

Frederick mentally reviewed the notes he had on the Massey family. "Your daughter is in her first season, is she not?"

"She is." Mrs. Massey nodded firmly. "She is set to make a very fine match."

"And your son? He is two and twenty, correct? Where is he?"

Mrs. Massey patted her hair. "He's on a walking tour of the Alps. We received a letter from him from Spiez not long ago."

Frederick watched her hand. "How long has he been gone?"

Mr. Massey cleared his throat. "Thirteen months now."

"That's a long tour." Frederick arched his eyebrows. "And when did you give Lady Richford the necklace?"

The pause was palpable. Mr. Massey's hand whitened around his wife's. "Thirteen months ago."

Frederick leaned forward, resting his elbows on his knees. "Mr. and Mrs. Massey, what did Lady Richford know about your son?"

"That doesn't matter." And by the look on Mrs. Massey's face, Frederick knew she would never tell. "We paid what that woman demanded, but if you are here to insinuate we had anything to do with her death, that's absurd."

"Can you tell me where you were Wednesday last, the night of Lady Richford's death?"

"At home," Mr. Massey said stoutly. "We haven't gone to any social event in many weeks."

"When did we go to the opera?" A line creased Mrs. Massey's forehead.

"Three weeks Thursday." Mr. Massey gave Frederick a hard look. "As I said, we don't go out much."

Frederick would confirm with the servants and the neighbors, but there was always the chance the household would lie, the neighbors prove unobservant. "And last night? About midnight?"

"Home in bed," Mr. Massey said firmly. "Both of us."

Nodding, Frederick rose, covered his sleepy stagger with a

small bout of coughing, and made his leave. Next on his list, he made his way to the offices at Parliament.

Lord Anglia was not around to receive him, or so the man's secretary told Frederick. He also told him it was highly improper for Bow Street to harass a member of the House of Lords in such a manner. "People might get the wrong idea."

"That Lord Anglia is a suspect in two murder investigations?" Frederick shrugged, his fatigue loosening his tongue. "Or they will get the right idea. Did the earl have anything on his schedule for last night? Any meetings to sit through, balls to attend?"

The secretary straightened to his full height, an impressive inch or so above Frederick's, but the move was hardly threatening. The man was naught but skin and bones, and Frederick had no doubt he could lay the young man out with one finger.

"My lord was here, in his offices, late into the night." The secretary lifted his chin. "We were working on the second draft of the hospital procurement bill."

"You were here with him?" Frederick poised his bit of lead above his notebook. "From when to when?"

"My lord had an early supper and returned to the office around eight." His Adam's apple bobbed. "I don't believe we left until at least two this morning."

"Can anyone else confirm that?" As the secretary couldn't refrain from shifting his weight every three seconds, Frederick had his doubts. He must be a very good secretary, because he was a very poor liar. It was almost heartening to know that Anglia didn't make hiring decisions based on an individual's skill in deception. Did that mean he was generally honest and didn't feel such skills were necessary to protect him or that he was so arrogant that he never thought someone would dare question him?

"No, we were alone. It was late," the clerk added defensively.

"And only your employer is dedicated enough to work such late hours." Frederick put away his notebook. "Thank you for your time."

Winding his way out of Parliament, Frederick pulled out his list of high-end jewelers, a copy of which he'd given to Eleanor. He could try to track her down, assist her with her questioning.

He paused on the street, swaying. He would fall asleep in the agency's carriage as he searched. And besides, he didn't want to assist with the questioning. He wanted to take her home with him, hold her as he fell asleep. That image lifted his lips.

"Sir?" His burly driver, who'd shown his use as a bruiser on more than one occasion, hopped down from the carriage seat and eyed him curiously. "Are you all right?"

"Fine." He handed the man the list of jewelers. "Let's make the rounds to these businesses. I'm looking for a woman."

He climbed into the carriage.

And he hoped he would never be too tired to find her.

Chapter Twenty-Eight

Eleanor

A FEW UNDERSTANDING words, some hints as to the urgency of her visit, and Eleanor soon had Miss Abbott's location from the woman who ran the lodging house where Miss Lydia Abbott rented her rooms.

Mrs. Morgan planted her hands on her wide hips. "That girl has no decency. If it weren't for my husband's good heart, I would have kicked her out years ago. First, she tried to start a *salon*, in her rooms, but me and the mister put an end to that right quick." She said the word salon like it was poisonous. "We weren't going to have those types coming and going in our building. Shabby, the lot of them." She sniffed and traced her finger along the print of a flower's stem in the paper covering the hall. "Unbathed. But the mister says we can't condemn her for still going to those things, as long as she don't have them here no more."

The lodging house was a lovely building, with fresh flowers brightening the side tables pressed against the walls and a patterned molding on the ceiling. Eleanor could understand the owner's reticence in having the unwashed masses to'ing and fro'ing all over the buffed hardwood floors. It wasn't a place an aristo would condescend to live in, but for the average Cit, the lodgings were luxurious.

"So she is at a salon? Do you know where?"

Mrs. Morgan frowned down at her, giving Eleanor the exact same look her governess had when she'd come up with the wrong answer in her studies. "Today's Sunday. This is her painting day. She takes lessons somewhere on Burton Street, with a Frenchman named Geerod. Says he's a great master." She rolled her eyes. "I'd think a good master would be able to teach his pupil to get the paint on the canvas, not all over herself. But every week she comes home with splotches on her neck, her hands. I told her it better not get on my furniture, or I'd—"

"Thank you so much, Mrs. Morgan." Eleanor backed away. "You've been most helpful." She reached for the handle to the front door and yanked it open. "I can tell Miss Abbott is most fortunate in her landlady." And with one last smile, she fled.

Her driver, Johnny, was chatting with two young women who wore flour-dusted aprons. When he caught sight of her, Johnny gave the women an impish tilt of his hat, then hurried to open the carriage door. "That didn't take no time a'tall."

"No, not enough time to court a pretty young miss." Eleanor smiled as she took his hand and climbed into the carriage. Ever since she'd found Frederick sleeping on the settee in her front parlor the night before, she'd had a feeling of giddiness, a lightness that made her want to tease everyone around her until they felt as happy as she.

Frederick hadn't looked upon their indiscretion with remorse. Hadn't looked upon her with the disgust she knew some men felt after having taken what they wanted from a woman. Every indication pointed to the fact that he wanted her in his life on a permanent, and formal, basis. They had only to catch a killer, one other than her mother, of course, to take the next step.

"T'were *two* pretty young misses," he said, an exaggerated mournful expression on his face.

She laughed and gave Johnny the directions to the artist's studio. Eleanor sat back in the creaking coach. It had been awhile since she'd felt happy in her own home. Protected. Last night, Frederick had brought those feelings back with just his mere presence.

Her high spirits stayed with her through the drive and up the narrow stairs to the third and top story where the French painter worked. Panting softly from the climb, Eleanor raised her hand and knocked.

When the door opened, she plastered a smile on her face. And stared into air.

"Yes?" A nasally voice asked.

Eleanor dropped her gaze. The Frenchman was shorter than she expected any man to be. He couldn't have stood five feet, but his body was slender and well-shaped even for its lack of height. He had golden blond hair that curled about his collar and startling blue eyes.

"Oh. *Monsieur Girod?*"

"*Giroud.*" He rolled out the vowels.

"*Bonjour, est Mademoiselle Abbott ici?*"

The painter sneered, covering his ears. "Please stop. I speak English."

Eleanor ground her teeth. There was no need to be rude. Her accent might need a bit of work, but her French was clearly understandable. She had felt a little badly about comparing him to a wingless fairie in her mind, but no longer.

"So is she here?" Eleanor asked stiffly. "I need to speak with her."

"Wait here." Giroud sniffed, and strode away as fast as his tiny fairie legs could carry him.

All right, he walked at a normal speed, but Eleanor was still annoyed he'd insulted her French.

He disappeared around a corner, and a few murmured words drifted to the doorway.

Eleanor shifted, considering her options. If she were denied entry, she could push past the painter and force Miss Abbott to speak with her. She valued her chances against the diminutive man.

A little to her disappointment, when the Frenchman returned, he gave her a low bow (it could hardly be otherwise) and invited her inside. *"Entrée, s'il vous plait."* If she didn't suspect he was poking fun at her, it would have been prettily done.

Eleanor stepped inside, the scent of turpentine and paint burning her nose. She followed Giroud around the corner and into a room splashed with sunlight. Large windows sat on both walls of the corner suite, and a high skylight added to the brightness. Nothing was hidden in shadow in this studio.

Including a very naked Miss Abbott curled provocatively on a nest of silk counterpanes and pillows in the center of the floor.

"Good afternoon, Miss Lynton," Lydia Abbott arched her back in a small stretch. "How industrious of you to find me here."

"Ooh, don't move." Giroud hurried to his easel. "Remain just like that."

Eleanor stared at the pillow above Miss Abbott's head. It was covered in a lovely purple satin with a black lace trim. "Your landlady told me you were taking painting classes. I didn't realize that you were"—she cleared her throat delicately—"sitting."

"Or lying, as the case may be." Miss Abbott rested her hand on her smooth belly, the movement drawing Eleanor's gaze.

She snapped it back to the pillow. "Yes. Well. I was wondering if you'd heard about Edgar Bannister. That he'd been killed."

"I had heard that." Miss Abbott tutted. "What is the world coming to? I am almost glad Susan died first. Her son's death would have devastated her."

Eleanor gripped her left elbow with her right hand. Miss Abbott was likely right. Losing a child must be the greatest pain that existed. She'd heard that Lord Richford had gone to his country estate, unable to face society with this second blow. Could a man recover from losing his wife and only child?

"I wanted to ask you about your argument with Bannister." Perhaps it was the thought of Viscount Richford crying and all alone in the country, perhaps it was the surprise of questioning a nude Miss Abbott, but she didn't try to ease into the subject. It seemed like the time for artifice was past. "What was it concerning?"

"At the cemetery? I already told that Runner it was of little account."

Giroud put down his brush and strode to his subject. He repositioned one leg, bending it at the knee slightly, exposing a dark shadow at her vee. His fingers lingered a moment longer than necessary, his eyes dropping to half-mast.

Oh. That explained how Miss Abbott went home with paint on her body.

Eleanor fixed her attention on that pillow again. She wondered where Giroud had bought it. It was quite lovely. "No, the other argument you had. In front of the Queen's House in St. James. You were seen having a heated disagreement."

"I was seen?" Miss Abbott dipped her chin. "By whom?"

"By me." She met Miss Abbott's narrowed-eyed gaze. "I saw you. As did Mr. Rollins of Bow Street."

It would be easy to dismiss Eleanor's account, but adding Frederick's name gave the accusation more weight. Miss Abbott would have to answer or else face the law. At least Eleanor hoped so.

Fire kindled in Miss Abbott's eyes and was quickly doused. She turned a bored look toward the easel that Giroud had disappeared behind. Perhaps that was the expression he told her to wear. "Edgar took a perfectly natural conversation and made it acrimonious. I only wanted to offer him direction, as a favor to my friend. He didn't appreciate my concern." She frowned. "He was a very conventional young man."

Concern or interference? "Conventional how?" By her tone, Miss Abbott didn't consider conventionality an asset.

Giroud called out a direction, and Miss Abbott shifted to comply. "He didn't approve of his mother's interest in modernity. Or politics. Or of any interest outside of the home. His body might have been in the nineteenth century, but his head was firmly in the eighteenth. He had very traditional views on society. He and Susan butted heads frequently."

"Perhaps we should send him a copy of this painting, *chère*." The painter leaned around his easel, a grin licking his lips. "Show him just how magnificent an untraditional woman can be."

"Did you miss the part in the conversation where we discussed that he was dead?" Miss Abbott laughed, but it was ugly, cruel. "Go back to your painting."

The man's cheeks flushed, and he ducked back behind his canvas.

Eleanor didn't like the gnome, but she couldn't help but feel badly for him. His admiration for Miss Abbott was obvious. She seemed merely to tolerate him.

But Eleanor had only seen the two together for a few minutes, and as one was naked and the other French, they could hardly be considered to be at their best.

"What was Lady Richford like?" She knew all the reasons her mother hated the woman, knew the pettiness and cruelty that had led to giving her mother the cut direct, but there had to be more to the viscountess. "How was she interested in modernity?"

Miss Abbott traced a fold in the counterpane beneath her. "Susan was an ardent believer in the free love movement. She devoured everything written by Shelley. Advocated for female empowerment. She was brilliant." She blinked rapidly, her throat working on a swallow.

Eleanor's cheeks heated. She'd read Shelley before and found his poetry needlessly indulgent. His morality formed on the indulgence of childish whims.

After spending time with Frederick, finally experiencing the pleasures Shelley wrote about, Eleanor had to admit that her criticism of the man might be ill-formed, as well. She had come to a conclusion without a full understanding of the subject matter.

She cleared her throat. "Her husband is a Tory. I don't remember ever hearing gossip that he was married to a radical."

Bitterness twisted Miss Abbott's face. "Sue could hardly express her opinions in that house. Her husband held too much power over her, which was one of the reasons she advocated in private for the abolition of marriage."

"The beautiful *révolution* has inspired much, *non?*"

Miss Abbott gave the painter an approving look.

Eleanor couldn't help but think he'd made the statement ironically.

"Sue loved her family." Miss Abbott scraped her teeth over her lower lip. "But it was the fondness one might feel for a benevolent jailor."

"Did Bannister know his mother viewed him as a chain?" Eleanor could hardly credit it. Lady Richford had appeared rash at times but not a radical. She'd been a viscountess, and appeared to enjoy every privilege that endowed. But Eleanor hadn't been her intimate. The woman could have hidden a subversive streak she only shared with those to whom she was close.

Miss Abbott shrugged. "He most likely didn't care enough to learn his mother's thoughts."

"Do you think Bannister hated his mother enough to kill her?"

Miss Abbott frowned. "As he was murdered as well, that hardly seems likely."

"One was strangled, the other shot." Eleanor lifted one shoulder. "It could have been two different people. Perhaps someone getting revenge on Bannister for his crime."

Miss Abbott pursed her lips, humming softly. "I hadn't considered that. I don't like to think of Susan being killed by someone she loved, but that is a possibility."

"Since it is a possibility, I must ask where you were Friday night, around midnight."

"Are you asking for my alibi?" Miss Abbott hissed out a breath. "I usually appreciate bluntness in a woman. In you, however, I find it most unbecoming."

Eleanor couldn't disagree. It was an unbecoming question, fit only for these unbecoming times. She knew only too well how insulting it was to be accused of such a heinous act, however briefly. Her shoulders dropped an inch. At least now Frederick no longer had any doubts. He knew she couldn't commit murder.

At times, though, she feared he still suspected her mother.

"Will you answer?" she prodded.

"I was home sleeping," Miss Abbott bit out. "I can't be out every night with friends only to provide myself with a defense."

A frisson of excitement warmed Eleanor's heart at the fact that the woman was unaccounted for during Bannister's murder. That Frederick would have another suspect besides her mother to look at. It was quickly followed by shame. She shouldn't wish Miss Abbott's life to be burdened by accusation and doubt merely to relieve Eleanor from worry. She should care only about finding the truth.

And the truth was, Eleanor didn't have any reason to accuse the woman. She went down her last avenue. "Do you make much money sitting for paintings?" She infused her voice with casual curiosity. "When I had to work, I never thought about it as an option."

"For some women, it isn't an option." Miss Abbott slid her gaze down Eleanor's body.

The back of Eleanor's neck heated. She might not be a diamond of the first water, but she was comely enough. Frederick seemed to appreciate her form. And it wasn't as though Miss Abbott was accounted a great beauty.

Giroud left his painting to pour water into a mug from a carafe on the side table. He gave Eleanor an assessing look. "I would paint her."

All gnome-related thoughts vanished from Eleanor's mind. She gave the painter a warm smile.

"You would, and have, painted a corpse." Miss Abbott snarled and turned back to Eleanor. "And he doesn't pay much, if you were thinking of earning some extra blunt. Not that you need it anymore I hear."

No, Eleanor couldn't pretend she needed financial assistance.

Her unbecoming bluntness would have to continue. "You are a member of The Minerva Club, and those fees are dear. You live on a lovely street. If you will forgive my impudence, how do you support yourself? Did you inherit money?"

Planting her palm on the floor, Miss Abbott rolled to her feet as gracefully as a cat, her lithe body tensing. "Most of us aren't fortunate enough to have a rich papa. Most of us have to earn our way. I model, I write for periodicals, I earn money wherever I can. How I spend it, or where I live, are none of your bloody concern."

Eleanor took a step back. The aggression in the woman's stance was unmistakable. Eleanor's leg still hurt from the burn she'd received. She would not add injury from grappling with a naked woman to her aches.

Even if Eleanor managed to do the injuring, she still wished to avoid a scuffle. Naked. Woman. Her cheeks heated from merely thinking of such a situation.

"Of course." Eleanor held up a placating hand, inching back toward the hall that would lead her out. "Not my business at all. Thank you for your time, Miss Abbott. Try not to catch a chill." And with that she fled, wondering just how violent Miss Lydia Abbott could be.

And whether she had it in her to strangle a friend.

Chapter Twenty-Nine

Lady Mary

"So GLAD THAT you could join me." I sniffed, put out that it took Mr. Rollins and Eleanor a full three hours to respond to my summons. It was past my usual tea time, and I become cranky without that repast.

I looked between the two, not failing to note that they had arrived together. And that Eleanor looked suspiciously flushed.

Leaning back in my office chair, I rested my linked hands on my abdomen, smiling for the first time in who knew how long. Young love was enough to pull anyone from a foul spirit.

Mr. Rollins held Eleanor's chair until she sat, then took his own. "Pardon me for not being immediately available, Lady Mary. I do have duties to attend."

I suppose I'd earned that. In a more reasonable tone, I said, "It is inconvenient to have to call you hence every time we need to talk. We could set up another desk in my office for your use for the duration of the investigation?"

Rollins paused while removing his notepad, his hand half in his pocket. "No, I think not. Sir John Stauncey would hardly look kindly on such an arrangement, and I don't want him removing me from this investigation."

"But Lord Richford has hired you personally." Eleanor

reached over and rested her palm on his arm. "You can't be replaced."

Rollins traced his finger over the back of her hand, the motion so quick and light it could have been accidental. But when he straightened and turned a guilt-laden gaze on me, I knew better. "With Richford fleeing to his country estate, I'm not certain where I stand. When I notified him of his son's death, he..." Rollins sighed. "He was a broken man. I don't know if he has the mental capability to remember he's put me on retainer, much less to continue to contract me. It would be an easy thing for Stauncey to assign another agent."

"Then we need to solve the murders before that happens," I said firmly. "What can you tell us about how Bannister was killed?"

Rollins flipped open his notebook. "You already know the basics. Shot with a small caliber pistol at close range. We found a ruby necklace in his boot with the initials A.M. engraved on the clasp." He looked up. "The Masseys reluctantly confirmed it was theirs."

I reached for the walking stick leaning against my desk and tapped the silver ram's head that topped this one against one palm. "So, it is confirmed the viscountess engaged in blackmail. And used my club to sell some of her ill-gotten gains." The knowledge of that still burned. I wondered if White's had to deal with being used as a meeting place for illegal behavior. One could only hope. "What about the other jewelry you found? Any luck tracing those items?"

Eleanor scooted to the edge of her seat. "No. None of them were distinctive enough for the jewelers I questioned to remember. Except for the posey ring. One man thought a former worker might have made it. He had no records of it, though. It didn't seem as though this jeweler was overly fond of record-keeping. He did give me the worker's name, however."

"And I have men trying to find him," Rollins added.

I nodded. "And what about the rest of the murder scene.

Anything else of note?"

Mr. Rollins hesitated a moment. "Except for the body, it was undisturbed." He shot a sidelong glance at Eleanor. "The door hadn't been forced. Which leads me to believe Bannister invited his killer inside. He knew her. Or him."

"But you think it was a woman." I trailed my thumb over the ram's head. The silver had been etched with rough hatch marks on the horns, the slight scratch on my skin helping to focus my thoughts.

"Judging from the angle the bullet traveled, the shooter would have been shorter than most men." He ran a hand up the back of his head, mussing his auburn locks. "The fact that Bannister was shot at all makes me suspect the killer was a member of your sex. Lady Richford was a small woman. It wouldn't take much strength to strangle her, but Bannister was a different story. The same method wouldn't work for a woman, not unless she somehow incapacitated the man first. A different weapon was needed."

Eleanor sighed. "I should have asked Miss Abbott about Lady Richford's blackmail. As her dear friend, surely she would have known."

"Or participated in it." Mr. Rollins gave a growl of displeasure. "It's a good thing you didn't ask her. By your own account, she was angry enough with your questions. I don't want to think what she might have done to you had she known you thought she was involved with the viscountess's crimes."

"If she was," I felt the need to add, not wanting to accuse a possibly innocent woman. Although with Miss Abbott's revolutionary feelings, would it be far-fetched to think she would take anything other than glee from stealing from the wealthy? She flaunted her disgust with traditional society and its rules, seemed to yearn for the impossible utopia her political leanings promised.

Eleanor pursed her lips. "It could explain how she affords her lodgings. They are quite nice," she said to me, "for someone who only seems to have odd jobs to support herself."

I frowned. We were getting off the point. "Yes, she might be involved with Lady Richford's blackmail, but she didn't kill her. We spoke with the host of the salon she attended that night, and with his staff. Miss Abbott was there until well after midnight. She didn't leave early."

Rollins cleared his throat, shifting. "Yes, I had already spoken with Mr. Poole and confirmed she was there."

The ram on my stick smacked into my desk, the sound making Eleanor start. "And you didn't tell us?" I asked, outraged.

He grimaced. "I'm not accustomed to relating my investigation to anyone other than the magistrate. I apologize."

Knowing the Runner didn't hand out apologies freely, I was slightly mollified.

"She said the argument between her and Bannister was because he took offense at the guidance she wanted to give him." Eleanor wrinkled her nose. "For once, I can understand Bannister's temper. I wouldn't want Miss Abbott giving her opinions on my life, either."

Especially if Miss Abbott was living immorally, as well. The hypocrisy would have rubbed anyone wrong. I slumped in my chair. If Miss Abbott had partnered with Lady Richford to blackmail members of the *ton*, were there others? How many members of my club were looting the wealthy? The silver knob dug into my skin. And using my club to help them do it.

There was one man who might know. Or be able to find out. "What about the connection between Edric Cooke and Lord Anglia? If Cooke is connected with Anglia, and Lady Richford was in Anglia's way politically, could the crime lord be involved?"

Mr. Rollins dragged his hand down his face and sighed. "I don't want to add another suspect now, and I don't think a man of Cooke's reputation would have a woman strangled in a women's club. If he wanted the viscountess dead, her body would never have been found. And what would be the motive for Bannister's murder?"

I held up my free hand. "All right, it was only an idea." And the fact that the Runner dismissed Cooke as their murderer so readily released a knot in my shoulder I hadn't known was there.

Eleanor tapped her knuckles against her lips. "Frederick, I know you think the killer is a woman, but I still think Lord Anglia is a strong prospect." She stared out the window at the burgeoning dusk, not seeming to realize she'd called the Runner with his Christian name. "He stands to make money if his bills pass while Lord Richford is out of the way, and his attack in the paper was quite vicious. I could see him choking the life out of someone."

"His secretary says they were together, working," Rollins said. "I didn't believe him, but I also don't know why Anglia would publish such a piece about the viscountess, putting his name on it, if he intended to kill her later. He didn't need to draw suspicion to himself."

I jabbed the walking stick into the floor and pressed to standing. I stalked to the window and peered out. No protesting crowd. No one with a flaming jug. "We're going in circles. What I wouldn't give to have all of our suspects in one place, available for all our questions, where they could be called on their lies by the others."

"Why can't we have that?"

I turned at the excitement in Eleanor's voice. "Have what?"

"A party." She stood as well. "Send out invitations to all our suspects. Gather them together. And with Frederick there, they'll have to answer us."

Ever the gentleman, Mr. Rollins also rose to his feet. "Why would they come?"

I toyed with the idea. "If the invitation is worded correctly. If it comes from myself and my nephew in conjunction, perhaps? Not many people refuse a party hosted by the Duke of Montague."

"Will your nephew come?" Eleanor's brows drew together.

"It doesn't matter. It will be too late as far as our guests are concerned." I rolled up on my toes, liking this idea better and better. "We can have it at my house. This Saturday. The short notice is incredibly rude. They will each think they are second choice guests only invited after another invitee has declined, but much is forgiven when done in a duke's name."

"We don't have a moment to lose." Eleanor rushed to the door. "I'll get the invitations drawn up now before the calligrapher closes. I can send them out tomorrow." She looked to Mr. Rollins. "Are you coming?"

He shook his head. "I have more work to do. Can I join you and your mother for supper again?"

She gave him a wide grin. "Of course. I'll see you then." And she was gone.

I arched my eyebrows. "Supper together? Again?"

"Yes." He adjusted his neckcloth, smoothing the ends under his jacket. "This party of yours will likely come to naught."

"Or we could learn something important." It was becoming too dark to see the road clearly, and I didn't like the idea of the lights in my window making me so visible. I pulled the heavy velvet drapes closed. "Each of our suspects is aware we are investigating. Once they are all gathered, they might be annoyed, but hardly surprised. I see no drawback."

"As you say." Rollins shoved his hands in his jacket pockets.

I waited. He'd said he had work to do but seemed content to stare daggers at my office wall. "Was there something on your mind?" I finally asked.

He opened his mouth. Closed it. Slowly released a deep breath. "Yes. I was wondering if I could see some applications to join your club. Those of Lady Richford, Mrs. Massey, and Mrs. Lynton. I might as well include Miss Abbott, as well. Assuming you've kept those papers."

The world was made up of records and red tape. Of course, I'd kept them. "Why do you want to see them?"

"I have a colleague who has studied graphic expression in handwriting." He cleared his throat. "He is always most eager to analyze the handwriting of suspects in our cases."

I narrowed my eyes. "To what end?"

"He swears handwriting can reveal a person's character. Simmons blathers on and on about some French blokes who've made a study of it. Or were they Italian?" Mr. Rollins pressed his notebook to his chest, his thumb tracing the edge.

"What a barrel of nonsense." To think evil could be seen in script. "You can't believe that bosh."

His cheeks darkened. "I understand it has been used as evidence in some trials on the Continent."

"But not England."

"No." He sighed, and opened his notebook, pulling a torn bit of paper from it. "I also want Simmons to compare the handwriting samples to this. See if he can match it to any of your patrons."

"Identifying a person based on their handwriting?" I pursed my lips. "That I can credit more."

"Unfortunately, our court system doesn't yet agree. It can't be used as evidence, but it might point me to the culprit."

"Where did you find that paper?" I narrowed my eyes.

"By Edgar Bannister's body." He pressed his lips flat. "It appears the killer tore the paper from Bannister's hand and destroyed the remainder."

"And you waited for Eleanor to leave before making this request." I didn't need to phrase it as a question. I knew why he'd waited. I just didn't know if I approved.

He turned his somber green eyes to me. "I hope Mrs. Lynton isn't involved, but I can't yet rule it out."

I didn't envy the man his position. I knew all too well what it was to make an impossible decision, one that could be seen as a betrayal.

I trudged to a cabinet in the corner of the room and opened the top drawer. I pulled out two thick folders and brought them to my desk. "The applications are filed alphabetically." I quickly shuffled through the papers, pulling out the ones he'd requested.

Rollins laid his scrap of paper next to the forms. I had a standard list of questions with room below to answer. Lady Richford's hand was bold and rounded. Mrs. Massey's neat and tight. Miss

Abbott's scrawl was barely legible. I remembered the headache I'd suffered trying to read her words.

It was difficult to tell if Mrs. Lynton's hand was a match to the few words Rollins had on his paper. It was by far the closest of the applications, but I couldn't swear they were by the same hand. But I wasn't a handwriting expert. I suspected this Simmons at Bow Street would be able to analyze the two samples better than I.

Mr. Rollins must have had the same idea. "Can I borrow these? I'll bring them back."

I tucked the applications back into their folders. "Why don't you take all of them? See if any others are possible matches."

"Thank you." He tucked the torn scrap back in his notebook and slid it in his pocket. Picking up the folders, he turned for the door.

"What will you do if it is a match with Mrs. Lynton?" I asked.

He paused, his wide shoulders drawing tight beneath his jacket. He didn't look back at me. "I'll arrest her."

I let him go without another word, praying that if Rollins found a match to his evidence, it wouldn't be Mrs. Lynton.

Because if Rollins arrested Eleanor's mother, I feared that neither the ardor nor zeal of young love would be strong enough to overcome it.

Chapter Thirty

Lady Mary

"HIS GRACE THE Duke of Montague paid a call, milady." Mr. Stavers's hands shook slightly as he took her light walking cape. "He waited for nigh on an hour before a previous engagement called him away."

I removed my cap and tossed it on the entry table. "Was he annoyed with my note telling him he was co-hosting my party?" Marcus was a dear boy, but even I knew I had been pushing the limits using his name without his express permission.

"I cannot say, milady." The butler gave the door to the entry closet a shove, fighting against the bulge of outerwear that stuffed it full. He finally won the battle, and the latch clicked shut. "His Grace did say he'd learned who wrote that rubbish about you in *The Times*. He asked that you call on him when you have the time."

Blast the man. Why couldn't he have told Stavers who the blackguard was? Or left me a note? I shoved my walking stick into the bucket by the door that held its brethren and turned for my library, knowing a fire would already be waiting for me there.

I knew why. He wanted to see me face to face, delve into why I and my club were being attacked, before deciding whether he should step in to help me. Whether I wanted his assistance or not.

I dropped into the chair next to my sideboard, reaching for the crystal decanter that rested there.

And I didn't fully understand why I would be so against his aid.

"A late tea, milady?" Stavers hovered in the doorway, his watery gaze taking in the brandy I was pouring, the slump in my shoulders. "Or it will take but an hour for cook to put out a nice supper."

"I'll wait for supper." I didn't take a sip, just held the glass between my two palms and stared at the ceiling. A spider had taken up residence in the corner near me. It wasn't moving, just sat there. Watching. Waiting. Perhaps it was dead.

Fabric rustled. Light footsteps drew near. "A tiring day?"

"Did Stavers send you?" I lifted my head and glared at Jane. Officially, she was my lady's maid, but the woman had been with me so long the lines between friend, family, and servant had long since blurred.

Jane poured her own glass of brandy. "He's worried about you. We all are. If you root around like a pig for truffles, you're bound to come up dirty."

A bark of laughter burst through my lips, surprising myself as well as Jane. "How very poetical of you. I'm afraid mud has already been brought to my doorstep." To my club's, at least. "You and Stavers need not concern yourselves."

Jane eased into the chair opposite. The skin on her face looked sallow, the flickering light of the fire casting shadows in the deep grooves of her forehead. "When will you go see his Grace?"

My household had been gossiping together. "Tomorrow," I snapped.

"He can help." Jane stretched out her legs, pointing her toes toward the heat of the fire.

"He has his own troubles to sort." Jane and I had never spoken of it, but she must know a bit of the secret life my nephew lived. She'd been around me too long not to. And while Marcus's history of assisting the Crown with delicate problems most likely did mean he would be an asset to my investigation, I was loath to include him.

He had his own life.

He had two young children and a wife he wanted to spend every free moment with.

I wanted to do this myself.

The truth of that hooked beneath my ribcage. I'd been a daughter, a wife, an aunt. Always an accessory of a man. It made no matter that I loved all those men in my life. In this society, they were the ones who made the decisions. Who were useful. It wasn't until I'd created my club that I'd ever created something that was just mine.

And it was pure selfishness that made me want to keep it, and even its problems, my own. Mr. Rollins's involvement didn't count. We didn't have a history, and he was merely doing his job. Frankly, I couldn't believe it had been as easy as it had been to convince him to accept my and Eleanor's involvement. But if Marcus became involved, then his friends would become involved, too, and I would be on the outside looking in on my own life.

No, when I went to see him to discover the identity of my accuser, I would need to convince the boy to stay out of it.

Except when I needed him to provide me with information about anonymous authors.

Or lend me his name on my invitation.

I blew out a breath. I was a hypocrite of the worst kind. I did want his help, but only on my terms.

"If you won't let him investigate, then you should have more protection when you do so," Jane said stoutly. "I can go around with you until the matter is resolved."

Jane was twenty years older than me if she was a day, and the drink she'd poured herself wasn't just to be companionable. Her bones ached, especially in the cold, and a nip now and then eased the pain. Making Jane trail after me all day, out in the elements, would be cruel. "Ernest is with me when I 'go around', as you say, and otherwise I'm at the club with several burly footmen."

"Ernest stays with the carriage when he drives you, and most of your footmen are no longer strapping young bucks." Jane patted the white lace cap over her hair.

"Do you make a habit of checking the physique of the men who work for me?" I couldn't hide my amusement. I suppose I also noticed when a young man was of good form, even though I was no longer attracted to men so much my junior. Aging didn't make one blind to male beauty.

Jane huffed, then lapsed into silence. We sat sipping our brandies, relaxing our bones.

"That poor man," Jane finally said. "Can you imagine losing both your wife and only child? To murder? How can he ever recover?"

I didn't think Lord Richford would recover. I hoped I was wrong. That his friends and faith would bear him through, or that in a couple of years he might meet someone who would revive the life in him. But his wife's death had nearly broken him, and the news of his son was most likely the quelling blow.

I ran my thumb along the rim of my glass. "Do you ever regret it?" I asked softly. "Staying with me all these years instead of making a family of your own?" Jane had been with me ever since I was a child. She'd helped me arrange my hair to the latest fashions the day Cavindish had asked for my hand. She'd moved to Cavindish House when I'd married, then come here when I'd become a widow. I'd never known her to show an interest in a man, not even a casual flirtation.

Shame burned in my chest. I knew what it was like to live with regrets, to feel the pain of never creating a family of my own. Had my narcissism sentenced my friend to the same pain?

Jane dipped her chin, the firelight shimmering through the lace of her cap. "You are quite dear to me, madam, but if I had met a man to love, I would have left you in an instant."

I grimaced. Well, there was me put in my place.

"I would have been at Gretna Green before you'd even had your first cup of tea, without one thought as to who would help you dress or style your hair."

I held up a hand. "All right, I understand your point. No need to relish just how little your service to me means."

Jane smirked, pulling a shawl from the ottoman near her and draping it over her lap.

A log popped in the fireplace, drawing our gazes. The mood turned somber once more as we stared into the flames.

"No one gets everything they want in this life," Jane said, "but we can't survive with regrets."

I swallowed. She wasn't just talking about herself. She knew the struggles Cavindish and I had to have children. Knew the emptiness I'd felt.

"It's best we focus on the gifts we did receive." She raised her half-empty glass to me as though in a toast. "And there are many."

I saluted her back. I didn't know if it were her words or the brandy, but my spirit revived. Self-pity was for the weak. It did no one any good to look back. Eyes forward, as Father used to say, though he had been talking about my and my brother's tendency to stare out the window instead of paying attention to our lessons, not metaphorically.

Still, it was a good reminder. Once we learned who'd killed Lady Richford and her son, I could refocus my attention on saving my club.

Which reminded me. "Jane, will you tell the rest of the household to prepare to host a dinner party? Not large. Twelve at most."

"Twelve is still a lot to clean and cook for," she said grumpily. "When is this party to be?"

"In four days' time." I lifted my glass to my lips, ignoring her muttered oaths. It might be short notice, but it was moving forward.

In four days' time, I just might know the identity of the killer.

Chapter Thirty-One

Frederick

FREDERICK FELT MORE resignation than guilt when he handed the letter over to Simmons, the agent who studied handwriting at his office on Bow Street. The letter written by Mrs. Lynton to a cousin that was supposed to go out in tomorrow's post.

The one he had stolen.

The agent had said the brief applications weren't enough for him to test against. There hadn't been enough letters in common to compare to the scrap found at Bannister's.

So, when he'd had tea with Eleanor again, seen the letters by the front door waiting for the morning post, he'd taken one addressed by Mrs. Lynton's hand.

It had been too easy. He didn't expect high security in a private residence especially as he'd been invited inside, but there didn't seem to be enough servants to watch over the house. No one looked askance at his presence nor when he and Eleanor were together unattended. Her mother rarely came down, even for meals it seemed. He couldn't deny he enjoyed the freedom that gave him and Eleanor, but his gut tensed knowing that she was so unprotected.

He wondered if their butler, Mr. Grosse, would notice that one of the outgoing post was missing from the silver tray in the entry. Would he tell Eleanor? Would she know it had been Frederick who'd taken it?

"Oy, Rollins, Lewis is looking for you." The agent at the desk next to his looked up from his paperwork.

Frederick tossed his greatcoat over the back of his chair. "And?" He hadn't spoken to Lewis in some months. He had been Frederick's partner on the Bow Street Patrol but had remained on the streets while Frederick had been promoted to investigator.

His neighbor blinked. "And what?"

"Where's Lewis?" Frederick tried to keep the irritation out of his voice. "What did he want?"

The man shrugged and turned back to his documents.

Lips pressed tight, Frederick looked around the office. Lewis wasn't in sight.

"Rollins!" Stauncey stood at the door to his private office. He waved Frederick over, then disappeared back inside.

Frederick went to his office. "Yes, Sir John?"

"Close the door and sit down."

Frederick did as he said. "I have Simmons analyzing a comparison sample from one of the suspects to the scrap of the letter we found with Bannister's body. I know that last judge called such evidence quackery, but one never knows if a different judge will be more receptive to the study. And Briley reported back. He thinks the bullet was a 13.2 caliber, most likely shot from a turn-off pocket pistol, or perhaps a pepper-box."

Stauncey acted as though he hadn't heard him. "Are you attending a party at Lady Mary Cavindish's with all of your suspects?" The magistrate steepled his fingers and stared over them at Frederick steadily.

Frederick didn't react. He hadn't wanted his employer to know that particular detail, not until the party was over and, hopefully, he'd learned more for the investigation. He had, however, told a few of his fellow agents when he'd asked for their assistance. He wanted to have men outside Lady Mary's house in case a suspect turned violent or ran. One of them must have snitched.

"I am," he answered. "This Saturday evening."

"To what end?" Stauncey frowned. "You think gathering everyone together in a social event will induce the guilty party to confess in front of their peers?" His scornful tone told him what he thought of the idea.

"A confession would be appreciated but not expected." Frederick tapped his fingers against his thigh. "I do hope that useful information might be let slip in a social situation where I'm certain the wine will be flowing. Lips are tight when questioned by an officer of Bow Street. It can't hurt."

Stauncey inhaled sharply. "I don't approve of using Lady Mary in your investigation. The first murder was at her club. She has a motive, and it doesn't necessarily align with ours."

"She wants to find the killer," Frederick said. "Our goals are aligned."

"You can't be that naïve." He pulled a snuffbox from his pocket and pulled out a pinch. "She's a canny woman, I'll give you that, but it isn't our policy to partner with civilians."

"Partner, no." Frederick shifted. This was delicate territory. Regardless if Frederick cooperated with Lady Mary and Eleanor or not, they would investigate. He didn't want them to have a go at it defenseless, but he also couldn't disregard a direct order from his superior. "The lady has been useful, giving me information and access to the *ton* I didn't have. That doesn't mean I provide her with information."

Stauncey gave him an approving look. "You *aren't* that naïve. That's good to know."

His good opinion made something inside Frederick wither. His self-respect, most like. He didn't normally approve of deception, but this misdirection seemed the only way to keep control of the investigation. Keep control of Lady Mary and Eleanor. And without that control, disaster could ensue.

"I've asked Briley and Quinton to watch Lady Mary's house during the party, just in case force becomes necessary."

The magistrate sniffed another bit of tobacco. "You sound confident this silly party will pay fruit."

"I don't know that it will; I don't know that it won't." Frederick ground his jaw. "I want to be prepared just in case."

Stauncey leaned back. "Understood."

As he remained quiet after that, Frederick stood to take his leave, thinking the interview over. His employer's voice stopped him at the door. "Just how prepared are you, Rollins?"

He turned. "Sir?"

"For the consequences?" The magistrate's dark eyes stared at him, unreadable. "You're determined to follow where the evidence leads, but have you thought about what will happen when you make an arrest? The killer isn't likely to be an unknown from the streets. The killer may well be someone with influence."

And with that influence came connections. Those connections would be embarrassed by the results of the investigation. Those in power would be happier if Frederick arrested a nobody, regardless of guilt or innocence. It would make them feel better, safer, to pretend that it hadn't been one of their peers who'd strangled a woman, shot her son to his death. It would be easier to stay wrapped in their cocoons, content in their ignorance.

Frederick's arrest would likely tear that sense of safety from them.

And they wouldn't thank him for it. If someone in power took particular exception, it could end his career.

He knew those were the consequences his magistrate hinted at. Knew that the offices at Bow Street were Stauncey's top concern. He weighed the justice in this one case against the future harm if this office lost its funds.

But Frederick's thoughts were of other consequences. Of someone else's sense of safety being ripped apart.

Of the pain he could cause Eleanor if the person he arrested was the woman he feared had committed these crimes.

As he left the magistrate's office, he swallowed down the

lump in his throat. Simmons would get back to him in the next day or two with an analysis of the writings he'd submitted. Perhaps he would show that the paper in Bannister's apartment wasn't written by Mrs. Lynton.

But Frederick didn't hold out much hope.

Chapter Thirty-Two

Eleanor

A S DINNER PARTIES went, this one was a disaster. Eleanor took a sip of her cream of watercress soup, the sounds of everyone's spoons against their bowls loud in the dining room. With their limited guest list, everyone had soon realized this party for the ploy it was.

And they were not amused.

Lord Anglia was on her left, his cravat fussily knotted, his sighs expressing his extreme displeasure that he had been bothered to attend. Next to him was Mrs. Massey, then her husband, who kept his eyes pinned to the bowl in front of him, not even raising them when Lady Mary spoke next to him.

She was at the head of the table, trying her best to make innocent conversation, her jaw clenching tighter and tighter with each rebuff. Lady Mary should know by now that innocent conversation wasn't her forte.

Frederick sat at Lady Mary's left, his hair slicked neatly back, making her fingers twitch to ruffle those auburn locks. He was always handsome, but never so much as when he looked like he'd come straight from her bed.

Miss Abbott was to his left. Eleanor didn't know if watercress soup wasn't to her liking or if the company had soured her appetite, but the woman leant back in her chair, thin arms crossed, and glared at each member of the party in turn.

The last member of the party was the one who knotted up Eleanor's insides. She shouldn't have spoken of the party in front of her mother, at least not while Frederick had been sitting with them at their own dinner table. In an act of unfailing politeness, when the subject of the party had arisen, he had invited her mother to join them.

Eleanor pushed away the errant thought that Frederick's action might not have been born from politeness. That he'd wanted her mother at the party of suspects because that's where he thought she belonged.

But they'd been over the timelines too many times. She'd been there when he'd spoken to their servants, and they had all confirmed her mother was home at the times of the murders. He couldn't still suspect her. Rolling her shoulders, Eleanor shook off her lingering doubts and tried to engage her neighbor.

"How is the bill for the national hospital faring, Lord Anglia? Do you think the full House will approve it?"

He tapped his spoon against the rim of the bowl before setting it down. "I believe it has a good chance. Are such public interest bills of particular concern to you?" he asked, his voice condescending.

"A fortnight ago I would have said no." Eleanor patted her lips with her napkin. "Now I find them endlessly fascinating. I never considered the power such a bill contained. The ability to reward numerous guilds and construction corporations, based not on their worth but their political alliances. And of course the funds that those guilds might return to some voting members as thanks."

Lady Mary snorted. "It is most unfair. Mr. Rollins subjected me to a lecture just this night on the wisdom of speaking delicately to best achieve one's ends. I have been biting my tongue for nigh on an hour." She gave Frederick a reproachful look. "He lectured the wrong woman." With a wave of her hand, two footmen stepped forward and began collecting the soup bowls. Plates of roast lamb and buttered carrots quickly replaced them.

Miss Abbott held up her wine glass for a refill. "Then this charade is over? We can all stop pretending we don't know why we're here?"

"Pretense has a time and place." Mr. Massey cut into his meat, his motions sharp. "I, for one, am happy to eat this good food, make pointless conversation, and return home early."

"Did the duke even know his name was on your invitation?" Anglia asked. He looked down at the other end of the table, presumably where Lady Mary's nephew would have sat. "When next I see him, I will tell him this was done in very poor form."

Laughter burbled out of Lady Mary. "I would very much like to be there when you do. Montague couldn't care less about *form*." She ran a finger under her eye. "If you must know, his daughter has a hint of fever. He and the duchess decided to remain at home with her instead of attending."

The party was supposed to have one more guest, too. They'd sent an invitation to Mr. Edric Cooke, hoping that by putting him and Lord Anglia together they might learn something new about the connection between the two. Lady Mary had said that seeing Anglia's reaction to the man could be instructive in itself.

But the crime lord had sent back a message that he was unable to attend, giving his thanks at such an *unusual* invitation. Lady Mary had been disappointed. She'd tried to hide it, but apparently her hopes that Cooke's appearance would loosen Anglia's tongue had been greater than Eleanor had thought.

"I can see why." Anglia leaned back, crossing one smartly tailored leg over the other. His cream pantaloons were snug across his thighs, and Eleanor suspected a bit of padding had been added to his calves. "I'd prefer the sickroom to this, as well."

Frederick's intent eyes had been observing everyone's interactions. He finally spoke up. "No need to be rude." His gaze toward the earl was decidedly unfriendly. "This is a night for dinner and conversation. Let's keep it pleasant."

"Yes, but why are *we* here?" Mrs. Massey pushed her plate away. "You have to admit we are a queer group."

"Isn't it obvious?" Miss Abbott took a large swallow of wine. "Each of us is a suspect. The Runner and his lackeys wanted to stir the pot."

Eleanor's mother paled.

Eleanor fumed at being called a lackey.

"Each of you is connected in some way to Lady Richford's and her son's death, yes." Frederick leaned forward, planting his palms on the table. "It doesn't necessarily follow that you are a suspect. I thought if we gathered all the players involved together, we might learn something new. Something that will help me catch the killer. That is what everyone wants, is it not?"

Anglia lifted his hands and clapped slowly. Obnoxiously. "You are quite the wordsmith. You should write fiction instead of work on Bow Street. If you are gathering us together in this desperate attempt, you are clearly unqualified to be a Runner."

"An officer of the Bow Street magistrate," Frederick gritted out.

"Are we truly suspects?" Eleanor's mother blotted her upper lip with her napkin. "I was sleeping. I couldn't have done it."

Eleanor frowned at Frederick. This was all his fault for inviting her. "Of course, you aren't a suspect, Mother. We just thought it would be nice for you to spend some time out of the house. Talk with friends."

Although there weren't many at the table who qualified as such. This had been a bad idea. All of it. Eleanor couldn't believe that Lady Mary had been able to convince her and Frederick to go along with this confounded suggestion. How trite to think that by gathering everyone together they might learn something new. And to invite her mother, of all things. In public, her mother seemed to keep her bearings more easily, not losing control of her emotions as she did in private with Eleanor. But every day brought new heartaches. If her mother lost control at a public function, she would never live down the shame, Eleanor knew.

Her mother shook her head, not seeming to hear Eleanor. "She deserved it, but that poor boy...."

The table went quiet. It was broken by Anglia's bark of laughter. "I take it back. This is most entertaining. My dear Missus...Lynton, was it? Why don't you tell us how you really feel about the departed Lady Richford?"

"She feels sorrow over any tragic death," Eleanor snapped. She gripped her fork tightly, her hand shaking from the effort it took not to stab the man with it.

"Was it tragic?" Mrs. Massey waited for the footman to refill her own glass of wine. It was her third, Eleanor thought. Or perhaps her fourth. "Or was it deserved?"

Her husband tried to draw the glass away from her, but she jerked from his grip, wine sloshing onto the white tablecloth.

Miss Abbott tossed her napkin onto her plate. "How dare you? Susan was a wonderful woman. She didn't deserve anything she got in life."

Eleanor pursed her lips. That was an odd turn of phrase. Did Miss Abbott mean that Lady Richford had hidden hardships that she didn't deserve or that she hadn't deserved the riches and status being a viscountess brought?

"You two were awfully close." Mrs. Massey narrowed her eyes. "Were you involved in her schemes, as well?"

"The only schemes I heard about were between Sue and your husband," Miss Abbott spat out.

Mrs. Massey gasped, pressing her palm over her overflowing bosom.

Mr. Massey only frowned, a deep groove lining his forehead. "What?"

"Everyone knows that's why you and Sue fought," Miss Abbott continued. "Were you jealous of her time with your husband? Is that why you killed her?"

Anglia leaned toward Eleanor, resting his hand on her arm. "This truly is more entertaining than White's ever could be.

Thank you for the invitation."

His breath was hot on her ear. Moist. She leaned away from the unpleasant sensation. Looking up, she saw Frederick's glare focused on the man. On his hand on her arm to be more precise. Things were already becoming heated. Eleanor eased her arm from under Anglia. She didn't need Frederick causing a scene over another man touching her.

"That's not why Mrs. Massey would have killed her." Lady Mary was the only one still eating. She cut a bite of carrot and placed it in her mouth, chewing thoughtfully. "I would have thought as Lady Richford's intimate friend, you would have known that."

Miss Abbott leapt to her feet, her hip knocking into the table. Glasses of wine trembled, and more than a few hands went out to steady them. "I will not be spoken to in this manner." And with a flounce of her skirts, she turned on her heel and left the room.

"We have dessert coming," Lady Mary called after her.

All right, Eleanor didn't want Frederick causing *more* of a scene. Although this night would be memorable regardless of what else happened.

Lady Mary stuck another bite in her mouth and shrugged. "It's a Bakewell tart. One of Cook's specialties. No one should miss it."

Mrs. Massey stood, wobbled, and grabbed for her husband's shoulder. After she'd steadied herself, she tugged him up. "Miss Abbott might be as infernal as her friend, but she was right about this. We don't have to subject ourselves to your…your…insinuations, either."

She pulled Mr. Massey after her.

He looked forlornly back at the table. "I do love a good Bakewell tart."

"I'll have our cook make you one tomorrow." And she stamped out of the room, dragging her husband after her.

Lord Anglia neatly folded his napkin. "There have been too many dramatic exits. I'm bored again." Standing, he gave a smart bow and started for the exit.

Lady Mary popped to her feet. "Lord Anglia, a moment."

He kept going, and Lady Mary disappeared after him.

Frederick and Eleanor locked gazes, then jumped to their own feet.

"Mother, stay here," Eleanor said as she circled the table. They trotted after Lady Mary, catching up in the entry. The door had just closed on the Masseys. Anglia was winding a woolen scarf around his neck and took the coat Lady Mary's butler held out.

Lady Mary stepped in front of the door, blocking Anglia's exit. "I wished to speak with you about your connection with Mr. Edric Cooke. I hear he has become involved in the passage of your spending bills."

"What of it?" Anglia shoved his hands into leather gloves. "As a private citizen, he has the right to advocate for bills he would like to see passed."

"Even if he, and the lawmakers involved, stand to profit from them?"

Anglia tilted his head. "You've surprised me, Lady Mary. I thought this conversation would be about something altogether different."

"You thought I called you here because of your anonymous piece in *The Times*?" Lady Mary said. "Or the threatening note you had delivered to my house?"

A smile curled at the edges of Anglia's mouth. "Neither as anonymous as I thought it would seem. And the note was a kindly warning. Not a threat."

"Not much is anonymous when I have powerful relations," Lady Mary said. She'd admitted to Eleanor and Frederick that she'd gone to see her nephew finally. He'd found out who the author had been. Not many newspaper editors could stand firm against a duke.

Anglia lifted one shoulder. "Just like Mr. Cooke, I have a right to say my piece."

"It was libel." Frederick took a step forward, his shoulders seeming to widen.

"Was it?" Anglia took his hat from the butler. "Speak to a solicitor. I think you'll find not many would take such a case."

"Did Lady Richford threaten you with a lawsuit, my lord?" Lady Mary crossed her arms. "Perhaps you weren't always so confident that you would win such a case."

Anglia's knuckles whitened around the brim of his hat. "I'm not the one who should take care with his words. Accusing me of murder is slanderous."

"We are merely asking questions," Frederick said. His body had tensed right along with Anglia's.

Anglia smiled, his teeth appearing pointed in the glow of the gas lamps. "Then I will tell you truly, I no longer had anything to worry about with Lady Richford. I know what Mrs. Massey was alluding to when she was shrieking at Miss Abbott. And I know that it is true. Lady Richford did have a light hand. I caught her wearing a pin that belonged to the wife of a colleague of mine. I told her I knew. And I told her what would happen if she continued to oppose me. That piece in *The Times* that morning had just been a reminder. One she understood."

"So the blackmailer became the blackmailee." Lady Mary shook her head. "Why do people make such a trial out of their lives?"

"Who was your colleague?" Frederick asked.

"None of your business." Anglia tugged at the cuff of his coat. "He has nothing to do with the matter."

"And he votes the way you want him to," Eleanor added.

Anglia's grin was genuine, and quickly gone. "Just so." He stepped to Lady Mary's side, looking from her to the door handle and back, eyebrows lifted.

With a sigh, she stepped aside. Her butler hurried between the two to open the door.

Anglia set his hat on his dark head, adjusted it. "It's ironic you brought up Mr. Cooke. While it has amused me to be thought one of your suspects, it has gone on long enough. Speak with Mr. Cooke. I was at his club, The Cagey Vixen, the night of Lady Richford's murder. There are several witnesses who can attest to the fact I cannot be the killer. Mr. Cooke chief among them." And without a nod or backward glance, he stepped out into the foggy night and disappeared.

Eleanor hadn't realized how tense their group in the entry had been until the door clicked shut behind him and everyone seemed to sag.

"Well, that was unpleasant." Eleanor pressed her palm to her abdomen. "And unfruitful. We learned nothing new."

Frederick took her hand, squeezed it. "Lord Anglia gave us an alibi. If I can confirm it, that eliminates one more suspect."

"We also learned just how ill-advised it was to gather all the suspects together into one room." Lady Mary pinched her lips tight. "It was like a plot point in a badly written Gothic novel. Truly, I can't understand how I let you convince me to do this, Eleanor."

Eleanor gaped as Lady Mary marched past her and back to the dining room.

Frederick gave her hand another squeeze, his palm warm and rough against hers. "She doesn't mean it." He leaned down to whisper in her ear. "And I, for one, am exceedingly fond of all your ideas."

The tickle of his breath on her ear, the low timbre of his voice, the heat of his nearness, all sent an army of ants marching through her stomach. She glanced at the butler to see if he'd heard, but he studiously avoided her gaze.

"Let's go have some of that tart." Frederick tugged her down the hall. "There should be plenty now for second helpings."

Eleanor traipsed after him. Dessert did sound good, but she couldn't just let the matter drop. She sniffed. "I could have sworn the idea was Lady Mary's."

Chapter Thirty-Three
Lady Mary

ROLLINS HAD WANTED to go alone to The Cagey Vixen. I had quickly disabused him of that notion.

I was only curious to see what a gambling hell looked like. I've been to quite a few places in my life that would make the society ladies gasp in horror, but a gambling den hasn't been one of them. Whether I saw Mr. Cooke there or not was of little consequence.

Except, of course, we had to see Mr. Cooke, ask him about Lord Anglia's alibi. A flutter that I felt much too old for batted behind my breastbone. If only the dratted man had come to my dinner party, we wouldn't have had to seek him out now.

"You can still stay in the carriage." Frederick stood on the coach's steps, his body half in and half out of the coach. "Our driver will make sure no one bothers you, even in this neighborhood."

I peered over his shoulder. The neighborhood was one of tall, sandstone buildings, only faintly stained by soot. The pedestrians striding behind Frederick looked like men of business, with a few tradesmen interspersed. As dens of sin went, this one was in a respectable location. I supposed men of consequence didn't want to be looking over their shoulders for a cutthroat or foist whenever they went to indulge in one of their vices.

"I think I shall be fine accompanying you." I started moving toward the steps, forcing Mr. Rollins to move back and offer his hand. On the pavement, I looked up. Mr. Cooke's building was shorter than the rest, only two stories high, with tall Corinthian columns stretching to the portico over the top floor. Potted boxwoods stood on either side of the deep red door of the entrance, their branches shaped into wide coils. A discreet sign was nestled against the alcove above the door: *The C. V.*

Rollins handed his card to the doorman, who told us to wait in a small room off the foyer.

"Do you think he'll see us?" Rollins asked, examining a painting of deep greens and blues, a quaint hunting scene in the countryside.

"He'd better." I thought about taking a seat to wait. Cooke would see us, he'd be too curious not to, but I wouldn't put it past him to make us wait longer than necessary. Just because he could.

But much to my surprise, the doorman quickly returned to show us to Cooke's offices. He took us to the main, central room, sunken a couple of feet into the ground and packed with gaming tables and a bar along the far wall. Only three men sat slouched at one of the tables, the rest empty, understandable at this time of day.

We went up one of the wide staircases that rose on both sides of the room up to the balcony on the first floor. Several doors ran along the hallways branching out in a T-shape, and the doorman took us to the right, to the door at the far end of the corridor. He knocked once, then pushed it open.

"Mr. Rollins and Lady Mary Cavindish, sir." He announced us with a small incline of his head, then left, closing the door behind him.

Edric Cooke sat behind his stained mahogany desk, his gaze flicking over Rollins before settling on me. I couldn't read his expression, and I had the first flicker of concern about arriving on his doorstep with a magistrate's agent in tow. I hadn't considered that he might think I had brought a government agent in order to prosecute him in some way.

I firmed my grip on my walking stick, a pure white one today, the shaft and knob all carved from a single piece of alabaster with the bottom end notched into a small piece of wood, its only nod to functionality. It had been a gift from my husband the summer I'd twisted my ankle, and I wondered why it had been the one I'd chosen this morning for this excursion.

Cooke indicated the two seats across from him. "To what do I owe the pleasure?" he asked, his voice making it sound as though it was anything but.

I eyed the chairs. They were squat, little things, and I could only imagine Cooke had chosen them as it would put his guests in a lower position, forcing them to look up to him. It was a savvy, and petty, move, one I decided not to play along with. A settee backed up against a side wall, and I strode over to pull up the three pillows that adorned it.

I plopped one on the seat of my chair and handed Rollins the other two. "Here. With your long legs, you'll need the boost."

A muscle ticked in the Runner's jaw, but he took the pillows. He probably thought it would make less of a scene if he just went along instead of arguing with me. I settled on the chair, wiggling a bit to even out the cushion. He would thank me later.

The flint had left Cooke's eyes, his lips twitching. There was no amusement in his voice, however, when he said, "Why are you here?"

Rollins sat, his backrest only rising to his lower back with his extra cushions. "I'd like to ask you about Lord Anglia. The earl's secretary says the earl was with him at the office the night Lady Richford was killed. Anglia says he was here."

"And you want to know who is lying?" Cooke pulled a leather-bound journal from one of the desk drawers and flipped it open. "She died what, almost three weeks ago? That Wednesday?"

Rollins nodded in confirmation.

"You keep a registry of everyone who comes in to gamble?" I would love to track the attendance behavior of my members, see which nights were favorites for different people, but it was more record-keeping than I even wanted to think about.

"I keep notes on my high-stakes players." Cooke ran his finger down a side column, then flipped the page. "And the Earl of Anglia doesn't play small."

"He has a problem with gaming?" Rollins asked. "Has he ever gotten himself into trouble?"

Cooke narrowed his gaze on something on the page. "You misunderstand. He plays for high stakes, but it isn't usually money. Anglia is smart. He doesn't risk much blunt, but he plays with the Quality in order to gossip. He wins in the information he gathers."

Yes, mingling with the giants of industry and learning about their different business ventures would be helpful for a man who put his own profits above the well-being of the nation. It also wouldn't hurt to know who had lost big and could be open to bribery.

Cooke huffed out a laugh. "I don't know why Anglia's man would say he was at his offices. It was no lie to say Anglia was working, but he was here while doing it." He looked up. "He was at the hazard tables, from about ten at night until two the next morning. He played with Virgil Baldwin and Ross Collins if you wish for secondary confirmation."

Knowing Cooke's reputation, I was sure Rollins would be following up with the two men. Baldwin was the owner of a large import business, mainly cotton from the former colonies. The other name I wasn't familiar with. But if Cooke hadn't thought they'd be in accordance with him, he wouldn't have mentioned their names.

"Do you know if Lady Richford's son was an accomplice to her blackmail schemes?" I asked. His murder still got under my skin. Why kill a mother and son? Unless they were both involved in the same misdeeds.

"Blackmail?" Cooke ran his fingers through his steel-grey hair, the locks falling strictly back into their place. "I thought the lady was a thief."

The look Mr. Rollins shot me could only be called reproachful. Yes, we were supposed to be garnering information, not giving it, but I thought it likely that the crime lord would know that information soon, if not already. He struck me as a man who wanted to know all the underhanded dealings in London.

"There's not much difference between the two," Rollins said, tapping his notebook against his thigh. "Had you heard that her son was involved?"

"I had not." Cooke leaned back, steepling his fingers before his chin.

"And what of the other women linked to Lady Richford?" I scooted to the edge of my seat. "If we could speak with that man you told me of, the one who buys and sells stolen goods, he might be able to tell us if he knew of anyone else working with the viscountess. And with Mr. Rollins with me, you need have no fear for my safety."

It seemed this night I was destined for disappointed looks. Cooke accompanied his with a heavy sigh. "I thought our conversations would remain private. But as it happens, you misunderstood me. I had only heard a rumor. I am a law-abiding businessman. I would never associate with a criminal such as that."

Rollins snorted. "Of course."

The door opened, and a beautiful young women entered. The burgundy of her dress was so dark it looked almost black, and the fabric clung to her body like a second skin. Without sparing us a look, she went to Cooke's desk and handed him a missive. "It's here."

Cooke's face remained impassive, but I caught the flare of interest in his eyes. For the news the woman brought or for the woman herself?

He stood. "If you will excuse me, I have business to attend." Raising his voice, he said, "Jocko will show you out."

The man must have been standing right outside the door, waiting for his master's instruction. The same man who had led us in stepped into the doorway. "Follow me."

Rollins looked at me and shrugged. We had no cause to force our presence on Mr. Cooke, and I didn't know what else he could tell us. He had confirmed Lord Anglia's alibi. That was sufficient.

"Thank you for your time, Mr. Cooke." Rollins slid his notebook away, inclined his head to the woman, and stood, one of the pillows sliding off his seat to the floor. He turned for the door, stretching his arm in front of him as an invitation for me to precede him.

I glanced once more at Cooke's face, the woman, the missive, then dipped my own head and left his office. A few more patrons filled a table on the main floor. I wondered how crowded the hell would become when night fell. Activities such as these were best done under the cover of darkness.

Rollins handed me into the carriage, gave his driver instructions.

"Do you believe him?" I asked, once the carriage had started to move.

"I see no reason why not to." Rollins turned his hat in his hands. "Lord Anglia was always a bit of a stretch as the murderer. It is good to clear him once and for all."

I made a noise in the back of my throat. Yes, we were down yet another suspect, but the true culprit still remained a mystery. I suppose this was what investigations entailed. Tediously going over everyone's alibis, eliminating the possibilities until only one person remained who could have committed the crime.

I looked out the window. I hated to admit it, since the entertainment value of an investigation should be irrelevant, but the routine procedure was dreadfully dull. I would have thought an investigator's life more interesting. At least I didn't have to complete the paperwork that Rollins complained about.

The carriage turned onto a familiar street. "We're going back to my club? Isn't there someone else we should speak to?" I had thought to pay a call to the Masseys, pretend to apologize for the dinner party, see if I could draw anything else out of them.

I didn't want to. At this point, I felt as though we were going in circles, repeating questions, hearing the same answers. But going in a circle was still going somewhere. It had to be better than standing in one place.

Rollins shook his head. "I need to return to my office for the afternoon. I have duties there I can't ignore."

The paperwork. I was happy to climb down from the carriage and leave the man to that task. I waved goodbye. I thought about calling for my own coach, making that visit to the Masseys.

I turned into my club instead. After all, going in circles made one dizzy after a while. No, what this investigation called for was thought. An analysis of all that we'd learned up to this point accompanied by rational deduction.

A spot of tea wouldn't go amiss, either.

Chapter Thirty-Four

Frederick

T HE DECEPTION DIDN'T sit right in his gut. Frederick stood across the street from Eleanor's townhouse, wondering if she was at home. But he couldn't trust Lady Mary to keep the information to herself that he still investigated Mrs. Lynton. Until he'd either cleared the woman or found evidence of her guilt, he didn't want Eleanor to know.

The door at his back swung open. "Can I help you, sir?"

Frederick turned. This was the fourth neighbor's home he'd questioned. He handed the butler his card. "I'd like to speak with the servants here. Can we meet in the kitchens perhaps?" He'd already spoken to the owners of the houses that neighbored the Lyntons. The servants, however, seemed more willing to gossip, and their knowledge surpassed that of their masters.

The butler was skilled at controlling his emotions. With just an incline of his head, he said, "Of course, sir. If you'll follow me," as though being questioned by an officer of Bow Street were an everyday occurrence.

Frederick was offered a cup of tea and a slice of nut bread while he waited for the remaining servants to gather. Their answers were similar to what he'd already learned from the neighboring houses. The Lynton servants were worried about their mistress. She'd always been such a kind, concerned lady, but lately she'd shown signs of temper. Of imbalance.

"She kept Mr. Grosse and Miss Olive on even through all that family's troubles," the cook said, pushing another wedge of bread at him even though he hadn't finished his first. "Treated like family, they are."

"Do you think her servants would lie to protect her? Tell me she remained at home when she might have left?" Frederick asked.

An uncomfortable silence met his question. "They're good people," the butler finally said. "They wouldn't lie to the law."

"But they don't know all the comings and goings," one of the maids added. "Mr. Grosse, sweet man, doesn't hear the best, and Miss Olive likes her sleep a bit too much if you ask me."

"No one asked you." The cook glared at the girl.

Frederick swirled the remains of his tea in his cup. "Is she wrong though?"

"No." The butler cleared his throat. "That household might not be as attentive as some. That doesn't mean Mrs. Lynton did anything wrong."

It didn't mean that she hadn't, either. "On the night of the murder, did any of you see anyone leave the house?" he asked.

"It's hard to remember," the butler said. "That was over a fortnight ago."

Something in the man's tone made Frederick grip his bit of lead a little tighter. "But you have seen someone going out at night. Mrs. Lynton?"

The servants gave each other uneasy looks.

"A woman and her son were murdered." Frederick turned a pointed stare on each of them. "This is not a time to withhold the truth."

The cook's shoulders heaved. "I have an achy back, you see. A bit of walking does it good most nights. I figure Mrs. Lynton might have the same problem. I see her sometimes leaving her house." She scooted forward on her chair. "But she's not going out for the night. She's in her night rail she is."

"One of her people always comes out to fetch her," the butler added quickly.

Frederick cocked his head. "Always?"

The butler scratched at a mark on the wood table. "Well, once or twice we've had to knock on their door. Let them know Mrs. Lynton was feeling poorly."

Frederick swallowed. The Lynton's front door wasn't as closely watched as Eleanor's servants would have him believe. And how could it be? The house wasn't a prison. If someone wanted to leave, she would find a way.

Frederick thanked them for their time and stood, feeling like a fifty-pound yoke burdened his shoulders. The story was the same elsewhere. Mrs. Lynton's alibi was easily punctured. Her emotional instability was well-known and her hatred of the victim likewise acknowledged.

He followed the butler out the servant's exit, ignoring the snub, and breathed in deeply. The sky was overcast and grim, a match to his mood. Perhaps it would finally rain, but he didn't hold out hope. There had been too many times he'd been led to believe the gathering clouds would bring relief. Too many times when hope had been dangled in front of him, only to be snatched away.

There were more neighbors to question, but how many times did he need to hear what he already knew? Eleanor's mother had a motive to harm Lady Richford and the opportunity. And after seeing the bruises and scratches on Eleanor's arms, he knew she had the ability as well. There was truth to the yarn that madmen had heightened strength. The same went for madwomen.

He felt dirty compiling a case against Eleanor's mother. Then he felt annoyed. It was his job, after all. More than that, his responsibility to protect society from someone who was prone to do harm. His duty to protect Eleanor.

But he knew she wouldn't feel the same.

Hoping to alleviate his guilt, he directed his driver to another suspect's residence, feeling fortunate when Miss Abbott answered his knock.

"I'm leaving in twenty minutes for a demonstration on electricity," she told him after seating herself in her large parlor. "They are going to reanimate a frog, and I won't miss that."

Her flat was open, the parlor and dining area sharing a space. One door led off the north side of the room to a small kitchen, peeking through the narrow doorway. Another door led from the east of the room to the woman's private chambers, he assumed.

"I'll make this brief." Frederick remained standing, gripping the back of the chair before him. "My associates are currently searching for the man I learned purchased stolen jewelry from Lady Richford." He considered jewelry obtained from blackmail the same as theft. "I am going to ask him what other women he met with. It will go better for you if you tell me you were involved in Lady Richford's blackmail schemes than if I have to learn it from him."

My bluff was convincing even to myself. Of course, if Miss Abbott never met with the man then it was all for naught.

Miss Abbott's shoulders were rigid. She smoothed her hands down her skirts. Her fingers, adorned with several gold rings, dug into the fabric. "I was with Susan when she sold a necklace or two. I thought they were her own. She wanted money her husband didn't know about, but she was scared to deal with a man of that sort on her own. She was my friend. Of course, I stood by her when she met with him."

"How noble of you."

Miss Abbott frowned at the sarcasm in his voice.

Surely, she couldn't truly believe he would fall for her nonsense.

He picked up a carved ivory statue of an elephant. Two small black stones formed its eyes. "Blackmail seems to have done well by you. A nice apartment. Pretty artwork. Days spent attending demonstrations instead of in labor."

"I have blackmailed no one."

"Did you let Lady Richford do all the odious work? Is that what caused the disagreement between you two?" Frederick ran his thumb over the elephant's trunk. "There are many ways partners in crime can become enemies."

"There was no disagreement." She stood, her hands clenched by her sides. "Do you know how rare it is to find a kindred spirit? If I were so criminally inclined as you seem to think, to find another woman who matched my machinations step for step? Such a friend I would treasure. I would never hurt Susan."

"If she was such a good friend, you should want the one who killed her caught. You should have protected her against those who threatened her." It was an abominable thing to say, but killers weren't caught with kind words.

But Miss Abbott didn't seem to take offense. Her shoulders lowered. "You mean Mrs. Lynton. I knew she hated Susan. Susan knew how much Mrs. Lynton hated her. We never believed she would make good on her threats, however, never believed she would turn violent."

Frederick stilled. It always came back to Mrs. Lynton. "What threats did she make?"

Miss Abbott cocked her head, her forehead creasing. "The letter. Susan kept it in the secret compartment in her writing desk along with some other personal items. I thought you must have seen it if you were asking."

"You saw a letter from Mrs. Lynton making a threat against the viscountess?"

She nodded. "Susan showed it to me. We laughed about it. Of all the people Susan had…crossed, she hadn't counted Mrs. Lynton amongst them. It had been a little snub, over a decade ago. So many people hated Susan for much worse."

"Hate is a strong word."

She shrugged. "Susan didn't care what others thought about her. It was the quality of hers that I loved most. Now"—she said, moving toward a coat rack by her front door—"I must show you out. I don't want to be late."

Frederick inhaled sharply. Every damned arrow seemed to point just where he didn't want. He stomped out of the apartment and out of the lodging house. Temple Church was only a block away, and he turned toward it as he pulled out his pocket watch and checked the time. He climbed into his carriage. He really did need to make an appearance at the office. And this way his words to Lady Mary weren't truly a lie.

The office was unusually empty, just two other agents hunched over their desks, the door to Sir John's office closed, the window above it dark. Good. He wasn't in the mood to deliver another progress report. The progress he'd made he didn't want to report. He hadn't told the magistrate that Mrs. Lynton was his prime suspect, and he didn't want to until absolutely necessary.

He would need to ask Lord Richford if he could search his wife's desk again. What he found there could be another nail in Mrs. Lynton's coffin, but perhaps something he found would lead him in a different direction. An easier direction. One that wouldn't crush the woman he was coming to love.

He'd barely dropped his arse into his chair, however, before it became necessary.

"Oy. Rollins!" Simmons poked his head into the office. "I looked at that letter you brought."

Frederick waved him in, dread filling his gut. "What have you got?"

The agent sauntered to his desk. "Preliminary studies show the author to have a fretful nature, clearly in high emotion at the time of writing. The Swiss physiognomist Lavater thinks that if the tail on an—"

"I can read a person's character on my own, Simmons." He planted his palms on his desk. "I wanted to know your opinion from your other area of study. Please, no lectures from the Swiss or French or Italians."

Simmons slapped the letter Frederick had taken from Mrs. Lynton's house on his desk and more gingerly placed the scrap of paper from Bannister's apartment. He sniffed before giving Frederick a broad smile. "They're a match."

Chapter Thirty-Five

Eleanor

"Mr. Rollins here to see you, miss."

Eleanor hopped out of the large wingback chair, setting her book aside, when Mr. Grosse made his announcement. She'd wondered if Frederick would come for supper tonight. Pausing briefly in front of a mirror, she tucked a strand of hair back into its twist, pinched her cheeks, then hurried for the door.

She drew her brows together when she saw him. His handsome face looked haggard, his eyes dull. "Frederick, what are you doing standing in the doorway? Come in. You look like you need a stiff drink."

"Eleanor." He stepped forward and to the side, revealing another man standing behind him. "This is Simmons, another officer of Bow Street." He swallowed, his Adam's apple bobbing. "I'm sorry. We've come to arrest your mother."

Eleanor stopped so abruptly it was as though she'd walked into a wall. She blinked. "No." She shook her head. "You're making a jest. A poor one."

Mr. Grosse made a motion as if to close the door, but the other agent pressed his palm against it, holding it open until he'd stepped inside. He gingerly closed it behind him.

"Miss?" Mr. Grosse wrung his hands.

Eleanor couldn't think of a thing to say. Her mind was blank, her body numb.

Frederick stepped before her and gripped her shoulders. Without breaking her gaze, he said, "Find Mrs. Lynton. Bring her down please, Mr. Grosse."

Eleanor opened her mouth to object.

Frederick squeezed her shoulders. "It will be worse if we have to restrain her or carry her out."

The reality of the situation rushed at Eleanor, like a monstrous wave surging for the shore. A whimper escaped her lips. She shook her head again. "You can't." She gripped the edge of his coat. "Please, you can't."

"We found a letter Bannister's murderer tried to destroy. It was written by your mother." Frederick raised his hand to brush a lock of hair off her cheek.

She slapped his hand away, rage filling the void. She stepped back, jerking out of his grasp.

His fingers twitched before he lowered his hands. "Her mind is troubled, Eleanor. You know this. I need to ask if you have a pistol in the house."

She tried to suck in a deep breath, but her lungs wouldn't fully expand. Black dots swirled in front of her eyes. She looked over Frederick's shoulder to the other agent. Frederick mentioning her mother's mental troubles in front of another person seemed a bigger betrayal than his coming to arrest her somehow. She'd shared her fears about her mother's mind in private. He couldn't kiss each scratch and bruise her mother had given her, then come here to tear her life apart.

"Eleanor." Frederick's voice deepened. "Is there a pistol here, maybe one your father owned?"

"No." She pressed her hand to her abdomen. Not anymore. It was still in Lady Mary's box of lost items. "Why are you doing this?" She knew the answer, of course. He believed her mother guilty. She didn't understand how he'd never spoken to her of these suspicions, not since they'd become intimate. How he could just show up on her doorstep and take her mother from her?

Movement on the stairs drew all their attention. Mr. Grosse had obviously warned his mistress of what awaited. She was pale, her eyes unfocused, but her steps unerringly carried her forward.

Eleanor rushed to her and gripped her hand. It was cold and gave no answering squeeze. "Mother, we'll sort this out. I'll go with you. You won't be alone."

"That's not possible." Frederick tugged her back and nodded at his associate. The man stepped forward and took her mother's shoulder, leading her to the door. "You can't stay with her."

His touch burned. She'd once craved it; now it made her sick.

"Simmons will take your mother. I'll stay with you."

"No." Her shoulders slowly rolled back. The panic was ebbing, leaving a grim sort of determination. And rage. "I don't want you here."

He reached for her. "Eleanor...."

Side-stepping him, she went to her mother and held her tight. Her mother's arms remained limp by her side. "Be strong. I'll speak with Mr. Lake. He'll know what to do." Their family solicitor had been wise when protecting their newfound assets. Whether he knew anything about criminal law was another story, but she needed to believe he could help. She needed her mother to believe it.

"I'm not going to leave you like this, Eleanor." Frederick raked his fingers through his hair. "You aren't well. I understand, but I can—"

"I want you out of my house, Mr. Rollins." She wrapped her arms around her waist. She felt like a vase that had been dropped. It hadn't broken but cracks fanned its surface from the impact. Unless she held herself together, she was going to break, fall into pieces.

A muscle ticced in Frederick's jaw. He looked almost as devastated as she felt, but she wouldn't let herself care. This was his doing.

He closed his eyes and blew out a breath. When he opened them again, they were resigned. "I'll make sure she's safe."

Safe? Frederick was arresting her mother for murder. The penalty for that was death. *Safe* no longer had a meaning. But she nodded. She needed him to leave. If he stayed, she wouldn't be able to hold herself together.

Her mother left without a sound. When the door closed behind them, Eleanor and Mr. Grosse stood unmoving, and at least on her part, unthinking. The back of her mind raced with everything that needed to be done, but the front part was blissfully silent. She stared at the door, as though expecting it to open back up, her mother to come back through as though she'd only been out for a day of shopping.

But that wasn't going to happen.

Mr. Grosse finally turned. "Miss?"

The expectation in his voice is what finally broke her. The realization that she was the one who would need to figure this out. Her father was dead, her mother arrested. There were no siblings. No uncles to call for aid. She was alone.

And she had no idea what to do.

Her lungs hammered in and out, her breaths harsh. She pressed her palm flat against the wall, praying she wouldn't fall. No matter how much she wanted to, now was not the time to come apart. Her mother needed her. And if Eleanor didn't know how to proceed, there was someone who might.

Decision made, she straightened from the wall. "Mr. Grosse, please tell the coachman to have the carriage brought round."

LADY MARY BARELY looked up from the ledgers on her desk. "Are you here to cancel your membership, as well?"

Eleanor stopped behind the guest chair in Lady Mary's office, her hands gripping the backrest. "No. Unless we find the true killer, however, my mother will no longer be a member." She swallowed, the back of her throat burning. "Fre—Mr. Rollins arrested her."

Lady Mary dropped her pen and lifted her head. "What? He did no such thing."

Eleanor nodded. "Just now. He and another Runner came to the house and took her away." She looked out the window, her eyes blurring. "She didn't even object. I think she feels guilty about hating Lady Richford so much, almost like her hate became a living thing that got the viscountess killed." Either that, or she hadn't understood what was happening. But being led away by two Bow Street Runners should be clear enough for even the most disordered mind.

"I don't know where she is right now," Eleanor continued. "Is she already sitting in a jail cell? Is she talking to the magistrate? Frederick wouldn't let me accompany them."

"At least he was right about something." Lady Mary stood and circled the desk. She guided Eleanor into the guest chair and sat in the one next to it. "You can't help your mother by following her around. You'll only make yourself sick, and your mother might not want a witness to her humiliation."

Eleanor leaned forward and buried her face in her hands. "What am I to do?"

Lady Mary rubbed soothing circles on her back. "There is only one thing that you can do."

"Find the murderer."

Lady Mary's hand paused. "Well, yes, that too, but I thought that went without saying. I meant find defense counsel for your mother."

"We have a man we used to help with my father's business and investments."

Lady Mary sniffed. "While I'm sure he is excellent at bills of lading and whatnot, I meant someone who specializes in criminal cases. I know a man. One of my nephew's friends is acquainted with him and has brought him to some parties I attended. I believe Summerset wanted to have a criminal defense counsel on hand in case one of his escapades landed him in hot water." She leant across the desk and dragged a journal in front of her. She ripped out a blank page and wrote down a name. "I believe his office is in Hanover Square. Call on him. Tell him I sent you."

Eleanor blew on the ink before folding the paper and putting it in her reticule. "Thank you."

"Now, how are you doing? Truly."

Eleanor huffed out a laugh. "It doesn't feel real. Not yet. But I'll be strong. I have to be, for my mother."

Lady Mary nodded, approvingly. "And how is your Frederick?"

Eleanor gaped. "How should he be doing? He arrested my mother!" She slumped back in her chair. Why should she care how that traitor was doing?

"Come now, don't be silly." Lady Mary frowned. "He must have had sufficient reason to arrest your mother. And if he hadn't done it, another Runner would have."

Eleanor started to protest, but Lady Mary held up her hand. "I'm not saying he was right, only that he would never do anything to hurt you unless he absolutely must. He feels his duties most heavily, that boy."

A steel coil wrapped around Eleanor's chest. She wouldn't feel guilty about how she'd treated Frederick. She wouldn't. He'd smiled at her mother over the dinner table and then arrested her. He'd held Eleanor in his arms and told her he wanted to take care of her forever.

If she closed her eyes, she could almost feel those arms now.

She blew out a shaky breath. He'd thought he'd had good reason for his actions. Eleanor knew this, but it didn't make accepting those actions any easier. In time, she might be able to forgive him, but she could never forget. If her mother was prosecuted, convicted... executed.

There was no way Eleanor could ever be with the man who'd had a hand in that. It would be too big a betrayal of her mother.

"Do you have any of that brandy?" Eleanor asked. She'd take the burning pain down her throat if it eased the ache around her heart.

Lady Mary stood. "None of that now. You don't have time for self-pity." Reaching down, she grabbed Eleanor's arm and pulled her to standing. The woman was surprisingly strong. "Go. Speak to that solicitor. The sooner he takes your mother's case, the better."

Eleanor knew she was right. It was something solid to do, a definite act. And with her mind in such a muddle, a sure direction to travel in should be welcome.

She kissed Lady Mary goodbye, turned her steps to leave the club.

But Eleanor had been taught when she was young that life was rarely fair. Bad things happened to good people all the time. And more often than not, the wicked suffered no consequences, in this life, at least.

She would hire counsel for her mother. She would go through all the motions of helping her.

All the while knowing anything she did most likely would have no effect.

Chapter Thirty-Six

Lady Mary

I SWIRLED THE brandy in my glass, watching its honeyed droplets cling to the sides. I'd told Eleanor that the liquor wouldn't help her, but I didn't see why I shouldn't partake.

Eleanor's mother had been arrested, a woman I knew in my heart didn't commit the crime. Any hope for a happy ending between Eleanor and Frederick seemed lost. And as for my own happy ending....

I glared at the ledgers. Over thirty percent of my members hadn't paid their dues this month. It was no longer speculative. I was bleeding membership. Revenue was down just as my expenses had skyrocketed with the fire repairs. I could keep the club running with my personal funds, but I hadn't wanted this to be a hobby. I'd wanted to succeed with a profitable business.

I stared into my brandy again, too morose to even drink it. We didn't always get what we wanted. At my age, I would have thought I'd have learned that lesson by now.

Perhaps it was time to ask for help. My nephew would be only too happy to provide it. He had real investigators who could uncover the truth. If I hadn't let my pride hold my tongue from asking him for assistance, how different the situation might be. The true killer might now be in custody. Mrs. Lynton would be safe at home. And I might not be losing members like a drunkard loses his last coin at the pub.

Bobby knocked on my open door. "That blighter Rollins is here. I told him—Oi!"

There was a scuffle, pushing back and forth, until Rollins ducked under Bobby's arm and sprang into my office. "I need to see you, and your servants are being most inhospitable today."

My lips curved. I couldn't imagine Eleanor unburdening her heart to Bobby or the others, but that didn't mean they hadn't heard just the same. Even closed doors weren't much of a barrier to the inquisitiveness of my servants. Apparently, they had taken sides, and it wasn't Mr. Rollins's.

"You arrested Mrs. Lynton," I stated.

Rollins adjusted his cravat. "I did."

Bobby grabbed the back of his coat and tugged him toward the door. "You made Miss Lynton sad. I don't like seeing her sad."

I had to agree. But when Rollins twisted, his fist pulled back and ready to bloody Bobby's face, I spoke up. "Bobby, it's all right. Leave him be. I'd like to hear what he has to say for himself."

Bobby grumbled but released Rollins's coat. He leaned against the doorjamb, crossing his arms. "Fine."

"This conversation is private," Rollins informed him, before grabbing the door and shutting it in Bobby's face.

"I think you'll find not much around here remains private." I watched as Rollins straightened his cravat while marching back and forth. My office wasn't large enough for such serious pacing. "Well?" I said, tiring on his behalf. "What have you to say? You can't honestly believe Mrs. Lynton killed Lady Richford and her son."

"Of course, I believe it." He gave me a disgruntled look. "I wouldn't have arrested her if I didn't."

True enough. "What finally convinced you?"

"The handwriting samples. The killer tried to destroy one of her letters that Bannister had." He punched one fist into the other hand. "Miss Abbott told me Lady Richford had a threatening letter from Mrs. Lynton. Bannister must have gotten ahold of it, probably the same time he took that sack of items his mother had blackmailed from her victims. He contacted Mrs. Lynton. To blackmail her, accuse her, I don't know. But it only makes sense if she went to confront Bannister, killed him, and tried to destroy any evidence implicating her."

I sniffed. "She didn't do a very good job of it."

Rollins twisted his mouth but continued with his case. "She has shown hints of violence. Eleanor knows this. She just doesn't want to believe it."

"What hints of violence?" I had seen no such thing, but it would explain why Eleanor had been so desperate to have her mother's club membership revoked.

Rollins stopped. He planted his hands on his hips and sucked in a deep breath. "You would need to ask Eleanor about those. The magistrate won't need to know about that to make his case," he muttered to himself.

"Her servants give her an alibi," I reminded him.

The look he gave me was full of derision, and it was well deserved. The word of the people one pays could hardly be considered reliable.

"Her mind is becoming fractured." Rollins gripped the back of his neck. "Perhaps the judge will take that into account."

I tapped my fingers on the desk. The memory of how we'd found Lady Richford's body rose to my mind. That image was never very far. "It wasn't a fractured mind that devised these killings. Nor a fractured mind that had the sense to escape without detection. A vicious one, yes, but not fractured."

Rollins shook his head. "It all fits," he repeated.

"What of this letter Miss Abbott told you about? Where was it?"

"Lady Richford had a secret compartment in her writing desk that I didn't find." He narrowed his eyes. "Apparently the viscountess showed her friend Mrs. Lynton's letter and they had a grand laugh about it. I've sent a note to Lord Richford asking for access to his townhouse here in London to see what else she kept in that secret drawer, but it hardly matters at this point."

He flexed his fingers. "Have you seen Eleanor? How is she doing?"

"Yes, and how do you think?" A secret compartment in her desk. I examined my own. It felt deficient knowing it only had the standard drawers that everyone could see. "You arrested her mother. That is hard to forgive."

"Hard I can handle." Rollins set his jaw. "If there's a chance, no matter how small, that Eleanor can forgive me, I will make it happen. But if it's impossible...." His voice broke on the last word, and I stood and circled the desk to stand before him.

"Nothing is impossible." Well, not if they found the true killer. If Eleanor's mother was hanged, her forgiveness of Rollins would stretch the bounds of even my optimism. "Nothing will be accomplished by you standing here chattering with me, either. If you want something done, you must go after it."

Which went for myself, as well.

It wasn't difficult to herd him to the door. With a subdued farewell, he exited my office.

Leaving me to take my next step. Because while he had been talking, I'd been plotting. Mr. Rollins might not think Lady Richford's desk no longer held anything important to the case, but I needed to be sure. And gaining access to her writing desk required a specialized set of skills.

I would be asking my nephew for help, after all. I could only hope he wouldn't lord it over me indefinitely.

Chapter Thirty-Seven

Lady Mary

.

THE MAN STANDING in front of my fireplace sipping my twelve-year-old whiskey was a dashing figure. Then, most of my nephew's friends were. Julius Blackwell, Earl of Rothchild should be the last person one thought of when one needed a spot of burglary committed. Rich, handsome, witty, he was the epitome of the ideal man in the Quality.

Except for the skills he possessed to gain entry anywhere he wanted, and his irritating habit of moving without making a sound.

I looked at the booty on my tea table. I'd closed the curtains to my back parlor. The chances of anyone lurking in my garden to see Julius bring me the items were small, but not impossible. "You're certain this is all there was?"

He pressed his hand to his chest. "Your doubt wounds me, Aunt May. I didn't just check the lady's personal writing desk, but all the desks. With Lord Richford in the country, his remaining servants have taken to drinking his better wines. I could have spent all night there without worry."

"Hmm." I poked at the desk drawer's contents. A signet ring, a women's bracelet, some cash, and two letters. I picked up the first, my eyebrows rising. "Did you read this?"

Julius inclined his head. "That one was a bit concerning. I will have to tell Castlereagh that one of his officials was most likely being blackmailed."

Knowing the Foreign Secretary's reputation, I pitied his official. But to put such things to paper was the height of stupidity and much deserving of a set-down, even if the letter was directed to a friend. I wondered how Lady Richford had gotten ahold of it.

The other letter was similarly indiscreet, though the consequences of it becoming public were much less dangerous. Most everyone in the *ton* knew the woman had liaisons with men not her husband. The proof would have infuriated her husband but could hardly come as a shock.

I tapped my knuckle against my mouth as I examined the stash again. Maybe it wasn't that there was too little here; maybe there was too much.

"Are there any other homes you'd like me to…" He delicately cleared his throat. "Gain entry to? It was good practice. I fear after leaving the Crown's service my skills are becoming a bit neglected."

He looked at her eagerly, and she was almost sad she didn't have more homes for him to burgle. "Not at the moment, no. But thank you for this. You and the rest of the boys are always so good to me."

A wicked grin crossed his face. "Anything for you. Summerset was most put out that I got the task of housebreaking for you. Even though you are only blood to Marcus, you're family to us all."

I was not going to get sentimental over one of the lads thieving for me. Marcus and his four close friends had filled a void, one that I doubt they even knew existed.

I flicked my hand at him. "Away with you. I'm sure your wife is eagerly awaiting your return and cursing me for putting you in danger."

He swallowed the rest of the whiskey and brought the glass to the table. He bent over it and kissed my cheek. "I would face any danger for you," he said gallantly. "Now, if you require any further assistance, you will let one of us know."

I smiled at his order. Dear, overbearing man. "Go. I know you have better things to do with your time."

When the door snicked close behind him, my smile fell. I tapped my knuckle to my lips again, my mind spinning over everything I'd learned. There was a hole somewhere in my knowledge. A mistake. A false assumption. Something that hid the truth from me.

How did Mrs. Lynton's letter come to be in Bannister's possession? That part made no sense. Lady Richford had no reason to give it to her son. And if Bannister knew about the secret compartment in his mother's desk, why hadn't he taken everything from it? Why just that one letter?

The fire in the grate popped, and still I sat, staring at the wall.

Until only one option made sense.

I pushed to standing. I had sent Julius away too soon. There was still one more thing I needed from him.

Chapter Thirty-Eight

Frederick

"I REPEAT, MISS Lynton is not receiving callers." Mr. Grosse glared at Frederick before slamming the door.

He rocked back on his heels. He was becoming tired of doors being shut in his face. Tired of having to explain why he, an officer of the Bow Street magistrate, arrested a person suspected of murder.

And more than anything, he was tired of not knowing how Eleanor fared. Was she crying? Was anyone making sure that she ate? He needed to know these things, and closed doors weren't going to stop him.

Making sure no one was watching, Frederick went through a gate into the yard on the side of the house that was more wilderness than garden. If he were a gentleman, he wouldn't know which window on the first floor led into Eleanor's bedroom.

But where Eleanor was concerned, he wasn't a gentleman. He'd made no claim to be one. And she was going to learn that tactics like refusing callers, while successful on the men of her station, did nothing more than delay him.

Unfortunately, there was no handy trellis that led to her window. No covered portico he could climb onto and from there gain entry to her room. There was, however, a ramshackle shed in the corner of the yard, and inside that was a rickety ladder whose strength he decided not to ponder as he leant it against the wall of her home.

The fates were with him. Her window was unlatched, a fact he would scold her for later. After all, if it was easy for him to break into her house, anyone could do so.

The window pulled open without a sound. He pressed his palms to the sill and hefted himself inside. The room was silent, still, and he had a moment to wonder if she was in a downstairs parlor. He could have broken in at a much easier location.

"Climbing through windows seems most improper for an officer of Bow Street. Some might say its criminal."

Frederick swung his head around. There, on her back on her bed, hands folded across her abdomen, Eleanor lay staring at the ceiling. Her gown's lavender color almost matched the counterpane.

"I know you feel duty bound to arrest criminals," she continued, "but I see logistical problems trying to arrest yourself. I suppose you could turn yourself in."

He went and sat down on the side of her bed. He placed his palm near her thigh, the edges of her skirts just under his fingers. "I know you're angry. I understand it, but there are things we must discuss. I can help you through this process. You don't have to face this alone."

"Without my mother, I am alone."

He curled his fingers, dragging an inch of fabric into his fist. "You might feel that way, but it isn't true. Eleanor, I...." How did he express all the feelings he had about their relationship, the expectations he had? His hopes? Yes, he was the instrument that had brought her sorrow, but he could also be the one to comfort her. "I want to be your husband. The one you turn to in times of trouble. I know the timing isn't ideal—"

She barked out a laugh. Finally, she turned her head to look at him. "Husband? You want us to marry?"

The back of his neck burned. She didn't have to make it sound outlandish. After what they'd done, of course he'd thought they'd marry. She should have assumed as much, too. The fact that she didn't only served to heighten his irritation. Had she really thought so poorly of him? "You could be carrying my child at this moment, one who will need the protection of a father. Yes, we will marry."

And, God forgive him, he hoped she was with child. He hadn't thought he'd need something to bind Eleanor to him besides the feelings they had for each other. Now, he realized he'd been naïve. Feelings weren't enough. Love wasn't enough. Because she loved her mother, too. And he'd taken her mother away.

Her throat rolled as she swallowed. She turned her gaze back to the ceiling. "I won't marry you on a chance. I'll wait to see if I'm…well, you know."

"You will tell me." She didn't answer, so Frederick gripped her thigh. "Eleanor, you will tell me as soon as you know."

Her chin jerked down in a quick nod.

Even though she'd agreed, Frederick wasn't satisfied. How could he be when he didn't see a path to his and Eleanor's happiness? He loosened his fingers on her leg, but didn't remove them. He needed the connection, and until she told him to release her, he wasn't letting her go.

Clearing his throat, he tried a different tack. "You hired a solicitor for your mother?"

"Yes." She tapped her thumb on the bodice of her gown. "Did you know defense counsel can't call their own witnesses or address the jury in felony cases? He will only be able to cross-exam the prosecution's witnesses and evidence. I hadn't known that, not until today. The attorney informed me of all sorts of limitations that prejudice the court system against the accused."

"It might not be perfect, but—"

"How many innocent people do you think have been convicted in our courts? Have been hanged?" Eleanor's chest heaved up and down. "I'd accepted that a few sacrifices might have to be made to keep our system running, but one feels differently when it's one's mother on the altar."

Frederick traced the slight quiver of her chin with his eyes. Saw as her hands clenched into fists. "I spoke with the magistrate. He knows your mother isn't well. He'll ask the prosecutor for leniency. She can be sent to an asylum for the mentally ill."

"An asylum for the rest of her life might be worse than hanging."

"The evidence is there," he said softly. "I know you don't want to believe it, but you've seen with your own eyes the rages she can fly into. And if she can harm her own daughter, what wouldn't she do to a woman she considered her enemy?"

She said nothing.

"I couldn't turn a blind eye." The back of his throat burned. "You can hate me. I can even hate myself, but I won't let a killer roam free to hurt others, even if that killer is someone you love."

She muffled a sob, the sound a dagger to his heart. "You're wrong. You've arrested the wrong person."

He could take it no longer. "Move over," he told her, his voice gruff. Not waiting, he pressed his hands to her sides and pushed until there was enough space on the bed for his body, as well.

"What are you doing?" She glared at him as he lay next to her, facing her on his side.

"You can be angry with me again in an hour." Wrapping an arm around her waist, he rolled her until she was tucked against him, his chin tucked over her head, her breath hot against his throat. "Right now, let me just hold you."

He expected her to object. To push at him. Pound him with her fists. When she gripped his shirt and pressed her cheek to his chest, he knew just how badly he'd broken her heart.

"Only an hour," she whispered.

Frederick gripped the nape of her neck, holding her close. One hour to hold her in his arms, to feel her heart beat against his.

An hour wasn't enough.

Chapter Thirty-Nine

Eleanor

FINDING THE FENCE hadn't been as difficult as Eleanor had anticipated. She'd spoken with the groom of the house she'd been a governess at, knowing he had light fingers. He didn't know anyone who bought and sold stolen goods, but he had a friend who might. And that friend had another friend, who had given her three names of men who worked the area around The Minerva Club.

The first fence had died six months ago. The second had never dealt with "swells," as he'd told her with a sniff. With the third, she struck gold.

"She let me in the back door, she did." Mr. Hill twirled the brim of his cap around his finger. They stood on the corner of Long Acre and Garrick Street, his office, as he'd joked to her. The fence was younger than Eleanor would have expected, not more than thirty with a sallow complexion marred with fever scars. He didn't strike Eleanor as a dangerous type, but she was glad it had been cool enough that day for her to bring her muff without suspicion. The dagger concealed within was reassuring in her right hand.

"I'd never 'ad a lady as fine as 'er bringing me trinkets to buy. 'Er gown alone cost more than everything she sold to me. I think she did it for the fun."

"Did you ever deal with her associates?" At his blank look, she said, "Did you ever see any other women working with her? Any friends of hers whom you also bought jewelry from?"

"Oh, sure." He slapped his cap against his trousers, dust and dirt billowing up from the contact. "There were a couple of lasses that came with. It wouldn't be smart for a fine lady like that to meet someone like me on 'er own." He gave Eleanor a pointed look.

She ignored it. "What did these women look like?"

Mr. Hill described a woman who could only be Miss Abbott. That wasn't a surprise. Eleanor was certain any escapades Lady Richford was in, Miss Abbott was neck-deep in, too. "And the other woman?"

"Pretty little thing. She only came up yea 'igh." He indicated his chest level. "Light 'air, big blue eyes. Didn't say nothing, but nice to look at." He gave her an appraising look, and Eleanor felt that she didn't rate as highly in his eyes.

Her heart thudded dully in her chest. There was a man who did rate her highly. One who looked at her as though he couldn't bear to part from her. One who'd cared enough to hold her until she'd cried herself to sleep.

And had been gone when she'd awoken.

Thanking Mr. Hill, she trudged back to her carriage, giving her driver the direction to her next stop.

She hadn't expected Frederick to still be in her bed when she'd awoken as dusk was settling the night before. Their truce had been temporary. He was still the man who'd arrested her mother.

But she'd missed him all the same.

Eleanor tried to attend to her next conversation, to the woman whose description she'd recognized all too well. Another member of Lady Mary's club. Another woman she would never have thought would break the law. But thoughts of Frederick kept intruding.

Why did he have to feel his duties so heavily? Why couldn't he have turned a blind eye to the evidence against her mother?

And why did Eleanor love the dutiful man? She knew herself well enough to know she could never respect Frederick if he had turned a blind eye, and she could never be with him if he hadn't. It was a situation that she could only lose.

The woman's next words broke through her grief. "What was that? Say that again?" Eleanor asked.

Mrs. Sanders huffed out a breath. "You promise you won't tell the authorities my name? My husband would send me to one of the colonies if he learned I'd blackmailed anyone."

"I'm only concerned with the person who killed Lady Richford." Though if it would save her mother's life, Eleanor knew she would readily break that promise. "And if you don't wish *me* to tell your husband of your activities, you will repeat what you just said."

Mrs. Sanders tucked a golden curl behind her ear. "No need to be nasty." She sniffed. "All I was saying was that it wasn't about the money. It was about love."

Chapter Forty

Lady Mary

THIS MODE OF investigation was far superior to dull paper-work. I was tempted to pull the drapes closed to block out the sun. The day was bright, without a cloud in the sky, which in one respect, made my stint into housebreaking easier. Anyone who saw me entering this apartment would only think that Lady Mary Cavindish had come to pay a call.

But the bright light made me feel less furtive, which diminished a bit of the fun.

I slid the set of skeleton keys back into my reticule. It had taken some effort to convince Julius to lend them to me, and he'd stressed that they didn't fit many of the newer locks or those that came from the Continent, but the rooms I needed entry to were neither new nor French.

It had taken more effort to convince Julius not to accompany me. I didn't quite know what I was looking for and was too embarrassed to tell him I wanted to break into someone's lodgings only to poke about. I'd convinced him I didn't need his protection in the middle of the day, when my quarry was safely engaged elsewhere for at least two more hours, leaving the apartment empty.

I was certain, however, Julius had immediately gone to report on me to my nephew. I should tell Cook to expect a guest to dinner tonight.

I started at the small desk wedged into the corner of the parlor. It contained only stationary, ink, and a couple of quills. No incriminating letters. No unused spaces that could contain hidden compartments.

I moved to the bedroom. Something thumped against the wall connecting to the next apartment, making me start. A woman yelled. A man answered, then it went quiet again. Heart beating just a bit more rapidly, I went through the drawers of the dresser.

There was another thump against the wall. Another. Then a long screech. The neighbors must be moving furniture. Good. It should cover any noise I might make. I checked the small trunk at the foot of the bed, running my fingers over the edges looking for anything that could be hidden behind the paper.

When I finally found it, I was a bit disappointed. There hadn't been a loose brick on the mantel to search behind. No floorboards that weren't nailed down. The letter had been casually tossed onto the bedside table, the only attempt at concealment was that the cream paper matched the lacy, eggshell-colored cloth that covered the table.

I took the letter to the window and pushed my spectacles higher on my nose. It was addressed to "Mrs. L—." The author apologized for her past actions, herself "deeply wounded" that her selfishness had caused such hurt. She had decided to start anew, rededicating herself to her marriage and to a more righteous life. It ended: "I hope you can understand and forgive me. Sincerely—S."

The neighbor yelled at her husband to "use your bloody legs", followed by a particularly loud screech.

I drew my finger over the letters that had been squeezed into the margin. It was the final nail in the coffin and made my chest ache. Lady Richford had truly had a change of heart, decided to be a better person, and it had gotten her killed.

The next knock was so loud, I looked up to see if a hole had been punched through the wall.

I stilled, the hair on the back of my neck rising.

The wall remained intact.

But Miss Abbott stood in front of it, holding a pistol pointed straight at my chest.

Chapter Forty-One

Lady Mary

I TRIED TO steady my breathing. "The gun is hardly practical. Even with the racket your neighbors are making, a shot would be heard and investigated."

Miss Abbott tilted her head, the cerulean blue feather in her matching bonnet quivering. "Bannister's death proves that wrong. I had plenty of time to leave his apartment before any of his neighbors called for a constable."

"That was the middle of the night." I looked about for anything that could help. A weapon. A distraction. At the moment, I prayed that Julius had ignored my request and followed me here and would come climbing through the window. "There were candles that had to be lit, clothes to be put on."

Three loud bangs shook the wall between the apartments. Miss Abbott smirked. "I think I'd be fine. No, it isn't the noise. I don't know how I would explain your body found in my home, however." She looked at the space at my feet. "And I quite like my rug."

I folded the letter and tucked it up the cuff of my sleeve. "Well, then. Since we both agree you can't shoot me, I'll be leaving." I started for the door, annoyed that today of all days I'd left my walking stick at home. I'd wanted both hands free to snoop, but I now felt the lack of such a solid weapon.

I pulled up short when Miss Abbott stepped in front of me, raising the pistol to my face. It was a pretty thing, I saw. A glossy silver with a polished-wood handle. The shaft of the gun was made up of four small barrels joined together. Four barrels meant four bullets. One was enough to end me.

"I don't want to kill you here, but that doesn't mean I won't." Miss Abbott's eyes were flat. She almost looked bored. Like killing me wouldn't be any more bother than stamping on an insect. "I think I'd shoot you in the arm so you can still walk out of here with me, but I can wait until night falls and drag you out, if need be."

My shoulders lowered. Even getting shot in the arm didn't sound pleasant. And I certainly had a better chance to escape once we got to the street. "Where shall we go?"

She pursed her lips. "Your club, I think. It's fitting to have this end where it began." She stepped to the side and jerked the gun, indicating I should go ahead of her. When we reached the front door, she slipped the pistol inside her reticule, the cloth hiding its existence from outside observers.

It never left off pointing at me, however.

The noisy neighbors stayed inside their lodgings. The landlady didn't come out to investigate as we went down the stairs. The street wasn't busy, but there were a few carriages rolling down it. And a pair of men hurried down the pavement heading right for us. If I could just—

The muzzle of the pistol pressed into my back. "If you call out to them, I'll shoot one of them in the face. I might be caught, but he'll be dead. Do you want that on your conscience?"

My body flushed with heat. She was using my own morals against me. As Miss Abbott didn't have any morals, it was especially aggravating. And effective.

I let the men pass without making eye contact. I waved at my driver who had parked discreetly further down the street, and we waited as he pulled up in front of us. "The club, Ernest."

He barely looked askance at the additional passenger. And why should he? I hadn't told him of my suspicions, nor the purpose of my visit. He would merely think Miss Abbott an acquaintance to whom I was offering a ride.

The journey to the club seemed both eternal and over much too soon. Sitting with a killer made each second feel an hour. Especially as she never turned her eerie, hard gaze from me, even for a moment. But knowing that I would have to act or die when we arrived at my club, made me long for the ride to never end.

Bernard opened the door to the carriage, helped us down, then hurried for the door of the club. I thought about telling him some clever remark, one he would understand meant to get help but would be beyond Miss Abbott's understanding.

I was all out of clever remarks. I pictured Bernard with a hole in his head, and my mouth dried up.

"I believe Miss Lynton is in your office, milady." Bernard nodded to me, gave Miss Abbott a pleasant smile. "She seemed most anxious to see you."

My shoulders drooped lower, as though another weight had been added to them. I stomped toward my office, nearly tripping when Miss Abbott kicked my heel. She was so close to me, keeping that pistol jammed into my side, our feet nearly tangled.

"Careful, Lady Mary." She gripped my elbow with her free hand. "I wouldn't want you to injure yourself."

Not before she could kill me. "Whatever you're planning won't work. There are too many witnesses who saw you accompany me to my office. Bow Street will know just where to look if you kill me now."

"You've made me change my plans, but I can still make it work." She called a greeting to a woman in the newly reopened Tea Room as we passed. "I had hoped someone else would be blamed so I could remain here, but now I only need time to make it to the Continent. I have friends in France. I can live there."

"Of course, you have friends in France." I sniffed. "That ribbon you wore, and lost in your struggle to kill your friend, it was a symbol of the guillotine, was it not? A slash of red about your throat to show your childish support for the murder of thousands of innocents? You are such an admirer of their revolution it makes sense you think you can order life to your liking via bloodshed."

"You know nothing," Miss Abbott spat. "You have your title, your wealth, without a care in the world for the plight of others."

"You speak as though you were a commoner, yet you don't labor for a living. I bet you have a tidy sum to live upon." I raised my voice as we approached my office, hoping Eleanor would have some warning, perhaps be able to throw a potted plant at Miss Abbott's head. "How much money did you make from your part in the blackmail scheme?"

The gun jabbed into my ribs, stealing my breath. "Enough." She pushed me through the door, stepping inside, then quickly sidestepping to press her back to the wall. She must have suspected an ambush, as well.

Unfortunately, my hopes and her expectations were both unmet. Eleanor popped up at the sound of our entry, turning to face us as she spoke. "You'll never guess what I've learned. I...."

Her voice trailed off when she saw Miss Abbott, who drew the gun from her reticule. Eleanor shrank back, her hip bumping into my desk. "Oh. I see you already know."

"That Miss Abbott is our killer?" I looked around the office, frowning. Darn it, why did I have to be so tidy? There was no handy broom, no pair of scissors carelessly left out, that I could grab. "Yes, I do."

"Sit." Miss Abbott pointed at Eleanor's chair for Eleanor to sit in, then pointed at mine behind the desk.

We sat.

Miss Abbott pulled the servant's bell. "When your footman arrives, tell him to close the club and send all your workers home. You don't have many members left to remove in any event."

My heart beat faster. This would be unusual. My workers might become suspicious. It was a chance. A small one, but a chance.

She dropped gracefully into the other guest chair, pointing the gun at Eleanor and resting her reticule over it. "And make it sound convincing. I have very good aim."

And just like that, my hopes sank. I couldn't risk it. Not Eleanor. Not Bernard, nor Bobby, nor Timothy. They were like family. And I had no doubt Miss Abbott wouldn't hesitate to put a bullet in them.

So when Bobby appeared, I *was* convincing. I told him that with so few members, I wanted to give the workers a day off to spend in leisure. Paid, of course.

His eyes lit at that last bit, and with barely a glance at my companions, he trotted out of my office and went about emptying the club.

"I'm pleased you both are taking this so calmly." Miss Abbott slid to the edge of her chair. "When I pulled this gun on Bannister, he was far from tranquil. He kept repeating the question, 'Why?'" She mimicked weeping sounds. "'Why are you doing this?' He went on and on. Don't you want to know?"

I looked at the gun again. How much time did it take between firing one bullet and another? If I got out of this alive, I really must make a study of firearms. If I rushed her, would Eleanor be able to escape? Or would she be shot, as well? "Since it seems you wish to tell us, I'll ask. Why?"

"I know." Eleanor shifted, sliding her second hand into the muff she carried. "It's what I came here to tell you," she said to me. "I spoke with Mrs. Sanders. You remember her? Short, blonde, has an irritating laugh? Well, she's another member of their little blackmail gang. She told me."

"Edna doesn't know anything," Miss Abbott spat out.

"She knew enough." Eleanor's shoulders trembled, but she kept her voice even. "Enough for me to piece together the true reason you killed Lady Richford. She said that you were…closer than friends." Eleanor swallowed. "That you were in love with her. And Lady Richford didn't love you in return."

I sat back. I…hadn't been expecting that. I'd deduced that

Miss Abbott was the guilty party because no one else had had the opportunity to obtain that letter, excepting Lord Richford and his son. In their grief, they'd let Miss Abbott into their home, into Lady Richford's bedroom, to choose what clothes the victim would be buried in.

That unrequited love was the reason for the murder had never crossed my mind.

It should have. Just because Sapphos weren't common didn't mean they didn't exist. I had just been too blind to see it.

"The letter I found in your apartment." I tapped the folded paper in my sleeve. "I knew it was addressed to you, that the MRS had been added later. What were you planning on doing it with it after you'd added to it to make it look as though it were addressed to Mrs. Lynton?"

"Leaving it somewhere that the Runner might find," Miss Abbott said. "I wanted to press the point home that Mrs. Lynton had been wronged by Sue."

I cocked my head. "I'd thought Lady Richford was expressing her apologies that she wouldn't continue the blackmail scheme any longer. But she was ending the relationship with you, wasn't she?"

"She didn't mean it. Sue was confused." Miss Abbott waved the pistol about as she waved her hands. "It was that husband of hers. That son. They made her feel guilty for being her true self. But she was an exceptional woman, one who didn't bend to fit society's rules. She would have come around."

I couldn't stop the laugh that burst from my lips. "Come around? You're the one who ensured that could never happen. You killed her."

"I didn't—She wouldn't listen!" The gun bounced in the direction of my chest, and my lungs stalled. "I told her what they were doing, told her she couldn't leave me. She wouldn't listen."

"The viscountess wanted to renew her relationship with her husband." I couldn't think of a reason to keep her talking beyond prolonging the inevitable, but it was all I had. "They were planning a trip to the Continent."

"She got scared when Lord Anglia threatened to tell her husband about her activities," Miss Abbott said. "She said she'd come too close to ruining her family's reputation."

I dug my thumb into my breastbone, my heart aching. "Because she loved them. Often, it's only when we come close to losing something that we realize just how much."

"She loved me." Miss Abbott's face mottled with anger.

"I'm sure she did," Eleanor said, her eyes urging me to join in appeasing the killer.

It was the smart play, but I couldn't bring myself to do it. Miss Abbott struck me as someone who'd lived most of her life without anyone telling her she was wrong, that her behavior wouldn't be tolerated. If these were to be my last words, I didn't have the stomach to let her continue in that delusion.

"No, the viscountess loved the excitement of the forbidden relationship, of the blackmail, but she didn't love Miss Abbott." The viscountess barely knew how to love. I didn't know if it made the situation more or less tragic that Lady Richford had decided to try to learn how to love her family right before her death. "And Miss Abbott certainly didn't love her. It wasn't her rejection of your relationship that cut so deep, was it? It was the fact that the viscountess was rejecting the kind of person you are inside, your lifestyle of selfishness and deceit that made you angry enough to kill."

"You don't know my mind." Miss Abbott stood, her body moving jerkily.

"Perhaps not." I pursed my lips. "But I'm not certain you know it, either."

Miss Abbott went to the door and peered out. "If you didn't know about my special relationship with Susan, why did you break into my home?"

"The other letter, the one written by Mrs. Lynton." I slid my fingers underneath the lip of my top desk drawer and inched it open. "The one you told Mr. Rollins you saw in Lady Richford's home. The one you took and placed in Bannister's apartment to implicate Eleanor's mother."

"What about it?" She leaned against the doorframe, letting her arms drop to her sides.

A sliver of sharpened brass met my gaze in the drawer, the letter opener a tantalizing weapon. "Lady Richford would have no reason to bring it to her son's home before she was murdered, and if Bannister had found the hidden drawer in his mother's writing desk, he would have taken the other letters, cash, and jewelry, as well. You had access to the Richford's home as a close family friend. Did Bannister figure out what you and his mother had been up to? Is that why you killed him?"

"Stupid boy." Miss Abbott snorted. "He found one of Susan's stashes hidden in her closet. He knew we must have been working together and thought to turn the tables and blackmail me." She twisted her lips. "He even guessed that I killed his mother. He didn't care, except to the extent he could get more blunt with that information. You understand why I had to kill him."

I suppose I did, at least to her mind.

"And implicate my mother." Eleanor's body vibrated with outrage.

"That almost didn't come about. I'd intended to leave the entire letter your mother wrote, crumpled at the edge of the grate. Edgar tore it from my hand, came at me. I had to shoot him. And when he collapsed, the letter fell into the fire. I only had the small portion. It was fortunate Bow Street had such competent agents to compare the handwriting as your mother's signature at the bottom had been destroyed." Miss Abbott shrugged. "If it makes you feel better, your mother may end up free. After you kill Lady Mary, the suspicion for the other murders should shift to you, as well."

Eleanor had no answer to that, only stared with her mouth gaping wide.

Miss Abbott raised the gun. "Close that desk drawer, if you

please, Lady Mary. Whatever trinket you think will help you from there, I can assure you it won't beat my gun."

I ground my back teeth and did as she'd ordered.

"Stand up, both of you." Miss Abbott smiled, sending a shiver down my spine. "I'm feeling nostalgic. Let's adjourn to the Great Room, shall we?"

Eleanor and I locked gazes. We both knew what waited for us there, and, if I read her expression correctly, neither of us had any idea how to avoid following her orders without being shot.

I stepped around my desk, my chin raised. There was only one direction to go and that was forward. I could only pray an idea would come to us before it was too late.

Chapter Forty-Two

Frederick

"I'VE TOLD YOU. She is being well taken care of." Quinton tipped onto the back two legs of his chair and glared at the ceiling. "With that maid of hers in there with her, she'll likely have a more comfortable bed then either of us will tonight."

Those were the words Frederick wanted to hear, but they didn't reassure him. How could they? The mother of the woman he loved was in a cell. No matter it was a room kept for higher-class arrestees, that it boasted a bed, dining table, and fire grate, it remained a cell.

And Eleanor still couldn't forgive him.

Quinton brought his chair down with a thump. "Have you caught up with Lewis? He's still got a knot in his smallclothes about talking to you."

"Not yet." Frederick gripped the back of his neck. Lewis and he hadn't spoken much since Frederick had been promoted to officer and left patrol behind. The man most likely wanted to drink an ale or two and talk about old times. They'd patrolled the streets together for nigh on two years, and as Frederick had nowhere else to go, he might as well join the man in a pint. "I'll go find him. He still working Lincoln Inn Fields?"

Quinton nodded. "He's got a girl that lives near there. He

doesn't want to leave."

Frederick knew the feeling. With feet dragging, he found a hackney on the street and took it to the neighborhood. It wasn't long before he saw the scarlet waistcoat that the Bow Street Patrol were known for. He called out to Lewis before hopping out of the cab and shoving a coin in the driver's direction.

"Oy! Freddie. You finally remembered your old friend." The smile on Lewis's face took the heat out of the statement.

They shook hands. "I hear you wanted to speak with me," Frederick said. He turned up the collar on his coat. Night was falling, and all the day's heat seemed to have fled with the sun.

Lewis leaned back against the pole of a gas lamp. "I heard you was working the case of that high in the instep hoyden we stopped a while back. That *Lady* Richford."

Frederick's brow furrowed. "That's right."

"Too bad about her. She looked right nice in a pair of breeches."

Frederick pressed his lips together. If all Lewis wanted was to gossip about the death of a member of the *ton*, he wasn't interested. "Yes, and I've arrested someone for the murder. If you want to discuss the case, it will have to wait until after the inquiry." Or never. This was one case Frederick never wanted to think about again.

"Oh, well, if you've already caught yourself the killer, I guess it don't matter."

Frederick turned his gaze from a search for another hackney and narrowed it on Lewis. "What doesn't matter?"

"The information I had. About that night."

Frederick shoved his hands into his pockets so he wouldn't shake the man. "What night? What are you talking about?"

"The night we picked up Lady Richford. She weren't alone."

Frederick thought back. He and Lewis had broken up a small shoving match between some young bucks and who they'd discovered to be the viscountess. There had been a few people observing the scuffle, but at that time of night it hadn't been many. "Who else are you talking about?"

"Well, after you left with the lady, I started interviewing the witnesses." He sniffed. "Wanted to see if anyone else had noticed it was a woman's arse in those trousers that could make trouble for her. I knew you wanted to help her keep it secret."

Frederick's shoulders inched toward his ears. He'd forgotten how long it took Lewis to tell a story. Forgotten just how frustrating a conversation with the man could be. "And?"

"And one of the gentleman I talked to wasn't. A gentleman that is." Lewis glanced about before leaning forward. "It was another woman in trou. A friend of the viscountess. This one's hips didn't fill out the trousers quite so much, so it was easier for her to pass herself off as a buck."

Another member of the blackmail ring? It made sense that Lady Richford wouldn't be the only woman of the group to pretend to be a man. The same reasons that made it appealing for the viscountess to go about London unattended would apply to another of the lot. So why hadn't he considered it before?

"Do you know who it was?"

Lewis flapped his hand. "She gave me a false name. I knew as soon as she said it." But he gave Frederick her description, and it wasn't surprising.

"Why didn't you tell me this before?"

Lewis took off his navy cap and banged it against his thigh. "Well, the thing is, she asked me not to mention I'd seen her."

"And?" He knew there was more. There always had been with Lewis.

"I didn't ask for nothing, I swear. She offered. And, well, what she was offering was…." His blush was clear under the gas lamp. "A man don't turn down what she was offering, but I knew it wasn't looked on as quite proper for me as Runner, so…."

Frederick wanted to punch him. And kiss him. Because if Miss Abbott could convincingly appear as a man, then she no longer had an alibi. The doorman of the salon she'd attended hadn't seen a woman leave the premises at the time of the first murder, but he had seen men.

Putting his fingers to his lips, he whistled, hailing the cab down the street. "Thank you, Lewis. You may have saved an innocent life."

It was time to bring Miss Abbott in for another conversation. And search her rooms. If he found male dress, he would have enough to convince even Sir John. Mrs. Lynton might be free by midnight.

Chapter Forty-Three

Eleanor

Lady Mary was devilish at tying knots. But with the threat to put a bullet in Eleanor's face if the knots weren't to Miss Abbott's liking, Eleanor could hardly blame her friend.

Eleanor twisted her wrists, hoping to find a weakness in the bonds, but only managed to scrape her skin. "No one will believe I killed Lady Mary." The muff she'd set on her lap when Miss Abbott had directed her to sit in this hard, wooden chair and put her arms behind her back for Lady Mary to tie slid to the side. Eleanor tucked both legs up to steady it.

Miss Abbott finished her own knot around Lady Mary's wrists. They sat in the Great Room before the stage, two chairs pulled from their spots against the wall for them to sit in, the rest of the floor bare. Full night had fallen, and the only light came from the candle in the wall sconce that Miss Abbott had lit.

"I think they will." Miss Abbott tied one of Lady Mary's ankles to the chair leg, just as she'd had done to Eleanor, then stood. She plucked her reticule off the ground and slid her pistol inside. "Poor Miss Lynton had already suffered the loss of one beloved parent. She wasn't going to allow her mother to be victimized by Lady Richford. Not when the viscountess had already caused her mother so much distress years ago." She shrugged. "It's perfectly

266

believable."

Lady Mary snorted. "Only to your deranged mind."

Something warm trickled down Eleanor's thumb. She swallowed, the back of her throat aching. Perhaps if she covered her hands in blood she'd be able to make them slippery enough to escape her bonds. "It won't work. I have an alibi for the night Bannister was killed. I was with someone, and he'll know the truth."

Even in these circumstances, Eleanor's cheeks heated at her admission. It wasn't from shame. No, now that she faced death, she could look at her actions with Frederick from a different perspective. Now when she knew the chances of ever seeing him again were slim, she knew that pushing him away had been foolish. He was a good man, forced to make a horrible choice between loyalty and duty. She had no regrets about the man she'd taken to her bed.

She only regretted having to bring up such an intimate matter to the woman who was going to kill her.

"Were you now, you jade?" Miss Abbott smiled slyly. "And here I thought you were ever so proper. But that does hinder my plan." Pursing her lips, she hummed lightly. She looked for all the world as though she were debating what to have for supper, not how best to kill two more people.

Miss Abbott sighed. "I might not be able to blame you for the murders, but with you two gone, at least I'll have time to sort my affairs before traveling to the Continent. Your mother should hang, and then, when talk of the killings has become but a memory, I can return. It isn't optimal, but one must make the best choice from the options available."

"You've never made the best choice," Lady Mary said. "You've blackmailed and killed when the best choice would have been to walk away. You will be caught, because you're too reckless to remain unnoticed for long."

Miss Abbott bent over, placing her palms on Lady Mary's thighs. "I'll be gone. No one will catch me."

"Maybe not for this crime, but there'll be another." Lady Mary tilted her head, a snowy strand of hair escaping its knot. "You've always pushed the bounds of society, and now you've transgressed the ultimate one. You've killed. And you liked it."

Eleanor could see Lady Mary was right, that Miss Abbott would never be able to settle into a quiet life. She'd continue to hurt people, to wreak havoc, until she was eventually caught. She didn't know if pointing that out to the woman, irritating her further, was smart in this particular moment, however.

Miss Abbott straightened. "You've already had one fire. One of those protesters who started it has come back to finish the job." She lifted one shoulder. "It's such a shame you two weren't able to escape."

And with one last smile, Miss Abbott strode to the wall, took the candlestick, and left the room.

Leaving them in complete darkness.

"Well, this is a fine pickle. Any ideas?" Lady Mary asked.

"Can you turn your chair so you can reach my muff?"

There was a moment of silence. "Your what now?"

Eleanor rolled her eyes, the gesture pointless when no one could see it. "My hand muff. On my lap. There's a knife inside. If I try to maneuver behind you, I fear it will fall to the floor."

"Right." Lady Mary didn't even question why Eleanor had a knife in her muff, just set about scooting her chair.

Eleanor looked to the darkened doorway, praying the scraping noises wouldn't bring Miss Abbott back to investigate. Her worry was cut short when the leg of Lady Mary's chair smacked into her knee, making her eyes water. She gritted her teeth through the pain. "Can you reach it?"

"Yes." Lady Mary's voice was strained. "I just about.... Got it." There was a moment of silence. "How do I get the knife out of the muff? It won't do us much good covered in fur."

"Perhaps if I use my knees...?" Eleanor gripped the muff between her legs. "Can you scoot forward?"

More squeaking and thumping ensued until Lady Mary said

triumphantly, "It's free."

"All right. Try to hold it upright." Eleanor started her own noisy progress, turning her chair so she and Lady Mary were back to back. She felt around until something sharp pricked her arm. "Found it. Hold still. And don't drop the knife."

Lady Mary huffed. "Just get to work."

Eleanor tried to saw at her bonds. It was difficult. Her position didn't give her much leverage to work her arms up and down. The best she could do was hold her wrists pressed to the blade and try to rise up an inch or two before plopping down.

Her thigh muscles strained. She cut her skin as much as the rope. But eventually she felt one of the ropes around her wrists loosen.

"Hurry." Lady Mary whispered. "She's coming back."

Eleanor looked to the doorway. A dim glow framed it, and her heart sank. It was either Miss Abbott returning holding her candle, or the fire she'd set was getting close. Either way, it was too late.

Chapter Forty-Four

Lady Mary

I LEANED BACKWARD, increasing the pressure of the knife on Eleanor's ropes. She gasped in pain, but I ignored it. I couldn't concern myself with minor cuts and scrapes now. I'd feel badly about hurting Eleanor later.

If there was a later.

A sound I wished I wasn't familiar with met my ears. The whoosh and crackle of fire eating wood. The glow at the door brightened, and I knew the front of my club was in flames.

I swallowed. Something else I'd wait to feel badly about.

"Pull at your wrists," I hissed at Eleanor. We'd cut through more rope. I could feel the give beneath the blade. She must be close to being free.

"I am pulling." The heat in Eleanor's voice matched that of the fire. "It's just not…Oh!"

The pressure at the knife disappeared. Then Eleanor took the blade from my hand. "I'm free. Let me get the rope at my ankle then I'll free you."

I wasn't sure I appreciated that order, but I bit my tongue and waited for Eleanor to cut me loose. When she finally did, I shook out my hands as she freed my leg. I didn't object when she helped me stand. My legs felt unsteady, and I didn't know if it was from my muscles cramping from being tied up, from the traces of smoke I could now smell, or from fear.

I sniffed. It had better not be that last one. "The back door. Let's go."

We trotted for the exit, only to find it locked.

"I don't suppose you have the key on you?" Eleanor asked.

I inhaled sharply. "I do not."

"Then we'll have to sneak out the front." Eleanor turned and started forward. Her shin banged into the low stage, and a very unladylike word came from her mouth.

I pointed to the doorway, and the figure standing in it. "I echo that oath."

Miss Abbott held her candle high, blinking in disbelief at the empty chairs and then at us. "How...?" Her mouth clamped shut, and she fumbled to open her reticule.

I pushed Eleanor onto the stage, heaving myself up behind her. There were some rooms behind the platform, to hold sets and allow the cast to change for any plays they put on. We could barricade ourselves inside.

And be trapped for the fire that was coming.

It was one hell of a choice, setting oneself up to either burn to death or allowing oneself to be shot. My instincts screamed to delay the inevitable as long as possible. Time meant hope, and avoiding being shot gave us a few more moments of life.

Miss Abbott pulled her gun from her bag before we made it to the stage door. The wood of the door jamb exploded as a bullet smashed into it. Eleanor and I froze.

Miss Abbott stalked toward the stage, holding the candle in one hand and her pistol in the other. "I will be very happy to be rid of the pair of you."

Eleanor stepped in front of me, holding the knife out, the dear, silly girl. "It won't look like fire killed us. There will be holes in our bodies. The authorities will know someone killed us, and my mother is in custody."

Miss Abbott climbed the two steps onto the stage. "At this

point, I don't care."

I looked around, hoping a spear or sword from the latest play had been left out on the stage. I saw nothing. Except for a loop of rope.

Miss Abbott stalked closer, she and Eleanor facing off against each other.

I sidled toward the wall that held the rope. I needed Miss Abbott in just the right position on the stage. I needed Eleanor out of the way. And I needed this all to happen before Abbott shot us.

"It's no wonder Lady Richford ran back to her husband." Eleanor took a step to her left. "You're a soulless, heartless creature. No one could love you."

With a few flicks of my wrist, I loosened the figure eight shape of the rope, holding the weight of the stage curtain in my hand.

"She did love me!" Miss Abbott stumbled forward, the muzzle of her weapon centering on Eleanor's chest. "But she was weak. She listened to her family instead of her heart. And we all paid the cost. Just like you will now." She closed one eye, aiming at Eleanor.

A blur of black and white shot from stage left and collided into Miss Abbott just as I dropped the curtain.

A shot rang out, and Eleanor screamed.

Chapter Forty-Five

Lady Mary

"THERE'S ONLY SO many times I can apologize." I hadn't even wanted to apologize the first time, but the bruised and puffy skin around Mr. Rollins's eye had forced the grudging response.

Mr. Rollins held a slab of one of my very expensive steaks to his face as he sat back in the large wingback in my parlor. Eleanor perched on the armrest, her hand on his shoulder, seeming to want constant contact.

He glared at me from his one free eye. "Didn't you see me coming? I had her. There was no need to drop a weighted curtain on my head."

"Obviously I didn't." I drained my glass of brandy and contemplated another. It would be my third. On a normal night that would be excessive, but nothing about this night had been normal. I poured another.

"But how did you know to look for Miss Abbott at The Minerva Club?" Eleanor gazed upon Frederick like he was St. George after slaying the dragon. She brushed a lock of his hair off his brow. "You threw yourself on Miss Abbott right before she could shoot me."

I refrained from pointing out that my dropping the curtain

also saved her. Let the girl give all the praise to her beau. All the obstacles to their happiness seemed to have disappeared along with Eleanor's memory of everything she and I had done to save ourselves.

"Her landlady came out to investigate who was pounding on Miss Abbott's door." Frederick wrapped his free arm around Eleanor's waist and slid her onto his lap. "She said she saw her tenant get into a carriage with a….more mature woman."

I snorted. I was certain those weren't the woman's exact words. No matter. If my white hair caught the notice of the landlady and led to Frederick's precipitous arrival, then I was quite happy with its lack of color.

"It shouldn't have taken me so long to realize Abbott was the culprit," Frederick groused. "I knew there was something familiar about the posey ring found in the stash Bannister had taken from his mother's house. Miss Abbott had been wearing a matching one the day I questioned her."

I refrained from pointing out that if he had let me see all of his evidence I might have made the connection. "It also was inscribed with the words *Je t'adore?*"

"Miss Abbott's read *Je t'aime*. She says they exchanged the rings a year ago."

"I can't believe Miss Abbott also liked to dress as a man." Eleanor leaned back against Rollins's chest and sighed. "I wonder if they all did."

"How many members of my club do you think were involved with the blackmail?" My voice sounded peevish even to my own ears, but dammit, I had created my club so women could enjoy a bit of the freedom that men had, not so they could use it as their own little dens of iniquity. Perhaps Mr. Ryder was right. Perhaps by giving women the opportunity to romp and rollick, I had given them free rein to indulge in their baser instincts.

"Unless Miss Abbott or Mrs. Sanders talks, we'll probably never know," Eleanor said. "I'm happy to assume that no one else was involved."

I buried my disgruntled huff in my drink. If Bow Street couldn't bring prosecutions against the blackmailers, at least I wanted to know their names so I could remove them from my club.

If I even still had a club. The fire marshal wouldn't let me go in to inspect the damage, saying there could still be smoldering embers they needed to contain, and I hadn't been willing to stand another couple of hours on the street to wait, especially considering the weather.

It had finally begun to rain.

"I still find it hard to believe she could do it." Eleanor pressed her palm to her throat. "Choke the life out of a friend."

"She was strong." I swirled my brandy. "I saw the way she handled her horse. But she always had that alibi. I wonder why she had a cravat? Neither she nor Lady Richford were dressed as men that night."

Eleanor twisted her lips. "I didn't mean how she could have the physical ability. I meant how she could take her friend's life. And maybe she used it as a handkerchief."

Rollins rubbed his palm up and down her leg. "You don't understand because you can't fathom the mind of a killer, for which I'm grateful. She doesn't think the same way you or I would."

"Yes, she does." I rested my glass on my abdomen, feeling more tired than I could remember. "We've all thought that way, it's just been a long time."

"What?" Eleanor asked.

I rubbed my forehead. "She was like a child. A vicious, nasty one to be sure. All she thought about was satisfying her immediate wants. She desired something; she took it. Someone angered her; she lashed out. Most of us are trained out of such puerile behavior. She never was."

Eleanor frowned. "I'd rather think her mind was somehow defective."

"Oh, it was that, too. There has to be something wrong in the brain of someone who admires the Reign of Terror." I ran my thumb over the rim of my glass. "Miss Abbott didn't learn the lesson that most of the adherents of the Revolution did. That the search for freedom without an acknowledgement of our responsibilities, as well, only leads to a different sort of tyranny."

"Are you going to rebuild?" Rollins tossed the steak onto the nearby plate. "The damage seemed more extensive this time."

A part of me didn't want to. I didn't need the income, and building the club up the first time had been hard work. But when I did finally close its doors, I wanted it to be on my terms. Having someone else close it down was an insult not to be borne.

I smiled. I'd never shied from hard work, and I wouldn't start now. "I think I will." A new project. Yes, it would be tiring. It was also a reason to get out of bed in the morning. And it would make too many of the wrong people happy if my club failed.

"Good." Eleanor nodded. "London needs The Minerva Club."

"I don't know if all of London needs it," I said dryly, "but some of us do." It was good to push the bounds of society. Good to question the roles society placed on us. The trouble came when you pushed too far, when you forgot that some of those rules served a purpose.

Lady Richford had learned that the hard way. Miss Abbott would probably never learn it, but she'd feel its effects just the same. Reality had a harsh way of asserting itself, regardless of how one felt life should unfold.

The trick was in getting the balance right.

I looked at Eleanor and her man and wondered how they would fare. Between their different stations in life, their dissimilar temperaments, they would have a hard time finding balance. But I wouldn't bet against them.

"The blood is starting to seep through your bandages." I stood and went to ring for help. Eleanor's wrists had been a mess. My own only had slight pink marks around them, making me feel as though I hadn't tried nearly hard enough to escape my bonds.

"I'll just send for some more wrappings and iodine."

Rollins stood as well, earning a small squeak from Eleanor as she was lifted into the air then set on her feet. "I'm taking her home," he said. "You will need to come to my office to make a more thorough statement."

"I'll go on the morrow." I walked them to the front door, noticing their linked fingers, the soft press of Rollins's lips to the top of her head as he helped her into her coat.

There was something hopeful about seeing new love. It was a reminder that life went on, its never-ending cycles an argument against despair.

I rubbed my chest. It was also a reminder that part of my life was over. I was closer to the end of my cycle than the beginning.

Mr. Stavers closed the door behind the couple. "Milady, his grace sent this over." He handed her a folded page of paper. "He said his contact at *The Times* gave this to him to warn you. It's to be printed in tomorrow's paper."

I unfolded the page, a copy of tomorrow's opinion page.

"That nackle-ass dog." I stomped to my parlor, rereading Mr. Ryder's latest piece. "'…kindly lady led astray by the siren song of modernity…' Ha!" I held the page closer to my table lamp. "'…deceived by her naivety.' What balderdash!"

"Milady?" Stavers had followed me in, his face a mask of concern.

"This calls for more than brandy." I crumpled the page and tossed it into the fire. "Is there any more tart left in the kitchens?"

"I'll check." He left me to fume in silence.

Rebuilding my club would mean more than new wood and plaster. Its reputation had been damaged, too, and the continued opinion pieces from the president of the London Society for Morality and Decency wouldn't help my cause.

"Deceived by my naivety. Ha." I glared at the fire, the flames cheerfully devouring the vexatious words. It had been some decades since I had been burdened with naivety. Thankfully there were some compensations to aging. Wisdom was one of them.

The fire popped as I sank into a chair. Wisdom and acceptance. I couldn't force people to approve of me, just like Miss Abbott couldn't force Lady Richford to love her. The world wasn't made to accommodate itself around our desires. We had to find a way to live within the reality presented to us. And if you could find a way to live happily, even better.

Lady Richford had just begun to understand that. She had been killed before she'd taken more than a few steps on her journey to wisdom and acceptance. That was the true tragedy. We all died. I rubbed at a vein on the back of my hand. Some of us were closer to that eventuality than others. But Miss Abbott had robbed her friend of her chance to grow. To become a better person. Perhaps God could forgive that. I would have a harder time.

But the fact that the world was full of Miss Abbotts I had long ago accepted. My challenge would be to never let it make me cynical. And to that end I put all thought of murder and mayhem out of mind. I concentrated on the work ahead of me that I could control. My club. I would rebuild, and make it better than ever.

A charred corner of *The Times* lay on the stones before the hearth. Could I convince Mr. Ryder to stop targeting my club? Should I even try? He had gone from branding me a licentious libertine to now a witless dotard. The man most likely thought he was being kind by attributing what he considered the evils of my club to a feeble mind rather than malice.

I sniffed.

I think I preferred being accused of organizing an orgy.

The End

About the Author

Alyson Chase lives in Colorado. A former attorney, she happily ditched those suits and now works in her pajamas writing about men's briefs instead of legal briefs. When she's not writing, she's probably engaged in one of her favorite hobbies: napping, eating, or martial arts. (That last one almost makes up for the first two, right?) She also writes humorous, small-town, contemporary romance novels under the name Allyson Charles, and paranormal romances as A. Caprice.

My substack: authorac.substack.com
My website: www.alysonchase.com

www.ingramcontent.com/pod-product-compliance
Lightning Source LLC
Chambersburg PA
CBHW070535310726
48976CB00002BA/632